THIRD HOUR

NORTHWEST COUNTER-TERRORISM TASKFORCE - BOOK 3

LISA PHILLIPS

TWO DOGS PUBLISHING, LLC.

Trade Paperback ISBN: 979-8-88552-086-7

Published by Two Dogs Publishing, LLC.

Cover design Ryan Schwarz

Edited by Jen Weiber

1
_____

Talia breached the first firewall in minutes. That was disappointing.

In her peripheral, a slender figure moved closer.

"Can I get you anything, Ms. Matrice?" The bank manager's assistant had a perfectly blank face. Slim, though not from working out. She probably ate a quarter cup of almonds for lunch. Her blond hair didn't dare move out of the straight fall she'd styled it into, and her makeup was understated. Professional.

Talia said, "No, thank you. I'm fine here."

The assistant nodded. "I'm sure Mr. Crampton will be out momentarily."

Talia sent her a smile. She didn't mind sitting. The leather chairs in the bank's waiting area were comfortable, and her feet hurt from walking two blocks of downtown Seattle on three-inch heels because her Uber driver had decided to hit on her. She'd climbed out early and taken those few minutes to clear her head.

Talia looked down at the tablet computer in her lap. The screen was fourteen inches and the machine inside more powerful than several top-of-the-line desktop computers hooked together. She'd built it herself.

The bank had forwarded her a list of IP addresses for their

internal network, but she preferred to see if she could find that information herself. Later, she would compare the two. She tapped the screen and started a scan on their internal IP structure. That would tell her the scope of how their network was pieced together. Pockets. Layers. Sections. She was going to access it all. Then she would write a report, informing them of the vulnerabilities in their system.

Beyond the tablet screen, she swung her foot. Gold, strappy three-inch sandals. She'd owned them for nearly a week and had worn them five times already, just to adequately express her thanks to The Good Lord and His grace for allowing them to be on sale last Saturday. Nothing like retail therapy to distract her from the swirl of thoughts in her mind. Plus, she'd gotten a new matching gold purse out of it. That put her up to six gold purses. Her home computer was running a program at this very moment, searching the internet for sales so she could get her seventh.

Her mother thought her flashy style was *excessive*, though she agreed with Talia in giving due credit to God for her innate ability to find bargains. Mom responded to most things in life by regularly texting Bible verses on all kinds of things she thought Talia should know.

There were two unread on her phone from this morning. Later, when she'd shorn up her defenses, she would read them—maybe over ice cream. She hadn't exactly backslidden the past few weeks. She still believed. She just didn't want to deal with what had happened.

Not yet.

She was way too busy to cry.

The bank manager, Arnold Crampton, exited the hallway to his office on the far side of the bank lobby. The man who followed him wore a quality suit, but not so nice that it bragged of the tons of money he made as a Secret Service Agent. Because, yeah, he didn't make that much.

Talia had read the agent's whole file. Divorced, the father of a teenage daughter. The girl's mother, a psychiatrist, had moved to

Washington State a year ago and brought the girl with her. Mason had taken a position at the Seattle office of the Secret Service three months after. He rented a townhouse downtown but had recently been prequalified for a home loan.

What she'd read on her computer had not prepared her for the full impact of seeing him in the flesh, even from across the busy lobby of a snooty bank.

She actually gasped. Talia just barely managed to tamp down her reaction. Otherwise the old lady in the chair opposite was going to think she had loose morals. Everything about the man was...*thick*. He was like a California redwood. Tall. Barrel chested —she now knew what that expression meant. Long arms. Long legs. His head was shaved close, dark hair against his 95% cacao, hazelnut-truffle skin, smooth as it would taste...

The old lady across from her cleared her throat. "I think you might be drooling, dear."

Talia shut her eyes. She had to. The pull of him was too powerful, she had to look away. As much sensory deprivation as she could get. Though this wasn't a good solution, because now she could hear the low timbre of his voice. *Lordy be.* This wasn't going to be good at all.

She looked down at the steady tap of her foot. Fresh pedicure.

Her mind immediately flashed back to that cellar. She didn't dare close her eyes again. Not right now, when she would see it all again in full color, high definition. The screams. The cold floor. She could even smell it.

Don't.

Talia got up and swung her purse over her shoulder. No point in sitting here, watching them like a total stalker. She strode past the assistant, who called out, "If you'll wait..."

"It's fine," Talia told her. This woman didn't know who she was, or what she was doing here. She just knew that Talia was here to see Mr. Crampton.

He must've seen her strutting over. She never just "walked." Not if she could help it. He turned, saw her coming, and she saw it—the second his eyes widened. Did she care if she wasn't his cup of tea? No way. He might be an Earl-Grey-stuffy old man, but she was spicy Chai tea with milk *and* whipped cream.

Mason had a different reaction entirely. Eyebrows rose, and he shifted his stance. Appreciation? Maybe. She would *love* to be distracted by him, but too bad she was here to do her job.

She stuck her hand out to the bank manager for him to shake. Or kiss the back of her knuckles. A little sputtering and apologizing always made her feel better. "Talia Matrice, National Security Agency."

She would have sworn she saw Mason's lips twitch.

"Oh." There was the sputtering again. Crampton smoothed his tie with one hand and took hers with the other. Limp shake, slight squeeze. "Of course. We were expecting you."

Mason had shown up early.

Talia squared her shoulders and held her hand out to the Secret Service representative. "Agent Anderson?"

He held her hand with his warm, strong one as he nodded. His lips curled up and she got a flash of the kind of orthodontics bill her mother hadn't been able to afford. "I'm afraid you have me at a disadvantage, Ms. Matrice."

That was the way it was going to stay. If only for her peace of mind. "Talia is fine." She turned to the bank manager. "If you'll show me to the server room, I'll get hooked in."

She shifted her tablet computer, cradled in her left arm like she wasn't already working on the assignment, to assess the bank's computer system for vulnerabilities. He didn't need to know that.

"Of course." Crampton nodded. "If you'll come this way."

He strode back to the hall, and they turned a corner where the carpet met the double doors to his corner office. Mason glanced over at her as they followed. His head dipped to her shoes and back up.

Concerned she'd have trouble walking? She prided herself on never showing how much her shoes hurt her feet. Years of wearing heels and sticking those gel pads in, and they still weren't always comfortable.

His gaze scanned back up to her head. Intense, but more of a professional assessment. Trying to figure her out. She'd picked one of her more understated dresses, though it was bright purple. It hung loose, more loosely the last month or so at least. She'd lost twenty-five pounds since... *Don't think about that.* The team kept asking her out to lunch, or dinner, or both. Truth was, she had collar bones for the first time since junior high. She wasn't all that fired up to put the weight back on.

"Everything okay?"

She realized the manager had opened the door to the server room. Talia said, "Of course," as the obvious reply to Mason's question, and then strode in.

Liar.

———

MASON WATCHED HER WALK IN, then turned to the bank manager. "Thank you."

"Ask my assistant." Crampton waved a nonchalant hand. "If there's anything you need."

He nodded. "Will do. Thank you."

Crampton peered in after the NSA lady, probably curious as to what she was doing. No, the woman didn't match *any* expectations of what a computer geek, hired to do what they'd called a "penetration test" on the bank, would look like.

Some people claimed they didn't like surprises. He wasn't one of them.

Mason left the door open and wandered inside. Talia Matrice wore a dress that was at least a size, if not two, too big for her. It in no way detracted from the impact of the full package.

Considering it would be creepy to just stare at her, he walked over and looked at the screen of her computer. She'd plugged it directly into the computer terminal on the server rack. He knew some of the terminology, and how to breach a network, but was still learning all the ins and outs of the new things hackers were doing. Later, he planned to get certified in order to add to his resume. Maybe move into private information security work when he retired from the Secret Service.

Interesting, but not as interesting as the way her hair fell over her shoulders. Black curls were interspersed with bleached blonde ones that touched her shoulder blades.

Mason shifted his attention to the computer screen. "So how does this all work?"

Out the corner of his eye he saw her turn toward him. "Are you going to talk to me the entire time? Because I can get this done faster if I have quiet."

Decisive. Determined.

Beneath those qualities lay something else. *There it is.* It really was too bad that what was found under the surface never matched the persona a person showed on the outside. It might sound jaded to some, but it was the truth he'd learned over and over the hard way. No matter how appealing this woman might be on the surface, it wasn't reality.

Face facts.

Talia sighed. Then she reached out and braced a hand on his shoulder. She gave him a good portion of her weight while she pulled off one shoe, then the other, tossing them on the floor. She now stood three inches shorter. Her nose barely reached his shoulder.

He looked down at her. "I'll let you get to it."

"Thanks." She went back to the device. Her fingers flew across the keyboard so fast he lost track a few strokes in.

Mason turned away and wandered the room in a circuit that never took him out of arm's reach of her. The servers didn't need much more than a closet. He checked his phone and saw a calendar notification to meet his daughter for dinner. Like he was going to forget. She certainly wouldn't pass up the chance to let him pay for her food *and* give her some gas money.

Stella wouldn't like it—she never did like his generosity with his daughter—but if that was the worst he had to deal with from his ex-wife, he was going to take it. Some people had horror stories of their broken relationships. He had a strained, semi-friendship and a healthy, thriving daughter who was becoming an excellent negotiator. Rayna would make a great lawyer, but she wanted to go into public relations. The Senate wouldn't know what hit it if she ever decided to run for office.

Talia rolled her shoulders and paced a few steps.

"Done?"

She shook her head. "I'm waiting for the scan to finish."

Mason stowed his phone in the inside of his jacket. "How did you get into working with the NSA?"

"I hacked the school district website in sixth grade to change my F in PE to a B. The school's librarian caught me, because I was using the computer in there, and he sent me to the public library to take a class. The lady running it was a retired FBI agent. She told me I should do something legit with my abilities instead of ending up in jail."

She shrugged one shoulder. "So I did. Much to my mother's consternation, I did not major in fashion design or work to become a weather girl or some kind of TV news anchor with a fabulous collection of necklaces. Though, I got the bling." She spread her hand over the necklace she wore today, her fingernails tipped in a light pink.

Mason smiled. "Don't see eye to eye?" Who did, with their own parents?

"About the only things we agree on are gold, and Jesus." She hesitated there, at the end, waiting for his reaction.

Mason nodded. "My father is a reverend at a big church in Atlanta. They stream services now, so he has his own YouTube channel."

She smiled. "You subscribe to it?"

He chuckled. "The podcast, actually."

Her giggle had an alto pitch that sounded warm, instead of

high pitched and annoying. Her tablet thing emitted a series of beeps. She turned to it, and he took her in. A study in contradictions. The comparison to his ex-wife was evident, without him really even thinking about it.

Stella always pulled her black hair into a tight knot, so as to appear more professional. She was taller than Talia and worked to keep her figure as slim as possible. She had also frequently explained to him her views on any hair color that was not what God gave you.

Still, first impressions never panned out. Not in his experience. In fifteen years of marriage to a therapist, he'd been analyzed and diagnosed more times than he could count. Enough he'd absorbed some of it.

He'd thought that he and Stella would be in love for the rest of their lives. They'd both been working on their careers, and he thought they'd be going strong until Rayna was out of the house and college was paid for. Then they'd have time to rekindle the romance they shared at the beginning. Take a second honeymoon, or retire somewhere warm. Meanwhile, Stella had different expectations. She considered him her first, and longest running—though not most successful—client. *Her client.*

When she'd told him that, he'd filed for divorce. He wasn't interested in a business relationship with someone who never intended to work on the love part of their marriage, and who seemed to only want to shape him into the kind of person she thought he should be.

He had a good feeling about Talia. He could already tell that she understood a little about facing up to people's expectations. And owning who you were, regardless.

"Huh." She tapped away on the keyboard, then lifted a finger to swipe at the screen of her tablet.

Mason checked the time on his smart watch. He should probably get the assistant to order in sandwiches for their lunch. These penetration tests usually took all day, sometimes two work days to finish. Then he'd have to spend half a day doing paperwork. It wasn't life as a Secret Service agent in Washington DC, where he'd been hoping to end up on the president's detail. But it was honest, and it meant something to the stability of the financial sector to have the Secret Service ensure things were all working as they should be; that no one was gaming the system.

Her shoulders straightened, and she peered closer at the screen. Tension outlined the muscles in her back and the angle of her head.

He took a step toward her, feeling the gun on his hip with the shift of his legs. But the danger wasn't going to be physical. Not with an assignment like this. "Is everything—"

"What on earth?"

He wondered if she'd even heard him. "Talia."

She turned to him then, wide eyes full of fear.

"What is it?"

2

Talia looked at the screen again, just to make sure what she'd seen was correct. The program, which she'd written herself, had flagged a line of code running inside the bank's internal network. A line of code with her name on it.

Literally.

"Maybe you'd like to share with the whole class?"

She shot him a look, too worried about what this meant to be annoyed with him. Though, at any other time, she'd have been seriously irritated by that asinine comment. Before she could explain, her phone went crazy in her purse.

She bent and pulled out the iPhone, her fingers sliding around the pop socket on the back her niece had covered with plastic gems. Talia had taught the girl everything she knew about hot glue gun usage.

The notification on the screen made her frown.

She swiped through, then logged in to view her bank balance. "What…"

"Talia."

Rather than form the words—and she wasn't sure she actually could right now—Talia showed him the screen.

"So you have two million and some dollars in your checking account." He looked about as irritated as she'd been at his comment a second ago.

"I'm not bragging. I'm saying that just came out of nowhere." The phone shook, gripped in her hand. "The seven hundred and change is mine. The rest was just deposited. From an account in *this bank.*"

"You stole from the bank?"

"Yes." Then she realized how that sounded, so she quickly added, "That's what it looks like from this transaction."

She stowed her phone back in her purse, pretty much just dropping it in there. Who cared if she cracked the screen? She needed to get rid of this money. And fast.

Mr. Secret Service Agent reached across to her left shoulder. He gently forced her to step away from the terminal.

How was that going to help? "Let me at the computer."

"No." He let go of her shoulder but stayed between her and the terminal. "Explain."

"Somehow it looks like I took two million from the bank's accounts and transferred it into my own. While I was standing here, working."

"But you didn't."

"I can't believe you—"

"Answer the question." His voice was strong, an even tone she'd heard her teammates use in interrogations.

"No," she spoke through gritted teeth. "I didn't steal money from this bank and transfer it to the same account the federal government deposits my paycheck into. And I didn't do it in a completely obvious way any amateur hacker wouldn't even do, thus making it stupidly obvious in implicating myself."

His face didn't change. No sympathy. No humor. Totally professional, as though he'd shut down when faced with a cunning adversary.

She wasn't his enemy.

"I'm not that dumb." Problem was, this argument meant she could do it. Of course she could. She was the best. But she'd have done it in a way that made it not obvious it was her who had stolen money. "And I would never breach ethics, or the law, like that."

"Like hacking the school district website to change your grade?"

"I was twelve." Her hands curled into fists by her sides. "My mother made me tell the pastor so he could pray with me when I asked for forgiveness."

He looked like he might've agreed with her mother's methods. Talia felt sorry for his daughter, even if he had moved across the country to work and live where he was close to her.

"Now let me get to the terminal, so I can fix this and figure out who just tried to get me thrown in jail. Or worse, kicked off the task force."

His jaw worked side to side. Then he stepped out of her way. "When you're done, you can tell me about this task force you speak of—the one that wasn't in your file."

She nearly tripped over the strap of her purse. Ended up with her fingers on the keyboard and her ankle wrapped up with the chain that normally went over her shoulder. Of course the task force wasn't in her file. That defeated the purpose of the work they did.

She typed, rolling through sections of their network as she tried to find out where the command originated from. Had to have been activated somehow. Internally. Maybe by her program initializing? A signal that their code should go live, taking money and transferring it to her. Which meant they'd have been in the system before she was.

She thought about calling in to the office. Former Navy sailor Haley was their go-to gal, and she could solve just about any problem Talia threw at her. She'd been trying to trip the woman up—metaphorically speaking—for weeks. Haley had told her to "bring it on." Probably because she felt sorry for Talia and wanted to help occupy her so she didn't spiral into a depression.

The rest of them just brought in donuts and tried to get her to eat two. She'd eaten four, and then thrown them up later. Stupid roiling stomach.

No, she couldn't call the task force. They would swoop in and try to save her, which she would let them do. The reality was that she had to stand on her own two fabulous gold shoes. After she put them back on.

Talia swiped on her tablet screen to her bank accounts.

"Moving the money already?"

She finished what she'd started, then turned to him. "I transferred it back to where it came from." She lifted her chin. "Because it's not mine, and I don't want it."

He just stared at her.

Talia turned back from Mr. Judgmental and tried to nail down the terminal where the code had come from. Whose computer had been used to implicate her in a bank robbery? Whoever they were, they were good. That was for sure…

She took a step back and almost tripped because the chain strap of her purse was still wrapped around her foot.

Strong California redwood arms wrapped around her, then steadied her upright. "Careful." Like she was deficient somehow, and he needed to keep her standing. As if.

She moved out of his arms.

"What is it?"

She shook her head. All this couldn't be because of him. Her hacker, the man who'd had her kidnapped. Nearly *sold* on the black market, as though life was a commodity to be traded. Bartered for.

Victoria had gotten her back.

There was no way he'd bother with a stupid transfer now, after a month of nothing. Especially not for something that was just irritating and not much worse than that. Yes, it was two million dollars. But it wasn't like she hadn't fixed the problem as easily as it happened. What would be the point, other than to continue to torment her with his power over her? She could think of worse ways for him to prove that. She'd lived through the "worse." To the extent that those were all the ones she thought of now.

Was this *his* doing?

"Talia." The voice was softer, but not compassionate.

She shook her head.

"Talk to me."

A knock sounded on the door, enough it slid open a few inches. The manager's assistant stood in the doorway. "Mr. Crampton has informed me that an incident seems to have occurred. Money appears to be missing." She directed her attention to Mason. Considering he was the "law" here, that made sense. Did the assistant want him to arrest her?

Would he?

Almond lady's eyebrows rose. "And it appears to have been transferred into this woman's accounts."

Talia said, "I already put it back." Just so there was no confusion. "I'm trying to figure out where the transaction originated from." She glanced over at them for a second.

The assistant touched Mason's arm. "I require assurance that you'll do the right thing here."

He nodded. "Of course."

Talia mimicked his voice inside her head. *Of course.* She didn't watch to see what else the woman did. Or how he responded to it.

She had bigger problems right now than watching him flirt back. Or not. Whatever. It wasn't like she cared.

The assistant was probably going to get security, so they could escort her out.

Talia got back on the computer. She worked her way through all the data. Definitely a local terminal on the network. Maybe a flash drive, plugged into someone's computer. She could probably figure out which one, and they could go retrieve it. That would mean physical evidence to prove she wasn't the one behind this.

Security footage would confirm she never touched the computer in question.

She was being implicated.

Framed.

———

THE MANAGER'S assistant had left, looking nervous. Maybe Crampton had told her it was her responsibility to fix the problem. Mason had reassured her before she left that it was *his* job.

"Ms. Matrice, I'd like you to step away from the terminal."

She didn't move. "I'm almost done."

"Ma'am—"

"Seriously?" He didn't know if she was talking to him or the computer. Then she turned to him. "Give me, like, two minutes before you go all cop on me, okay?"

"Go all cop?"

She started typing again. "I work with a task force. All of them are federal agents. Like, super cops. You wouldn't believe the stories I could tell you. Abductions and militia, and gunshot wounds." She shook her head and made a gagging sound. "So much blood. Crazy chemicals in the river, and that drone strike."

He frowned, remembering a briefing he'd read. "Are you talking about the lab in Oregon that was all over the news?"

"Uh, yeah. That was us." She shrugged one shoulder. "Who do you think got Haley and Niall out of the lab before it blew?" She pointed one index finger at herself. "Moi. Thank you very much."

"Okay, so I get you know what you're doing. But this is serious."

"I'm one of the good guys," she said.

"You still need to answer my questions about this." There were several things that required an explanation at this point.

"I should probably call Victoria."

"Is she your lawyer?"

Talia glanced over to frown at him. "No. She's my boss. Director Bramlyn, State Department. Look her up."

He pulled out his phone to do exactly that.

"But be prepared for the backlash when you do."

"I really need you to step away from the terminal, Ms. Matrice." He tried to soften his voice, particularly when he said her name. Hopefully that would convince her he wasn't a threat. She could trust him, talk to him. It worked with suspects on occasion. Helped to build rapport and calm a situation.

He touched her shoulder then, as he'd done before. "The money is really back where it belongs?"

She bent to retrieve her phone, logged in again, and showed him the screen. Just the seven hundred and some change.

"Very well." He nodded. "But I think we might have to reschedule the remainder of this test to a later date." Because there still needed to be a full investigation.

"So you can get someone else in to do it?" She cocked her hip, something he knew from having a teenage daughter didn't mean anything good.

"That's not up to me. But you can't deny—" He tried to look like he was shrugging off the worry. "—that this will make for an interesting report."

"Nice for you," she shot back. "I'm in the middle of an investigation. I was trying to move on with my life, but *nooooo*. He just drags me right back into the middle of it so he can freak me out and mess with me. Like it wasn't bad enough before."

Mason thought he might've seen tears in her eyes for a second. Before he could say anything, she continued, "So we're back to the middle of this case. Where I'm the technical consultant *and* the victim. Yay." There was nothing good in her tone. Not even self-deprecation. She looked like she wanted to cry.

She was the victim? "Tell me what happened."

Talia scrunched up her nose and shook her head like there was no way she would ever do that. Not if she could help it.

He shifted closer a fraction. "How can I understand if you don't tell me what I need to know?"

He wanted to help as well, but he should keep this professional first. If it got personal later, that was something entirely different —until he arrested her. This woman clearly wasn't telling him the whole truth—understatement—so she probably had plenty to hide. He'd guess it wasn't all lawful, despite her credentials.

Had she really thought she could pull the wool over his eyes?

Talia actually looked for a moment as though she might talk. But then she shook her head. "Go ahead and look up Victoria Bramlyn. Check her out, and maybe she'll read you in. I'm not sure you have the clearance to be told."

She turned away then, opting for the cold shoulder instead of opening up. That was fine. He probably wouldn't trust her either if their roles were reversed.

"If you could not get back on the computer," he started.

She cut him off. "I'm shutting down." She pulled the cables connecting her tablet computer to the terminal and hit a few keys on the tiny keyboard before she twisted it and stowed it back between servers in the rack. "I guess he won. Again."

He moved so he could see her face. She'd paled like someone who'd seen a ghost. Whatever that was supposed to look like.

War weary, so different from that confident woman who'd walked right up to Mr. Crampton and introduced herself. What had happened to weigh her down to this level of defeat?

Whatever it was, she'd pushed it aside and found her strength. From her relationship with God, maybe. Now she'd been swallowed up by the past again. Those defenses had to have been flimsy.

"I need you to talk to me, Talia."

They could do that here, or in his office. Probably both. He didn't like the idea of taking her in for questioning, though he had to. This involvement would go in her file. A permanent mark on her career that might cause damage at a later date if she applied for a higher position. But he needed to know what had happened.

He needed an explanation for the stolen money, even if she'd given it back.

She shook her head and reached for her shoes. "You might think you want to help, or that you want to know so you can put all the juicy details of what happened to me in your file but when you do know, you'll wish you'd never asked."

"That isn't the way it works and you know it."

She straightened, now back to her augmented height. The woman was the full package; looks and brains, and a broken heart. She made him want to wrap her in a hug, the way Rayna insisted he do, claiming it was better than chocolate. Whatever that meant. Teenagers were like an alien species sometimes.

Or maybe that was women in general.

It could be a testament to his trouble understanding women and his lack of success in that department. Never mind that the Bible said to dwell with one's wife with understanding. He'd been married, and he hadn't figured that out. He didn't suppose he'd manage it with a woman he'd met barely an hour ago.

Talia lifted her chin and pinned him with a stare. "There's nothing you can do to help. But if you need to know so badly, I can—"

Feet pounded down the hallway and an older suited man ran past them, breathless.

They both watched him disappear through a door at the end of the hall, then Mason turned to her. "Let's go find the manager. We should talk to him before we head out."

They would be going to his office, where she would explain everything to him. She seemed to know who had transferred that money. Returning it didn't negate the fact a theft had occurred. All that had gone on here today required a full accounting, otherwise there would always be suspicion—on both of them.

He led her down the hall with his hand on the small of her back. She held her body tight, tense with whatever she was thinking. Before they turned the corner, a middle-aged man barreled toward them. Red faced. His thick jowls shifted as he ran. His white shirt strained in the front by the expanding gut above his waistline.

"Gunman." He breathed and shoved between them. "In the bank."

"What…"

The man trudged away, racing his heavy frame down the hallway. He glanced back over his shoulder. "We're being robbed."

3

Talia took a step back. A robbery…and a robber? That didn't make any sense. First she'd had her identity targeted to make it look like she'd stolen money from the bank. She'd put that back. Once she answered questions for the Secret Service and gave a statement, all that would be straightened out. But this?

Mason had his gun drawn now. He glanced at her. "Draw your weapon."

Talia reached into her purse and pulled out a stun gun.

"That's it? You need a real weapon here."

She pulled out her tablet with the other hand. Awkward, but it would help prove her point. "This is my weapon."

She tucked the stun gun between her elbow and her side. Typed with her thumbs on the screen of her tablet. She sent a message to Haley and Victoria to tell them there was a robbery in progress at the bank.

Was it the work of her hacker?

Brute force physical action wasn't his style. He had hired gunmen for that. Most of his work was done electronically. Talia was the one who had to face the consequences of it, while he stayed secure in whatever bunker he was holed up in, causing havoc in her life.

She bit her lip.

"We have to go." Mason's voice was surprisingly soft. Determined to bring her in after he took down a bank robber? Maybe he'd realized certain things were past her purview and that was all right with him, because he could handle it.

Pretty much like every other federal agent she knew.

"Or you can stay in this hallway while I go in there. But I need to do it fast, before anyone gets hurt."

"Go." She followed him as he crouched at the door and eased it open with two fingers. Hopefully no one would run out the door and crash into them.

He looked beyond it, gun ready to take on whoever was in the bank lobby. She'd had extensive training when she'd come onboard to work with the Northwest Counter-Terrorism Task Force, so she knew how to use all manner of weapons and how to defend herself, if necessary.

She preferred her stun gun.

And really, when it had come down to it, what good had that training been? Not much against a group of armed men who had captured her, drugged her, and then dropped her off at an undisclosed location to be sold on the black market. She got on her knees every morning and thanked God that Victoria managed to get her back.

She was here. She was okay.

But that didn't mean she was whole.

Life went on. This assignment had been about getting back to her real life. Now the hacker had found her here, too. She bit her lip to hold back the flood of emotion. She wanted to scream, and cry. Maybe go to her mom's house and lay on the couch in footie pajamas, drink tea and tell her all about what had happened.

She would do it, if her mom wouldn't respond by having some kind of medical event brought on by stress. Considering her therapist hadn't even been able to hold back his reaction, her mom surely wouldn't manage it.

Mason turned back and whispered, "There's a counter close

to us. We're out of his line of sight. We need to crawl to it. Ready?"

Talia whispered back, "A minute ago you were going to arrest me for being a thief. Now you want me to watch your back?" How was he sure she wasn't just going to stun him and then run off with those millions? Maybe he just wanted her with him so he could arrest her later.

His eyebrow rose. "You transferred it back, right?"

Like it would be that hard to take it again? She rolled her eyes. They probably looked ridiculous, crouched on the floor in the hallway having a whispered argument. "Just go already. Before something bad happens."

He shot her a look like she was the one holding him up. Mason crawled through the doorway. Talia followed him, juggling her purse against her hip with her tablet and the stun gun in her arms. She shuffled across the tile floor to the spot where he'd gone.

"Down," a male voice boomed, loud like it was an order and he was mad. "I said *heads down*."

She couldn't hold back the flinch. Mason crouched behind the counter. He tugged on her hand and slid her across the floor, like it was no big deal, so that she stopped right next to him. Close to him. He'd pulled her all the way. Like she didn't weigh more than she should—although less than she had a few weeks ago—near enough she was now propped against his hip. Talia wanted to be strong on her own. She wanted to feel safe even when she wasn't sheltered against the body of a strong man.

But life hadn't done that. Life had destroyed her sense of safety.

Talia rounded Mason's back and crawled to the far end of the counter, where there was a break between two desks. Beyond them was a half door, which she huddled behind. She set down the stun gun and lifted the tablet so only the camera peeked out. She used it like a scope until she saw him, and then took a burst of shots so she got a good one of his face. All the while, notifications dropped down on the screen. Victoria. Haley. Victoria again. Then the others, as they found out what was happening. Dakota. Josh. Alvarez. Niall.

Talia ignored them all and lowered the tablet.

"Good," the bank robber yelled. "Now, we all just *stay calm* and no one will get hurt."

She figured they always said that, right before they shot someone.

There was no time to read the messages the team had sent her. Talia replied with the best photo she had of the robber, and then sent a bunch more in a string. She followed it up with a message.

Run this. Get his ID.

However this turned out, they would know who he was. If Mason needed to talk to him, then it would help to have information he could use to build a rapport with the guy. If they got out of this.

She looked down at the pictures then and saw something in the corner. Talia used two fingers to enlarge the image. Swallowing down the gasp, she slid back to Mason and tapped his shoulder. When he looked over, she showed him.

He glanced up, a dark look in his eyes.

She mouthed, "He killed the security guard."

Mason nodded. She could see in his eyes that he felt the loss like a blow. Any life lost was a precious thing gone from this world. Didn't matter who it was. One person's life was not more or less valuable than another's. They were all God's creation.

She saw him shove aside the emotion and move to look around the counter. From what she'd read about hostage situations, he wasn't supposed to jump in fast. That got people hurt. He had to go slow and be methodical. But given the line of his jaw and the flex in the muscle, she figured he didn't like that. This man of decisive action wanted to lift up, shoot the gunman, and have the whole thing be over.

Who robbed a bank alone?

Her tablet buzzed on the floor where she'd set it down. Talia looked at the screen.

TWO MINUTES TO ARMED RESPONSE.

She showed Mason.

They'd better get here before anyone else got hurt. Then again, Talia and Mason needed a plan to take this guy down before the breach, where armed response showed up, guns blazing. Could Mason and Talia do it in a way that was quiet and meant the lowest risk of people getting hurt or killed?

She tapped Mason on the shoulder. When he looked over, she mouthed, "What do we do?"

––––––––

MASON STOWED his gun back in its holster. He could pull it out quickly. It was a risk, but he couldn't persuade this guy he wasn't a threat if he came out gun first.

He had to do this himself. Yes, he'd insisted Talia come in here with him, but he would rather she stayed behind the counter. The stun gun she had meant she would have to be within arm's reach of the guy. That wasn't going to happen if he could help it.

Mason wasn't the kind of man who let a woman swing out there by herself, her life in danger. Had she been a full-fledged, law-enforcement-type federal agent *who actually carried a gun*, he'd have worked it differently. But she was right. Her strongest weapon was her tablet. That was where her strengths lay.

He cleared his throat as he stepped out from behind the counter. Pretty non-aggressive as far as noises went. He straightened as the man whipped around, gun pointed straight at Mason's chest. Mason flinched and lifted both hands a little higher, palms out to the guy.

"I said everyone down on the floor." Breathy. Louder than necessary. The man's neck flushed. Pale eyebrows. Mouse brown hair. Clammy skin, and a two-day growth of patchy stubble.

Mason saw the man catch sight of his badge. "Easy." He'd get shot before he could say anything else, just for being a federal agent. "Put the gun down."

The guy looked around, maybe to see if there were any other feds here.

"It's just me." Mason kept his hands raised.

The man was probably in his twenties, maybe early thirties. T-shirt and brown jacket. Did he have more weapons hidden under there? His eyes weren't crazed or bloodshot, so he was probably not amped up on a substance that would lower his inhibitions. The sweating could just be nerves.

It was a wonder he hadn't shot Mason yet. "What do you want?"

"I want you to get down on your face, like everyone else."

He shook his head. "I'm not going to cower."

"I'll shoot you."

"You don't wanna do that," Mason told him. "It won't go well after you're arrested."

Beyond the gunman, a heavyset man lay on the floor. He lifted up enough that Mason caught his face. He made a series of hand motions Mason figured meant he was going to try something. He also mouthed a bunch of words Mason couldn't decipher. Really? If you were going to do that in a high-stress situation, you'd better know what you're doing. The fact none of it resembled any law enforcement or military signals didn't give Mason confidence.

He shook his head, eyes hard. A message this bystander would not mistake.

Before the gunman could turn and see who he communicated with, Mason motioned to the security guard, who he was glad to see still breathing.

Maybe the gunman had hit him on the head with his gun, instead of shooting him. That was something. "You haven't killed anyone yet. Now isn't the time to start."

"Says you." He almost seemed like he wasn't bothered either way. Would he shoot Mason just to say he'd killed a fed?

Mason didn't work bank robberies or hostage situations. His

investigations were all white-collar, financial crimes—things like Talia's penetration test on the bank's system. Usually this stuff was the purview of the FBI. He didn't know what was normal in this situation, and what wasn't. What he did know was that he had the power to direct where it went. And he fully intended to do everything he could to make sure no one else got hurt.

"I'm the one in charge," the man yelled again.

"Yes, you are." Mason still had his hands up. He needed to shift the balance further in this guy's direction. "I have to tell you, I'm not really sure what to do now." He let out a laugh he hoped sounded nervous. "This isn't really my field of law enforcement. But that's why I'm at the bank. Too bad for me it's on the day all the money I'm supposed to safeguard gets stolen."

A test. To see if this guy knew about the transfer to Talia.

The robber reacted, just a tiny flex of the muscles around his eyes. Mason wasn't sure what the man was planning on doing, if this wasn't about money. "You're Secret Service."

"I am." Mason shifted and touched a hand to his chest.

The other hostages were going to think he was an idiot, but he had to get the gunman to think Mason was someone he could control. It was the only way he could turn the tables. Surprise the guy enough to get the jump on him. Would he have enough time to pull it off?

Mason let out a short laugh. "Wow, my heart is racing. This is crazy. A real bank robbery."

The gunman made a face, like he just realized Mason was an idiot. Good.

Mason said, "I signed up for the detail to protect the president, but they didn't accept my application. I heard it's all just like standing around anyway. Looking cool in those glasses." Yeah, he was laying it on thick, but he had to sell the story. "They sent me here instead."

"I wonder why."

Mason made a face. Like he was mad about it and didn't

know the guy had been completely sarcastic. "They relegated me to Seattle." He paused. "Does it ever quit raining?"

"You're stalling," the man said. "Buying time for all your cop friends to get here."

"I thought you were the one waiting for something." Mason looked around. "Don't you have a friend in the vault, grabbing the money?"

"You just want to know if I'm alone or not." He lifted a phone with his other hand and waved it. "Maybe I'm stealing all the money right now."

Mason heard a muffled exclamation from behind the counter. He wanted to smirk, but that wouldn't play with the persona he was creating here. He figured if he looked over at Talia right now, he would see her furiously swipe on her tablet. Did she know how to stop that kind of hack?

The trust he needed to have in her had to supersede his own tendency toward distrust. Despite what he'd learned through experience, she could very well be honest. People deserved the benefit of the doubt, didn't they? Innocent until proven guilty.

Mason tipped his head to the side. "You couldn't do that from your car on the street?"

This persona he was making up on the spot could be knowledgeable about data security and at the same time not a good fit for the president's detail. Most people didn't know the Secret Service duties stretched to more than protection of key government officials and their families.

The bank robber's lips twisted. "It requires proximity."

"As in, inside the walls of the bank?" Some hacks needed to be within Bluetooth range of a network. Not everything could be accessed via an online connection—such as an internal bank network like what Talia had been testing. They purposely safeguarded people's money and information. In this day and age there couldn't be too much caution taken.

Proximity.

He'd been hearing a lot of this type of talk today. First from the bank manager, then their top cyber security officer who he'd met with before they headed down to the lobby. To hear it from this guy now couldn't be a coincidence. There was no way it was random.

Even considering the likelihood of a connection, the fact that there had been two incidents couldn't be ignored. First, there was the stolen money Talia had put back and now a guy trying to steal money. They were two very different things, but had to be connected. He didn't think the statistical probability of the two being unrelated would hold water.

Mason had no idea where their backup was, or how long they would be. "So that's what we're waiting for?"

"That, and one other thing." The man's face took on a slightly smug look. He shifted his gaze over Mason's shoulder. "Talia?"

The tap on her tablet, the pad of fingers to the screen, and the occasional click of a varnish-tipped nail…ceased.

"Time to go, Talia. We need to leave."

4

Talia didn't move. There were probably words worth saying, but she couldn't think what they would be. She was totally speechless.

Her tablet vibrated in her hands. Money wasn't being stolen from the bank. Whatever device he had, he wasn't doing anything with it.

None of this made any sense.

"Talia." He yelled her name louder this time.

She flinched and her tablet dropped to the floor. The screen didn't shatter. And was worrying about that even the most important thing right now? She should stand up. Ask this guy how on earth he knew her name.

Did she really want to do it? Not especially.

Was she going to? Probably.

Talia bit her lip and stood. It was wobbly getting onto her heels and upright after being on the floor, but she managed to do it with her skirt in place around her legs. Her mother had instilled in her the need to be a lady. In stressful times, what else could a person fall back on but those core things? *Maintain grace always, no matter what.* She'd tried. God knew she'd tried.

This time things were going to be different.

Especially if it was her enemy again. Back to pull her strings. *Again.* She straightened and looked at him, the stun gun behind her back. "Who are you?"

"Get over here." The bank robber waved the phone. "We're leaving."

She wanted to fight it. Then she saw his gun drift, aimed right at Mason. Was the Secret Service agent wearing a bulletproof vest? Did it matter? He could get shot in a bunch of places outside a vest that could be deadly—like his head, for one. She wasn't about to gamble Mason's life on a guess of how good a shot this guy was.

Besides, she had to get close enough to use the stun gun she had tucked behind her back in the tiny belt. "Don't shoot anyone…else." She moved around behind Mason and held her hands up.

"Let's *go*." He waved the gun this time.

People on the floor were starting to lift their heads, one by one. Wanting to get a look at the accomplice who'd been with the useless Secret Service agent. She knew what he'd been doing, and it had made her wince hearing the lengths he'd been prepared to go. That this man would ruin his standing, even with strangers, just to get the situation resolved. She wasn't sure the other members of her team would have done the same thing. They'd probably have come up, guns blazing, accepting the consequences.

Talia couldn't let anyone else here get hurt. She wasn't built that way, and she could only be sorry for that fact. She had to try and take him down herself, if she could. But first he'd have to believe that it was working, and that she was willing to go with him.

Why was he doing this? She'd never met this guy before. Why call her by name and tell her to come with him?

Did he have some kind of connection with the hacker? That had to be the man who orchestrated the money transfer to her. What about this? It all made no sense.

"I will kill him," the gunman assured her.

"Okay." The alternative was watching Mason—and any of the other innocent people here—die.

"Talia." Mason made an attempt to grab her arm.

She shook her head and scurried away from him. He would see the stun gun tucked behind her.

There was no way she'd let anyone get hurt because this guy wanted her. Was it the hacker? Bile swirled in her stomach and threatened to rise up to her throat as she studied his face. She would probably choke. She almost wished she could, just to get out of this situation. If she thought about it anymore she wouldn't do it. She'd freeze up like she had when…

Don't think about that.

She stared at his face instead. Studied the lines of Mason's features in case she never saw them again. Why did he have to be that handsome? It was a serious shame she'd met him on a disastrous day like this. Everything had gone wrong, like game pieces falling one by one. Each knocked down the next. Cascading like an avalanche. Like her life.

Mason mouthed, "Don't go too far."

Then a hand grabbed her wrist. She nearly stumbled. Strong fingers squeezed the bones hard enough she winced. Did Mason think she had control over where this man took her?

Talia swung out with the stun gun. Finger on the trigger thing. It already crackled, even before she touched it to—

His arm came up between them and slammed against her forearm. She cried out and dropped the stun gun. It clattered to the floor with the sound of breaking plastic.

"Nice try." He laughed as he hauled her to the entrance where he pushed her body against the door. His weight against hers gave him the momentum needed to shove the door open. She cried out as the gun pressed into her ribs.

"You know I like it like that," he hissed. "Scream a little louder for me."

Ice washed over her and she stumbled outside. His grip on her arm pulled her shoulder back so hard she cried out again, even though that was the last thing she wanted to do. She turned to the robber. "Who are you?" The words came out like a whisper.

He laughed in her face and they moved. Far enough he was away from the people inside, the ones he'd kept hostage. Where was her team? They'd said the Secret Service and local police, and whoever else, were minutes away. She didn't see anyone. If they were waiting for him to be away from innocents, they should move in now.

Outside, the bank looked completely normal. Just another weekday morning. He pulled her down the street in an awkward run-walk. She couldn't keep up on her heels, her feet sending sharp pains up her legs with every step.

"What are you doing? I don't know you. We aren't in on this together."

He dragged her along.

Talia had gone up against someone with superior computer skills. She should have known what her hacker looked like by now, right? Maybe this was him. Maybe not. If he hadn't had her kidnapped and nearly sold to the highest bidder, she might have managed to figure out his identity.

She lifted her chin and tried not to break down. "Was it you?"

"I'd like to take credit for whatever you're talking about—" He shoved her toward a beater car. "—but I'm sad to say I can't."

"Let me go."

He shook his head. "Not gonna happen." The gun was waved toward her now. "That's not the plan."

Where was Mason? She'd expected him to run out after her, maybe already firing off bullets. That would have been good. As a Plan B, considering her team was late. Instead of rescue, the gunman…robber…whatever this guy was, opened the trunk of the car. Was he going to sell her again?

"Get in."

She reared back. "No way. You aren't taking me anywhere."

"You think he had nasty plans for you before? You ain't seen nothin' yet." He flashed teeth at her in a way that resembled a wild animal fighting for his piece of meat.

Talia scrambled away and tried to run. He would probably shoot her, but she wasn't going to just comply. Even if it resulted in her death, she couldn't just do nothing. Coming with him had been the worst idea ever. Why didn't she just let Mason take care of him?

Where was her team?

He grabbed her. Arms banded around her waist and he lifted her from her feet, then deposited her by the car.

Visions of that basement flashed in her mind, and she choked on a sob. The smell. The screams. She couldn't go back there. She wanted to be strong enough. But she wasn't.

Hot breath brushed her cheek. "Get in."

She felt the gun press to her side and hitched a breath. She had one move left. After that she would be dead, or she would wish she was.

She turned around. Talia grabbed his elbows and brought her knee up, fast. Where it would hurt the most.

———

MASON FOLLOWED the two of them almost right after they stepped outside. His phone buzzed in his pocket, but he ignored it and focused instead on his pursuit.

Snowed by a pretty face once again. His dating history—the relationship with his wife notwithstanding—should have taught him that much. But life, or God, seemed insistent on reminding him one more time. Because apparently he *hadn't* learned his lesson.

They were up ahead on the sidewalk. He'd had to frown. The gunman who'd attempted to rob the bank electronically dragged Talia along, all the way to a car parked on a side street. And she fought him the whole way to the rusty beater. She stumbled, clearly in distress. Wasn't she his partner?

Mason didn't know what was going on. He didn't even know if any money had actually been taken from the bank at this point.

He followed them and stayed out of sight at a discreet distance. The gunman had a weapon pressed to Talia's side. Running up behind them and loudly announcing himself, or just tackling the guy, might cause the gun to go off unintentionally. He didn't want to surprise the guy into hurting or killing her.

He moved after the two of them all the way to the car where Talia kneed the guy. Mason winced in sympathy. He'd thought she was in on it.

But now the gunman was bent over, recovering from the force of her knee. Or trying to recover.

Mason came out from behind the dumpster. "Talia!"

She whirled around and ran to him. He held out his hand for her but kept his attention on the bank robber. He could hear the breathy cry as she raced over on those heels.

The bank robber started to lift his gun.

"Don't!" He yelled the word as loud as he could, already taking steps toward the guy.

Talia grabbed his hand. He tugged her behind him, but then let go. She needed to stick close. He felt the touch of her hands on his back and realized she'd huddled behind him for protection. She was scared. A victim, and not the perpetrator in this incident. Only she snagged her hands in his shirt.

"Let go," he ordered.

But the gunman had already chosen his next move. The man turned and ran away, down the alley.

Mason glanced back. "Stay here."

He didn't wait around for her response. He had to trust the fact she'd do as he ordered. Or she would get picked up by whatever law enforcement personnel arrived on scene first.

He had to capture and arrest this guy.

At the corner, he slowed a fraction. He didn't want to get blindsided if the man had chosen to wait out of sight so he could attack Mason. A car horn blasted. Mason spotted the guy in the middle of traffic, two lanes going in both directions. He pulled his badge and prayed, even as he waited for a good-sized opening. Then he ran across the street.

The driver of a white construction truck honked his horn. Mason nearly glanced off the front bumper but managed to avoid getting hit.

Same on the other side. Narrow misses and honked horns.

He didn't have time to explain, or apologize. Something he'd never liked about anyone else, as far as characteristics went. Some people seemed content to do whatever they wanted and deal with the fallout later. That wasn't in his makeup. And yet now, he was the one doing it.

Mason jumped the curb on the far side and slid between two ladies. "Sorry."

He chased the guy along the sidewalk to the alley he'd ducked down.

It was empty.

Mason went to the far end and looked both ways. He checked hiding spots the bank robber might have used and then tried the doors to the adjacent buildings. Nothing. He'd run—and fast.

Now he was gone.

Mason made his way back to the bank, past the car where Talia was supposed to have waited. A crowd of law enforcement and civilians crowded outside the bank. The manager saw him, and as he approached, pointed toward a couple of feds Mason knew.

Mason talked to the Secret Service agents who had responded, two guys from the office upstairs. He told them about the car the bank robber had abandoned. It needed to be impounded and gone through with tweezers. Surely some evidence lay inside.

Witness statements. Physical—and electronic—evidence. The rest of his day was going to involve a whole lot of grunt work. Mostly he figured there were good and not so good parts to any job, and everyone had to endure that balance.

Then he spotted her.

Talia clutched a phone to her ear and gestured widely with her free hand as she spoke to whoever was on the other end of the phone.

He trotted around a police officer escorting Crampton's assistant. She clutched her hands to her chest, tissues balled in her grip. She spotted him. "Special Agent—"

He said, "One second," and kept going. Mason moved in front of Talia.

She flinched the second she saw him out the corner of her eye. Then relaxed when she realized who it was. Anyone would be jumpy after something like this. Still, given how she'd acted since he met her a few hours ago, he couldn't help thinking of the strong façade she showed the world. And that the reality underneath was comprised of something altogether more fragile.

He wanted to know what had happened. About as much as he wanted to know how to help her.

Mason needed to get her to open up to him. Would she tell him what she'd been through? He wanted to believe they could establish trust between them. But he had no idea if that would turn out to be anything. Maybe they would never see each other after today.

"I've got to go." She hung up her phone before the caller could even reply. "I need my purse, I think it's still behind the counter. My tablet…" She didn't explain. But then she didn't really need to, did she?

He nodded. "Let's get your things, and then we can head back to my office."

"I'm not going with you. My team is picking me up."

"You won't be here, because you need to give your statement to the Secret Service." She knew procedure. Still, he felt the need to ease off on her a little bit. "It's also lunchtime, and I'm hungry. So we're going where my sandwich is." Then he added, "I'll make sure you get something."

Just because she needed to provide him with a written statement of everything that had happened, and what she knew about it, didn't mean they couldn't both be comfortable during the process. And if she wasn't who she said she was—if she really did have something to do with this—then maybe he could get her to relax enough she would let something slip.

Incriminate herself.

Talia touched a hand to her stomach. "I don't think I can eat anything."

"Coffee?"

She nodded, then blew out a breath. "That was…" She shook her head. "I don't even know what that was." Her fingers shook, threatening to send her phone to the sidewalk at her feet.

"Who was that guy?" They were getting ahead of things, and he'd have to ask her later—in an official capacity—but he wanted to know now.

"I have no idea. I'd never seen him before in my life." Her face was open. No sign of subterfuge. Could he trust her expression as honest?

"He seemed to know who you were."

He'd called her by name. He'd had some of the same hardware—or just the same skillset—that she had.

She bit her lip. "I know. That's the part that worries me."

5

"What else did he say to you?"

Mason sat across from her in the conference room. The Secret Service office in Seattle was small—they didn't need a huge detachment. Talia had met his boss. The assistant director was a bald Caucasian guy in his fifties who looked more the part of a jaded old homicide detective than someone rising in the ranks of a cutting edge federal agency.

She smoothed down the fold she'd made in the sub sandwich wrapper, then slid it ninety degrees and made another fold. "That's all of it."

Not much, as far as he was concerned, but it had to be enough because she had no intention of telling him more.

She had to check her tablet again, to see if Haley had come up with anything on the ID of the man whose photo she'd taken. There had been no word about that when she'd checked all her devices on the way over. Only a whole string of messages about the bank robbery. Lots of concern, in all caps, asking what was going on. Nothing about the ID.

"Talia."

She didn't want to, but she looked up. "Yes?"

"There's more." He paused. "You can trust me with it."

When he looked at her like that, she wanted to. Talia had to bite back the urge to spill it all. But then she'd end up crying over the sandwich shop napkins. Her makeup would run. Mason would realize she was nothing but a horrifying mess. A blubbering lunatic who couldn't get over what had happened. He'd wrap this up, a total professional, and then watch her walk away.

She shifted her hand on the table and her watch clinked against the surface. She looked at the face of it. Where was Victoria? How could it possibly take this long to get to the bank, realize she wasn't there, and then drive here?

"Somewhere you need to be?"

She shook her head.

"Talk to me, Talia."

She didn't quit shaking her head.

Mason sighed.

She didn't like disappointing him. The weight of it rested on her and threatened to buckle her under its pressure. "I don't know who that guy was. I don't know who put that money in my account, or why anyone wants to target me."

"Maybe that's true."

He thought she was lying? Talia said, "I'm not lying." She just wasn't telling him the whole truth. She couldn't, not until after she talked to Victoria.

"Who did you call?"

She frowned.

"Outside the bank, when I walked up to you. Who were you talking to?"

"My boss."

"And he's someone you talk to?"

"She."

"Does your superior at the NSA know what this is about?"

Was he going to go above her head? "My boss isn't NSA. She's a Director with the State Department." His brow furrowed, but she waved off his question. "I'm attached to the Northwest Counter-Terrorism Task Force."

"So this is about terrorism?"

"I have no idea." They'd been chasing someone with computer skills. A person who had sold VX gas to a militia in the Washington backwoods. But they'd caught Clare Norton, neutralizing that threat. Then they'd traced the money to fake scholarships for a research college just out of Portland.

She'd gotten too close.

That had to have been why hired men kidnapped her and delivered her to traffickers. People who would post her for sale on the dark web. As a hacker with government clearance, she'd fetched a high price.

Victoria had brokered a deal that meant she was the one who bought Talia back. Did the hacker know her boss had rescued her? She figured the person behind it was tech savvy enough, he knew exactly what had become of her.

"How did you get this bank assignment?"

"I wanted to do something…normal."

The things she'd seen in captivity had stayed with her. In her head. She couldn't get rid of them if she wanted to. She'd wanted to use her qualifications to do something solo. Get her confidence back. A quick win that would set her on track to who she'd been before her whole world was shattered.

And now—

A loud crash from the office made her yelp and spin around. She twisted her head so fast her neck tweaked. She hissed and couldn't stop her shoulders from lifting as her body curled in on itself.

"Hey." His voice was soft and right beside her.

She looked over at him, crouched beside her. Compassion written all over his face. He didn't touch her, which was good. She wasn't sure what she would do if his warm, strong fingers wrapped around hers. She wanted to be brave all by herself. Confident.

If he tried to help her she would just crumble.

Her fingers shook as she swept hair back from her face. This was so embarrassing. He'd seen her lose it, and now he was going to have more questions. Ones she did not want to answer.

Talia had to do this herself. She'd been targeted, and he was still messing with her.

"I don't like that look."

She shook her head. "Sorry I can't make you feel better." Did she even want to? It wasn't up to her to relieve him of his concerns. He had no idea what had happened to her, and if she managed it herself, then he never would.

Where was her team? She needed to get out of here.

Mason stood. She saw the expression on his face before he turned away. Disappointed. But there had been no way to avoid that.

He was a strong man, one whose tendency was to protect and safeguard other people. Why else would he have become a Secret Service agent? She knew the type because she worked with agents like him every day. But in this, she didn't need the help. She wasn't about to let other people get caught up in the fallout of whatever this guy did next.

Mason pulled out his phone and occupied himself. Probably checking email—or Facebook messages from his mom. Then again, if that was his work phone then it probably wasn't about social media. Real-time update emails would be more like it.

Normal stuff. The kind of things her team hated because it meant they were part of the federal behemoth.

More people she wasn't about to allow to be hurt by this person.

She needed to do this alone. To solve it alone. Otherwise, she would never believe that she'd be strong enough to go up against him herself—strong enough to face her demons. And where would that get her? She'd be here in this place, stuck under the fear, for the rest of her life.

Talia couldn't live like that. If she did, she wouldn't survive it. She had to beat this, get past it.

She had to beat *him*.

Mason's phone buzzed, still in his hand. "I need to go speak with the assistant director."

Talia nodded. "Could I have my tablet?"

She needed to get going with this search. Bring the fight back to the arena where she had the most ability. Not to mention, ask her team what was taking them so long to get here. "I'd like to get to work while I wait."

"No." Mason turned, already at the door. "Sorry, but I can't give you your tablet."

She got up, fully prepared to argue her case.

He shut the door behind him before she could.

———

"Well?"

Mason met his boss outside the assistant director's office. "There's something going on, but it's not that she tried to steal money from that bank."

Assistant Director Elliot Stanton leaned back in his chair. "You'd stake your career on that?"

If he did that, it would be a personal move made on a case that was personal. This was not. "When we've collated all the information and put together a report, I'll let you know the findings."

Diplomatic, yes. But this was about evidence, not his gut feeling that Talia had gone through some serious trauma. It was almost like she had PTSD.

The alternative was paranoia, and he just hadn't gotten that sense from her.

"Very well." His boss nodded in approval and looked down his long nose. The man was six-four and probably weighed one-seventy-five. There was a pool going on in the office of when he would finally crack and partake of the break room donuts, but so far they weren't getting anywhere on it and the money was piling up. It could fund somebody's vacation at this point.

"And the money from the theft?"

Mason said, "Nothing was actually stolen from the bank, according to our techs. The two million that was transferred to Talia's account was put back, as she said it was, and the bank robber appears to have been bluffing. Our techs said there was nothing running on the phone he had that could possibly have penetrated the bank's computer system."

"So it was a nonstarter?"

"It appears that way." And where did that lead them? A man who'd done nothing except wave a gun around and implicate Talia. That meant she'd been specifically targeted.

If she'd put the money back, did that mean the bank robber enacted his plan after she did so? Possibly as a reaction to the fact she'd immediately sent the money back.

It was worth a thought.

"The National Security Agency finally called me back."

Mason felt his eyebrows rise. "Did they fill you in on Talia Matrice?"

"She joined the agency fifteen years ago."

The woman wasn't old enough for... "She—"

"Was barely eighteen. I know," Stanton said. "Seems like she was some kind of child prodigy, and they snapped her up. Evidently that's the case every once in a while when they can't afford to let someone slip through their fingers. Right out of school. Fresh from that California science, poly-technical, what-ever-it's-called college. She signed right on with them."

"And her team now?" She'd made mention enough he knew there was something unusual about it.

Stanton nodded. "The Northwest Counter-Terrorism Task Force."

Was that what she'd called it? Mason had forgotten in the confusion...and the footrace. He was still angry the guy had gotten away, but he'd been assured their techs were on it. Hot on the surveillance trail. Running his ID, locating him from ATM and traffic cameras.

He couldn't hide forever.

"I've never heard of it," Mason said.

Stanton nodded. "And that's apparently the way they like it. The Director, Victoria Bramlyn, keeps it that way, though she's managed to build herself a reputation. She's well known as a maverick. Once they mentioned her name, I put it together. Word has it she's been working on a team that stays under the radar."

"She has an agenda?"

"The team is legitimate enough, and they've closed some big cases lately." Stanton shrugged. "Whatever her goal is, though, isn't known. She's been running her team for about five years, and Ms. Matrice is part of that. The rest of the group are from different agencies. Homeland, the Marshals service. Even NCIS."

Mason shook his head. Agents from different federal branches working together? That made no sense.

"It's an interesting model, but I can't say I have enough information to assess whether it's effective." Stanton motioned to the conference room. "Maybe she can tell you."

He thought about that. Now he'd concluded Talia had gone through something that made her jumpy and nervous, he'd figured the bank incidents were a result of her being targeted. Now that he knew more about this task force, he was even more certain she was hiding something.

His boss wandered off, and Mason checked his email again even though his smart watch would notify him if a new message came in from the technicians, or other agents still combing through the events of that morning.

Then he poured two fresh cups of coffee.

When he moved back to the conference room, he saw she clutched her big gold purse on her lap. The phone and tablet she'd used at the bank were part of what the techs were working on. Going through her devices and looking for evidence that would either indicate what she'd done, or clear her of any suspicion.

He was nearly at the door when a rush of feet startled him.

"Special Agent Anderson!"

Mason spun around. The tech nearly ran straight into the coffees. Mason took a step back, and some splashed on his shoes. "What is it?"

The tech sputtered, then swiped back a chunk of hair that had come loose from his bun. The guy had skinny jeans, a T-shirt ripped on his left hip, and he wore boating shoes with no socks. Why the assistant director let them dress like that, Mason had no idea.

"Speak."

The guy took a breath, then said, "I need to talk to her." He jabbed a finger over Mason's shoulder, in Talia's direction.

"Yes?"

Mason turned to see if her expression matched her tone. His lips pressed together. "What's going on?"

Before the guy could answer, Talia said, "I'm guessing they're having some…problems with my devices."

"It happened the moment we connected them to our system," the tech said.

Mason turned to Talia. "Whoever hacked the bank and transferred that money can get into our system here?"

Her eyebrows rose. "You think he used my device to access the bank's internal network?"

"I don't know. Do I?"

She glanced from him to the technician. "Well?"

Apparently she didn't want to talk about what Mason thought.

The guy flushed. "Your devices triggered some kind of failsafe we think is designed to keep us from accessing anything."

"She unlocked it." Mason had personally requested that she unlock the device and allow them access. He'd taken the passcode off before he handed it over to the techs, just so it didn't lock again before they got the chance to plug it into their system.

The tech shook his head. "Ms. Matrice." He sounded nervous. "We know who you are. We'd like to respectfully request that you come down to the lab and allow us to disconnect your tablet from our system in a way that doesn't delete everything on our system permanently."

Talia shook her head while a wry smile played at her lips. "Of course you tried just unplugging it."

"The whole thing is...ingenious." The tech looked like he was about to bow to her.

Mason had to wonder if this was some kind of nerd ritual, or meeting of the minds. He turned to Talia. "What did you do?"

She lifted her chin. "You asked me to hand over my device. You also asked me to unlock it."

"On the understanding that we use the access to help you provide evidence which will back up your statement."

She scoffed. "We both know you're only trying to get to the bottom of it all. Not that you're trying to help *me*. And I'm not going to give access to my system to just anyone, am I? There's no way I'd be that stupid."

Mason shut his mouth. But he was stupid, because he'd assumed just that? He folded his arms. "Let's go." He tugged her toward the elevator while the tech trotted behind them. "You can fix what you did, and then I have more questions for you."

"Joy." She sounded anything but happy.

They were almost to the elevator when the doors opened and a slender blonde woman stepped out wearing heels and a skirt suit, a purse hanging from one elbow. Her eyes narrowed on his hold on Talia's arm. "Not so fast."

Mason could have sworn he heard Talia chuckle under her breath.

6

Victoria was here. Talia's whole body relaxed, though she didn't move. Mason's hand on her back imparted warmth where she still shivered inside. Behind Talia's boss,—the woman was tiny, but assuming that small stature implied weakness was a mistake—their friend Welvern stepped out of the elevator.

Talia grinned. "Gang's all here."

Mark Welvern wasn't even part of their team, he was an FBI assistant director she figured had a major crush on Victoria, though he'd never done anything about it. Together they were like a page from a fashion magazine. The perfect young upwardly-mobile couple.

Welvern grinned. "Talia."

She held up her fist, which he touched with his.

"Causing trouble?"

She flipped her hand, palm up. "Would I do that?"

Both Victoria and Welvern said, "Yes."

They glanced at each other. Victoria actually *flushed*. Which, if you'd asked Talia an hour ago, she would have said was impossible.

Talia introduced them both to Mason and the technician, then faced the fact she had to tell them what was going on right now.

She sighed. "We were just headed down to the lab. They plugged my tablet into their system."

Victoria winced. "Please tell me there isn't going to be permanent damage."

Welvern laughed aloud. "If there is, I'm sure it's justified. No one messes with our girl."

And no one missed the look on Victoria's face. A war between not liking what he'd said—at all—and being blown away that he seemed to have inserted himself in as part of their team. Victoria was...flustered. Talia could hardly believe it, even though she was looking at her boss and watching the whole thing.

Victoria recovered quickly enough, turning to face Welvern. "I'm sure Assistant Director Stanton wants to speak with you."

It was clear from Welvern's face that he knew exactly what she was doing. He glanced at Mason and stuck his hand out. "Nice to meet you."

The Secret Service agent said, "Sure." Like this whole thing was utterly confusing, and he had no idea who these people were.

Welvern wandered off toward the assistant director's office. Victoria watched him go, her face void of expression. She chose now to not give anything away? The director motioned to the elevator she'd just stepped out of with a polite smile. "Going down?"

Mason said, "Yes."

She hit the button. When the doors slid open, the four of them stepped inside. Victoria, her and Mason, and the lab tech.

They rode the whole way down in silence. No one pulled out their phone or looked at their watch. Talia didn't even tap the toe of her shoe on the floor. Her mother would have been very proud.

Victoria wasn't about to start a conversation that would lead to them speaking about task force matters in front of non-task-force personnel. Mason wasn't who worried her, though his loyalty was to the Secret Service. She didn't think he'd be the type of agent to get into a turf war. She also didn't know how far into this he wanted to get.

He would participate in the case, but she wasn't sure he'd want to get into *her* case with Victoria calling the shots.

When the doors slid open, they all stepped forward. Mason put his arm out to waylay the tech, so she and Victoria stepped into the hallway first. Talia's boss shot a sideways glance at her. An entire exchange occurred there in that one long look.

Talia smiled, and Victoria reached over to touch her elbow.

Behind them, Mason said, "It's this way."

Victoria turned to him. Surely her boss knew she'd just made Talia feel better than she had all week. But she still acted nonchalant about it. "Lead on." She spoke as if she was some refined lady, and the manservant had just announced appetizers were to be served in the casual parlor.

Talia coughed to cover her laugh. The tech glanced over. The two men led them into the lab, and she let out a low whistle. "This place is nice."

The tech bounced on the balls of his feet. "You like? We just got it." He walked over to the huge table in the middle and swiped on the surface of it. He sent a file to a TV screen hung on the wall. Behind the document was an image, one that she'd bought from a stock photo site. She loved cute cat pictures.

"It's pretty sweet." She circled the room. Most of her setup at the task force office was what she'd cobbled together from pieces bought through private online sales. This was the best the government would purchase for its techs.

"Do you want one of these?" Victoria peered at the computer table screen, then looked at Talia. "I could get you one."

Talia had been kidnapped from her lab in their last office. Although she'd set up the new one, she hadn't spent much time there. "Not super portable." The way their task force was going, it'd be a few months before they would move again.

"We're done relocating."

Talia lifted her brows. "Really?" That worried more than intrigued her.

Victoria nodded. "We're in Seattle for good now."

But didn't that just mean every month spent here made it more and more likely he would find her again?

Maybe he already had.

Fear raced through her like nanites rushing to stop a heart.

"Talia." Victoria laid a hand on her arm. "They need you to disconnect your tablet from their system."

She pushed aside the fear and the questions, leaned forward and swiped between the cat's eyes. So cute.

"That's it?" The tech handed over her tablet.

Talia shrugged. "Not everything in life has to be difficult." She swiped the screen of her device and sent them the image she'd taken of the bank robber.

The tech saw it pop up on his screen. "Thanks."

"If I have anything else, I'll get that to you as well." She glanced between the tech and Mason. "Did you get access to his device, the one he said he was hacking the bank with?" He'd confirmed what she thought. The man hadn't been hacking at all, but there could've been something else they'd learned.

The tech said, "We pulled prints from it. We're running them through our database now."

"Great."

Victoria's phone rang, so she stepped into the hallway.

Mason said to Talia, "Ready to go back upstairs?"

That was it? "I'll need my cell phone as well."

The tech handed her an evidence bag containing her device.

Talia ripped the bag open and took her phone back, then initialed on the bag. It was her phone. Nothing on it was going to tell them anything about the money sent to her account—money she'd put back, like, two seconds later. She wasn't a thief.

"Let's go back upstairs."

He almost seemed...disappointed. Because of her reactions?

She was going to have to tell him what was going on. This was probably bigger than an attempted bank robbery. When he filed his report and they both went their separate ways, she'd feel the loss. The missing piece of what she wondered *could* be.

Mason would go back to work, and so would she.

Back to her fear. Back to trying to figure this out herself.

Talia wasn't all that sure she was ready.

————

HE LED her from the lab the same way they'd entered it, with his hand on the small of her back. Mason didn't want to think about why it felt like the right thing to do. He'd never been this way with a woman before. Probably it was just because she'd so clearly had something happen to her. Who wouldn't want to help, or support a person so clearly upset? There was nothing unusual about that.

They waited for the elevator while Victoria paced behind them on her phone.

"No." The director gestured widely with a slender arm, her fingers splayed. "Tell the governor that's unacceptable."

Mason glanced at Talia, his eyes wide. She smiled and leaned her face close to his to whisper, "She's just getting warmed up."

Mason locked gazes with her. She didn't move back straight away and instead gifted him with an up-close view as she bit her lip.

Victoria said, "Yes, you relay that message for me."

Talia started, and the moment was broken.

"I'll be waiting for his call."

She moved away, and he glanced back to see Victoria hang up on whoever she'd been talking to.

The director stowed her phone in a leather purse his daughter had told him was the color "blush." As though that information would help him live a fuller life.

Mason glanced between them. He could see that they wanted to speak, probably without him present. They were clearly friends as well as having a boss/employee relationship. Still, they needed to get through the debrief of events at the bank this morning. Reports would be filed, and they would all go back to their regular life. This day of crossing paths nothing but an anomaly in their lives.

His phone buzzed before he could even think how he felt about that.

Two texts from Rayna, who should be in fourth period about now—she might be late for dinner with him tonight. He sent back a Bitmoji of him giving two thumbs up, so she'd see it on her smart watch screen and wouldn't have to get her phone out during class. The third notification was from his assistant director, who wanted Mason in his office to speak with Welvern.

He replied to Stanton that he'd be right there, and the elevator doors slid open.

"If I had a dollar for every hour of my life I've spent in the elevator of a federal building," Victoria said.

Talia shifted her weight. "Right?"

The women shared a smile. Two very different ladies, but it was plain they were close. He wasn't sure he was all right with Talia walking away, though soon enough it would happen. "It would be good to coordinate our hunt for this bank robber."

Victoria said, "Will the FBI attempt to relieve you of the case?"

Mason shrugged. "They'll probably try. But if your team is working with us, then we can unequivocally argue we don't need their help on it."

"True." Though, Victoria didn't commit.

Talia tensed. What was that about? Close enough to touch, though they weren't. The elevator doors opened and they stepped out.

"I need to speak with my boss," he said. "The two of you can take the conference room."

Talia nodded.

He walked away without any more emotionally-charged glances. The whole office was observing the three of them, interested in the woman who'd co-opted the whole computer system with her tablet. Then there was Victoria, who would turn heads even if you didn't know she was a State Department Director.

Mason knocked on his boss's glass door. Welvern opened it. They shook hands again, and Stanton said, "Both of you can sit."

Mason blew out a breath as his weight compressed the chair.

"Long morning?" Welvern grinned.

Mason made a face. "Wrong shoes to chase a suspect on foot."

The FBI assistant director chuckled. He seemed to find humor readily. A good characteristic, especially for someone who'd been an agent for years. He didn't seem to have allowed the job to make him cynical, or jaded.

Since his boss's attention was on his computer screen, Mason said, "Have you worked with them for long?" He motioned toward the conference room over his shoulder.

"The ladies, or their task force?"

Mason shrugged.

"I've known Victoria for a few years. The task force works somewhat closely with my office, as our cases occasionally overlap, and they don't have the personnel to do a huge takedown. We're the largest armed-response team that's usually close enough to help."

"How many agents in the group?"

"Used to be five. They lost a guy to medical retirement about a year ago, I heard he's up in Alaska now. Recently, they took on a new office manager and an additional agent, plus his dog." Welvern counted off on his fingers. "Talia, who you know is NSA. Niall is an NCIS special agent. Haley used to be a Navy petty officer. Alvarez is a US Marshal, a legend actually. Dakota is Homeland Security, and her fiancé Josh is DEA. The dog is USMC, retired."

"Wow."

Welvern nodded. "It's an eclectic group, and Victoria took them all on."

Kind of sounded like Welvern wanted Victoria to take *him* on as well. Though, maybe not in an official capacity.

His boss chimed in. "Word through the grapevine is that there was some bad blood between Victoria and the powers that be at the state department."

Welvern made a face like he disagreed. "I'm not saying she isn't...unique in her style. But she also has the experience to back it up. Victoria Bramlyn has earned the right to be as maverick as she wants."

"Like keeping her 'director' title?" Stanton asked.

"And the way she went about earning it in the first place." Welvern paused. "Though, I wouldn't look too deeply into that. It's so classified, it would be a waste of your time."

"We'll see." It sounded like Stanton was prepared to try.

Mason's phone buzzed. He looked at the screen and saw there was an email forwarded from his boss. Looked like the daily update from their other case. One that was highest priority. He stowed the phone. Mason figured it probably had higher classification than anything about Victoria. It was probably the biggest government secret of this administration, and they were tasked with keeping it all under wraps until they could get a result.

The door flung open and Talia rushed in, breathless. "I found something."

Victoria was right behind her. Welvern stood. Mason looked at Talia while his boss said, "What is it?" He sounded peeved at being interrupted, but it wasn't like they'd been in the middle of something.

Talia sucked in a breath. "I had my program look at the origin of that transfer. Because it had to have come from somewhere." She glanced at him, so he nodded to encourage her to continue. "The code originated from a terminal at the bank. I think a flash drive or other storage device was plugged in. That allowed someone to access their database and make it look like I stole money."

Mason said, "You know whose terminal it was?"

She nodded. "I know which one of the bank's employees let him into their system."

T alia leaned against the wall in the hallway outside Sarah
Palmer's studio apartment. The bank manager's assistant
had lived here quietly for two years, according to the building's
manager. A uniformed police officer waited at the door. The
younger, red-headed man didn't hide his curiosity as to who she
was or why she was there. Talia just ignored him and waited for
Mason to come back out.

She didn't want to know what he would find inside.

Victoria had stayed behind at the Secret Service office, along
with Welvern. Though not without her first telling Mason that he
had *better* keep Talia safe. He seemed to have taken what
amounted to a threat seriously enough, telling her with a grave
look that he would. Talia had just looked at Welvern, and they'd
both rolled their eyes.

Their perpetrator might be targeting Talia personally, but she
wasn't sure she was in physical danger. Not that she would wander
off alone right now. She'd nearly been kidnapped earlier, and they
had no clue where the guy was now. Her facial recognition
program was running his image through surveillance picked up by
traffic cameras, ATMs and any other video feed that uploaded to

the cloud. She was going to find him. It was just a question of how long it would take.

That was why she had to access the woman's computer directly. Normally she only needed general proximity to the computer—if it was on and connected to the internet, she'd be able to get into it. Look around. Pull what she needed.

But right now her tablet was busy. So she had to be here.

It took only minutes for Mason to emerge from the apartment with the officer's partner who'd accompanied him inside. His face was grim. "Ms. Palmer is dead." He glanced at the officer who'd met them there. "If you'd call it in?"

It was probably good he didn't suffer from an overblown case of empathy. Likely that wouldn't serve him well. Kind of how it had been so detrimental to her lately. He probably didn't see many dead bodies in his line of work, though. Talia had seen one. And that was enough for the rest of her life.

The officer had already reached for his radio. "I'll get homicide here." He only stepped away a couple of paces, not leaving his post at the door as he radioed in to his dispatch what Mason had found.

He moved closer to her.

She studied his face. "Is it bad?"

Normal people wouldn't want to see a dead person. Especially not if it was gruesome. Talia didn't actually work with anyone who could be classified as "normal," but that didn't mean she had a strong stomach. The last thing she wanted was to do something embarrassing like pass out. Or hurl.

"There's a clear path to the computer. She's on the bathroom floor. Want to look at her system?"

Talia nodded. She had to know how the person behind this had contacted the bank manager's assistant to give her the flash drive—or whatever she'd used. If they could figure out how and with what reasoning they'd persuaded her to do it—or what they'd bribed her with—it would all be additional evidence that could help them find this guy.

She followed him inside the studio apartment. Kitchen island to the left. Small table and two chairs. Bed directly in front. Bathroom door—she didn't look over there. The couch was to the right, tucked in an alcove beside the front door. Talia turned her back to the bathroom door and pulled out Sarah's chair.

It seemed disrespectful to sit in a dead woman's chair and go through her private computer files, but she needed answers.

Mason stood close to her.

"I don't think he left anything that will lead right to him." She entered a series of codes that got her through the password. Sarah's desktop loaded. "He's proved himself extremely skilled so far."

The officer tapped on the door. "Detectives will be here in a few minutes. They said not to touch anything."

Mason answered for her. He pulled his badge out again. "Secret Service, remember? And we're nowhere near the body."

She could have told the officer all her credentials. Why she was the best—maybe the only—person here qualified for computer forensics who could also get an answer quickly. Some people didn't appreciate speed, but basically every case she worked had a time-is-of-the-essence vibe to it. They didn't want the bank robber hurting anyone else.

But she held off on throwing her weight around with the officer. She would save that for the detectives, if it was needed. Talia just got on with her work. She might even get done before the detectives showed up. The last thing she would do was look in the bathroom, let alone disturb a crime scene.

When the officer stepped back out, she glanced over her shoulder at Mason. "Was she murdered?"

A muscle in his jaw flexed, making the dark skin of his face shift. Whatever it was, he didn't want to say. But he did. "Pills on the floor beside an open prescription bottle. As for cause of death, I can't say. I've seen crime scenes before that were staged to look like an accident, or an overdose, to cover up a murder. Who knows what the truth is?"

She knew he couldn't make a judgment based only on seconds of having observed a scene. He wouldn't have touched anything either, except maybe to see if Sarah Palmer had a pulse. Did that bother him, finding someone who was too late to help?

She'd have to ask him later. If they got time to talk.

Mason shifted his weight from one foot to the other. "She told Crampton she was headed out to lunch, presumably right after she confronted me about the money. He never even knew it went missing. Or that you put it back."

"That was a few minutes before the robbery."

He nodded. "She slipped out the back exit of the bank and came home. Now she's dead."

Talia went through the woman's files. Mason leaned down and pulled a waste paper basket from under the desk. Inside was a manila envelope that had been ripped open. "Could be this was how she got the flash drive."

Talia nodded, most of her attention on the computer. She didn't know how they could confirm that for sure. Unless she found something… She clicked through two more folders. "Huh."

"What is it?"

Talia opened the command window. Yes, there was a line of code running in the background.

Before she could think too hard about what it meant, Talia pulled the top sticky note off the stack and folded it over the web cam at the top of the screen on Sarah's computer. Then she turned to Mason and mouthed, "He's been watching her."

Whether he could hear them or not, she didn't know. Which was why she'd made no sound.

He nodded, then touched her shoulder lightly.

She turned back to the computer and found an email sent to Sarah's personal address. Shortly *after* Talia and Mason had started their work at the bank.

Sarah had been lured back to her apartment under the guise of a romantic lunch, and now she was dead.

Had her lover killed her?

Or someone else?

———

Mason had no intention of letting Talia in on the state of Sarah Palmer. Just as he had no intention of allowing anything even remotely similar to happen to her. There was no way he'd let her get in the path of the bank robber if this was what had happened.

Yes, it looked like a drug overdose. He hadn't lied about that. However, it was also clear just from looking at her that Sarah had been in a serious physical altercation before she died. Whether or not the drugs were supposed to explain her death away, or just provide the police with the idea she'd been unstable, or even if she had been murdered, he wasn't sure. But she'd also been attacked.

The homicide detectives strode in. Mason met them over by the door and shook both their hands. They didn't seem all that impressed by his Secret Service credentials, or Talia's NSA ones when he told them who she was. But they seemed content to work this case with the two feds present. Especially when he'd implied he did not consider them to be working *for* him. He would provide whatever support they needed.

Mason said, "Even if that involves getting out of the way."

Talia got up from the computer and walked over.

"Anything?"

She said, "Just that email from her boyfriend, or whoever he is. I'll have to look into the email address. See if I can link that to a person." She didn't look too hopeful about it. Nor had she really given details about the person they were going up against.

A killer.

A hacker.

A bank robber.

One person, or three. Or two.

Did Talia know who it was? She had been specifically targeted. That meant there was reason to believe that if someone killed Sarah just to clean up a loose end, then Talia could very well be in danger, too.

Mason gave them both his statement, and then handed over his business card. The detective said, "Thanks."

He checked his watch. Time to get Talia back to the office.

She glanced at him. "Did we stay too long?"

Mason walked her outside, scanning the area as they moved. Hand on the small of her back. "I'm supposed to meet my daughter for dinner. We try to do it every two weeks."

He held open the passenger door and she climbed in. Mason trotted around to the driver's side. When he got in, Talia had her eyes closed, her head back against the seat.

"Tired?"

Her lips curled up before she opened her eyes. When she looked over, she said, "Yes."

"Long day." He started the engine.

"Long month."

"Yeah?" He let the word hang between them. Waited to see if she would take up the invitation to tell him what was on her mind. Maybe even what had happened to her that made her the target of someone who could hack a bank.

This was bordering on a conspiracy, considering the flash drive used to give the hacker physical access to transfer money to Talia's account. Using the bank manager's assistant and then killing her after. Every hour it seemed there was another moving piece added to this case. It was getting more and more complicated as the day went on.

Talia had closed her eyes again. He drove them from the apartment in the suburbs, back downtown through afternoon traffic. Not much better than rest-of-the-day traffic.

She sighed, long and loud. When he pulled into their underground parking lot, she said, "What now?"

Mason found a parking spot. "If we can find that bank robber, maybe he can shed some light on all the rest of it." He paused. "Maybe he's also the hacker, or maybe not."

She winced. Probably because she'd seen him, and the bank robber had called her out by name. Was she afraid of him? From the way her hand shook as she reached for the car door, he'd say she was.

"Do you know of any associates whose names we could run?" He was in the mood to kick in some doors and tighten the screws on an uncooperative interviewee.

Probably he would just knock, and follow procedure, but the mental image was satisfying enough.

She said, "I've been trying not to think about it all day. Because I've just been going around and around in my head. There's nothing. We know *nothing.* And it gripes me to say it, but if he hadn't walked into that bank and used my name, we'd never have even had anyone to chase down."

"Cue, manhunt."

Her brows flickered. "That's actually a great idea." She reached into her purse, by her feet.

"What?"

"I need to make a call." She tapped and swiped the screen, then put it to her ear. "It's me." She paused. "Because I'm *not* having a good day, that's why." She sounded like she had to fight back tears.

Mason reached out and touched the fingers of her free hand. She didn't jerk her hand away, so he entwined his fingers with hers and held on.

She bit her lip. "I need your help tracking down this bank robber guy."

He'd thought she was already running searches. Who had she called?

Her face flushed with relief. "Thank you." She flushed again and smiled, her gaze on their hands together on her knee. "I know."

Talia hung up. When she looked at him, she said, "Alvarez."

"One of your teammates?"

She nodded. "The US Marshal."

"You think he can find the bank robber?"

"He said he was already on it." She gave him a small smile, the first glimmer of relief he'd seen on her face all day. Because of her teammate. "Which is the best news, because Alvarez can find *anyone.*"

Mason said, "Good." Even though he felt anything but. She didn't need to take on his hang ups about who she relied on to help her. If this Alvarez guy was already on the hunt for their bank robber, then it was good. "Let's head upstairs."

They made their way through security to the floor where his desk sat in the sea of cubicles. Victoria and Welvern sat in Stanton's office, chatting with the man. Looked like they were drinking coffee.

"Dad!" Rayna slammed into him. A blur of pink sweater before her head glanced off his chin. She was getting bigger every week, it seemed.

"Baby girl." He gave her a good hug, then loosened his hold on her.

She leaned back and grinned. "You're busy, right?" When he nodded, she said, "I figured. That's why I grabbed Chinese takeout and came here." She glanced at Talia, then at him. "I got enough for a crowd, just in case."

Mason narrowed his eyes.

Her smile faltered.

"Rayna."

"What? I can be nice. Just because I brought Chinese food doesn't mean I *want something.*"

Mason shook his head. Yeah, except that it totally meant she wanted something. Behind her, an agent who also had a teen chuckled. Mason just prayed it wasn't something that was serious —or something that would cost him thousands.

Mason said, "This is Talia Matrice. We're working together today."

Rayna lifted her hand so they could shake.

Talia took a step to the side, out of reach of him and his

daughter. Her fingers were clenched on the strap of her purse. "I should get to work. There's a lot to do." She turned away and hurried to Stanton's office, but not before he saw a look of pain flash across her face.

Rayna let her hand drop. "Was it something I said?"

8

Victoria shut the door to the conference room. Talia heard it click. She couldn't turn around, or they'd all see the look on her face. No, that wasn't right. *Mason* would see the look on her face. That was the last thing she wanted to deal with right now.

"Talk to me." She'd followed Talia into the conference room almost immediately. Which meant she'd seen that beautiful young girl. Mason's *daughter.* Seen her reach out to shake Talia's hand.

Seen Talia's reaction.

She sucked in a breath, then turned and perched on the edge of the conference table. "I need to leave."

Victoria knew. She was probably the only friend Talia had who actually understood what'd happened to her. The director said, "I got you out of there, remember?"

How could she forget?

"You've had a long day."

"It's five o'clock," Talia said. "Not midnight."

"You're not hungry?" Victoria didn't eat until the afternoon.

"Do you need dinner?" she asked her boss, instead of answering.

"Don't worry about me. Welvern wants to go to this steak place he always talks about."

"Yeah?" Talia could actually smile, except for the reality of what was happening. "You should just go." There was no point in her sticking around just for Talia.

"We're not leaving until you do. In fact," Victoria said, "you should come with us to dinner."

"You are so chicken."

Talia didn't know how to describe it, except that it was like the director had sucked on a lemon. "I'll have you know I've faced down men a whole lot scarier than Mark Welvern."

"Yeah, but you didn't have feelings for them."

"And Mason? Would you like me to bring up your feelings for him?"

Talia shook her head. She didn't want to wave her hand. She'd never fool Victoria by acting blasé about it. "I'm not talking about that."

"Then talk to me about this bank robber."

Talia pulled out her tablet and looked to see if the scans she was running had pulled any results. She forwarded three things to Alvarez. All were possible sightings across town of the man she'd gotten on surveillance. The images were in profile, or the person had a hood on so it was only the lower half of the face. Could be him.

She felt sick at the idea that he was out there. "Hopefully Alvarez will pick him up soon." She glanced at Victoria. "I'm relying on him to catch the guy."

"You think this bank robber is the guy who targeted you?"

"I don't want to think it is, but I have no proof either way."

Victoria waved her into a chair, and they both sat facing each other. They'd talked like this so many times. Lately Talia hadn't been able to face the director. Yes, Victoria pulled her out of that pit. Calling it a pit was the nicest way she could describe it. She should just be thankful. Instead, it was like her head was still there.

As though part of her mind hadn't been rescued, and it was still in that basement. A nightmare she couldn't get out of.

Trapped.

Talia shut her eyes and leaned her head back, but she'd glanced at the window before she did. All she could see behind her closed lids was the sight of Mason leading his daughter to the break room, with that bag of take-out cartons in her hands. The same way he'd led her. Protective. Caring.

She didn't want to be coddled. She'd been trying to be strong.

Then one tall, gorgeous federal agent with a gun wandered up to her. Now, she was just as helpless as ever. No, actually she wasn't helpless. He hadn't treated her like she couldn't do this by herself.

He'd wanted to be there to help her. And she'd run off like a scared little rabbit.

Now he was leaving. Would she even be back here tomorrow? Probably not. Talia most likely wouldn't ever see him again. *Nice to meet you. Good bye.* She'd like to have said it had been a pleasure, but given the bank robbery and the murder, she wasn't sure she could.

Talia opened her eyes. She needed to ask Victoria a question. "Why did he kill Sarah Palmer?"

Victoria's attention never softened. She knew Talia couldn't absorb that emotion on top of her own. That she'd break even knowing Victoria was suffering on her behalf, a simple case of empathy. They'd been through too much together. It was enough just to know her boss understood.

Victoria kept her voice soft. "I don't know, darling." She was only fifteen or so years older than Talia, but that endearment was nice. Victoria had told her that she could count the people she cared about on one hand, and that Talia was one of them.

"Is he going to come after me again?"

"You think the team will allow that to happen?"

"They aren't here," Talia pointed out.

"Welvern and I came over as the ranking agents in their place. It holds more weight and means Stanton can't co-opt us into assisting him."

"Because no one gets to tell you what to do?"

Victoria flashed straight white teeth. "Not if I can help it."

Talia figured her plum lipstick had long since worn off. She'd actually put it on this morning after weeks of not bothering, because what was the point? And for what; nothing but a bank robbery. Though, the fact Mason had seen her looking her best made her feel at least a little better.

Too bad about the rest.

She shook off that line of thinking. "What about when the President calls?" Victoria might like to think no one told her what to do.

"I try not to let that happen too often," Victoria said. "Otherwise he gets upset when I remind him that it's he who owes me a favor."

Talia actually laughed. It felt really good. Fatigue fell off her like scales. *Thank You, Lord.* "I worry about working for you."

Not just because of the reason the NSA had allowed her to be transferred to Victoria's team.

"That day will come," Victoria said. Because she knew. "Right now we have to deal with what's right in front of us."

Talia figured she was right. There would come a day, probably not far off, when she'd have to answer for some things. Victoria had promised to stand with her then, as she did now, but Talia could only pray that everything they'd built withstood that storm. Instead of it all crashing down.

Talia nodded slowly. "This guy put a target on me." She thought it through. "Maybe because you got me back, he's decided to mess with me again. The money, the bank robbery. Could all be his plan to destroy my career."

"Because of his attempt to make it look like you took the money?"

Talia nodded.

"But you were easily able to reverse it."

She didn't want to nod again. Her neck was starting to hurt. So Talia said, "Yes, and he's too good to not be able to make something like that stick. He could have made it so damaging I'd have never been able to get out from under suspicion."

That wasn't fear talking but the knowledge that this guy was exactly that good.

Victoria had a thoughtful expression. "Instead, he chose the human element. He called you out by name, in front of the Secret Service."

"It wasn't the hacker." Talia sat up straight. "It was someone who wanted me to think it was him. Someone who wanted to do his work, maybe even impress him for whatever reason?" She had no way to prove it.

Still, someone capable of hiding a server on the dark web, and then make it nearly impossible to hack, would never be that sloppy. Right? Her enemy had beaten her. This guy who'd transferred the money, not so much. Why hadn't she seen that before now?

She'd been so overwhelmed with Mason, and nearly getting kidnapped, and also Mason...she just hadn't seen it.

"We need to find that bank robber."

Talia nodded. "We really do."

———

MASON THOUGHT about saying goodbye to Talia, but she seemed to be in a pretty deep discussion with her boss. There wasn't much point in staying late tonight. Half the team had come in and loaded a paper plate of Chinese food, then left before clean up.

Rayna caught the direction of his gaze. "Did she not like me?"

Mason reached over and squeezed the back of her neck as they headed for the stairs. "That's not it."

She twisted toward him, dipped her head and touched her forehead to his collarbone. When she leaned back, he said, "I spent time with her today, and it gave me the impression something happened to her. Something serious. Maybe even traumatic."

They took the stairwell down. It was their thing, jumping two at a time together in a race. The way they had when she'd been training in soccer. Then volleyball. Then basketball. Then volley-ball again. The girl could not manage to pick one sport and actu-ally stick with it.

Halfway down to the basement level where the parking garage was, she glanced back to where he trailed her like an old man. Having a seventeen-year-old daughter certainly made him feel old.

"Mom says PTSD can affect anyone, and then also all that stuff about how you never know what a person has been through."

"I hate when people pour my cereal for me," he intoned, using his grandma's voice. "They don't know how much I want."

She finished it for him, equally as high pitched. "They don't know what I've been through."

Mason grinned and she laughed. Not that they laughed about people who had suffered serious trauma. That wouldn't be cool. But with his ex-wife's constant litany of people's serious and heavy problems, he'd *had* to provide Rayna with some kind of outlet. A place where stress could bleed off, and she could maybe even laugh a little.

So they'd laughed.

Stella, not so much. It was like she wanted them to be serious all the time, when life was way too short for that. Way too short for Mason to live his life with a woman who insisted she knew how to "fix" him.

Rayna hauled the door open, huffing like it weighed a thou-sand pounds. "I don't think you could ever be with a simple woman."

Mason stopped before he stepped through it. "What does that mean?"

"Kerri has this guy. He's a lead guitarist for some band over in Breckenridge—his dad is in the Navy—but he wanted to rebel so he has these sleeves of tattoos, even though he's only a junior."

Mason had to fight letting a reaction slip out. He'd taught himself to stay stoic. If he jumped on her with an overblown reaction every time she told him something, eventually she would stop confiding in him at all. So he said, "Uh-huh." Like that was only mildly curious information.

"She gave him the total runaround. Like, crazy town. And he's still calling." She frowned with her eyebrows, nose, and mouth. It was his favorite expression of hers. As though the world exasperated her even as much as it confused her. He felt the same way. "She said it's like he gets off on the drama of it."

"You think I'm like that?"

"No." She let go of the door, and they headed for the car. "I think you'd get bored with someone simple. Or someone who has it all together. You need a woman you can...help. Someone who wants you to take care of her."

"As opposed to a woman who needs nothing from me?"

"Because she's *fine*." Rayna laughed. They'd both heard him and her mother have this conversation before. "She's not fine, by the way."

"Is she okay?"

"I don't know." His teen sighed, like all teens sigh. So much weight of the world. "She has a new client. I tried to get on her computer and look at the file, but she changed the password."

"Uh...good."

Rayna waved a hand. "I have to know how to help mom."

"She's fine, remember?" At least, he knew his ex-wife wanted to be fine. Maybe that was just what she told the world. Or she had a therapist of her own, a shrink for shrinks that she could talk to. Did they do that?

Mason said, "Where'd you park?"

She looked up at the row of cars in front of them, which included his six-year-old SUV with a hundred-fifty thousand miles on it. The brand new Camaro Rayna's mother had bought her was... She turned around. "Uh." Leaned around his back. "Over there." She smiled, triumphant at being able to locate her car.

He walked her to it. "Thank you for bringing dinner. Today was crazy."

"You're going home now?"

"Yes, *Mom*," he said. "I'll go right to sleep like a good boy."

"I'm gonna tell Gramma you said that."

"Don't." She wouldn't, would she? He might be a grown man, but his mother would still threaten to get her spatula out and teach him some manners. "Please, don't."

Rayna grinned her perfect little angel smile.

Mason shook his head. "Go on now, trouble."

She kissed his cheek. "Goodnight, Daddy."

Rayna didn't often call him that anymore, but once in a while it slipped out. He shifted the backpack with his laptop in it on his shoulder, and waited to watch her pull out before he headed to his car. She knew to wait for him by the exit, and he followed her home just to make sure she was okay. He thought about stopping in and saying hi to Stella, but didn't. Instead he thought about Talia as he drove on to his townhouse.

Was she really the kind of woman he needed in his life? Some women, as he well knew, wanted to be strong in a way that factored out a man. His opinion was that no one should be weak. People were people, and they each had hard—and soft—parts to who they were. He had a whole lot of respect for people who had faced awful situations and yet could still hold their heads high. Stand up. Keep going.

He'd been raised hearing tales of his grandfather in the south. Strength had been bred into his genes in a way that made him take that mantle proudly. To live the life so many before him hadn't been given the chance to.

Talia understood that. She'd fought beside him today, even without a gun. Her skills were evident. But so was her fear. He'd seen her push through it, though. Stand for what was right, despite how she'd fled from meeting Rayna. He had a feeling that was because of what had happened to her.

He had to admit, at least to himself, that he was disappointed. He'd have liked for them to meet. Maybe next time. He could find out what Talia's panic had been about. He could make it good for her. Nonthreatening.

The fact he even wanted to do that work was interesting. She was the first woman who'd piqued his interest in months. He didn't want to waste the chance. Didn't want to let it slip through his fingers. It might be something worthwhile—or did he just want someone to take care of, as Rayna had said, because he was lonely?

Mason parked in his garage, walked down the drive to retrieve his mail, and headed inside. He dropped the mail on the counter and set his backpack on the floor.

The blow came from behind him.

Before he could register what had happened, his body dropped to the floor.

9

Talia didn't want to eat the crust of the pizza, but she'd skipped lunch so she finished the whole thing. Welvern had wolfed down three slices while Victoria stabbed a plastic fork into a chicken salad.

"Sorry you guys didn't get your steak."

Victoria glanced at Welvern. He said, "Don't sweat it. We have time."

Talia wiped her hands on a napkin, wondering if he meant tonight's dinner or a time where it was just him and Victoria. Maybe it was both.

"There's another slice." Welvern nudged the corner of the pizza box.

Talia blew out a breath. "I'm stuffed." She didn't want to get into all that. With the weight she'd lost in the past few weeks, the team insisted she finish every meal they shared. And then have dessert.

Victoria eyed her over the salad. "That piece is mine."

Talia motioned to her. "There you go." She was all for salad, but when there was pizza instead? No way. Apparently Victoria was in the mood for both.

Welvern leaned back in his chair. "Are you guys okay?"

"Why would we be?" Talia asked. "Today was weird."

Victoria nodded. "So weird."

"Okay, that doesn't reassure me." Welvern eyed Talia, then Victoria. "Both of you are acting bizarre. Is this about the hacker?"

Talia glanced at Victoria. Had she told him everything? Her boss nodded in answer to the unspoken question. Talia said, "I may or may not have come face to face with my nightmare this morning. How I feel about that, I didn't really get the chance to process, considering he then tried to kidnap me. Although, honestly, seeing him in the flesh—if it was him—felt a little anticlimactic. I mean, how does reality ever measure up with the monster in your head?"

Welvern took a sip from his bottled water. "You want me to punch him in the face for you?"

"Yes."

"After Alvarez finds him."

She nodded. "Although, if you could also get the US attorney to file so many charges he never gets out of prison for the rest of his life, that would also not go unappreciated."

"I prefer the punching."

Talia actually smiled, even though Mark wasn't that kind of FBI agent. Mark did things by the book, but she also understood his feelings. He would be professional about this. Not just because Victoria would insist on it, or because his oath demanded it. They all wanted this guy to go down.

He'd caused so much chaos already, trafficking in a deadly weapon and funding scary medical research at a lab that had turned a Portland college into a war zone. Mark had been on the ground to clean up the aftermath of what had happened at that research college. He'd seen first hand the damage this guy had done.

Mark had done his part, while Victoria had done hers— getting her alias name in a dark web sale. She'd been the one who purchased Talia back. The only way she'd been able to find her and get her home before she was lost forever to some psycho.

"Hey." Victoria touched Talia's knee.

Talia shut her eyes for a second and shook her head. "I'm okay."

She just had no desire to go home alone. Working wasn't the problem. Going to church wasn't the problem. Eating, and trying to get some—but not all—of the weight back on, was a challenge, but it wasn't the problem.

Closing her eyes and trying to sleep was.

"He's still messing with me." Talia needed to say it out loud. Not that she'd thought after he tried to sell her, he'd then leave her alone. But she'd at least thought it would give her more than a few weeks of peace to figure out she was back with the team.

Victoria said, "I called a CIA contact of mine and gave them everything we had. They're looking into it."

More people knew what had happened to her? Talia pushed aside the embarrassment. They had to catch him. "Thanks."

"And the FBI is still running forensics on the…" Mark hesitated. "…place where they held you."

Talia started to tell him thanks as well, but her tablet chimed with an incoming video call. She tapped the screen. "Maybe it's Alvarez with an update."

Welvern grabbed the pizza box and walked out with an armful of their trash.

Considering Alvarez had a flip phone that did nothing but make calls and text—which he didn't do—she wasn't sure how that would work. But it was possible he'd found a place to make a video call.

She said, "Hello?"

The screen loaded. A living room, with Mason tied to a chair. Blood dripped from the side of his mouth and down his chin.

"Mason?"

Victoria shushed her. She leaned over to see. "Hit screen record."

"Hello?" Talia couldn't hear anything, but the video was live. Who was on the other end? "What's going on?"

A man spoke, his face never coming into view. She stared at Mason's bloody face, his head tipped to the side—out cold, while the man told her what he wanted.

———

MASON'S HEAD felt like it was about to explode. He could hear the guy talking. Could make out a tall dark figure in front of him through the blur. *Lord, don't let there be permanent damage.*

"...access."

He heard a few more words but couldn't make sense of them. He'd walked into his kitchen and been attacked. Now? Mason tried to move. His arms were tied to the chair, behind his hips, one on each side of his body. His feet felt like they'd been tied as well.

A moan escaped his lips.

The man looked over. Mason heard, "...or he dies."

Then the guy touched the screen of the phone or whatever it was he held in his hand. He walked over and moved so his face was right in Mason's. No problem focusing now.

"You." It was him, the bank robber.

The man chuckled.

"Sarah Palmer."

"That's what you wanna talk about?" The man moved behind him and snipped the ties holding Mason's arms to the sides of the chair.

Finding his hands suddenly free, Mason pulled them to the front. A sharp pain at his neck stopped him.

The man said, "Easy, or you overdose like that secretary did."

"She was an executive assistant." Why that came out of his mouth at a time like this, Mason wasn't sure. There was so much roiling through him. Anxiety. Fear. He wasn't sure what to do with it all, so he was talking nonsense.

This was about Talia, wasn't it? She'd been targeted. He'd

been worried she would continue to be targeted, but it turned out it was him that was the weak link in all this. The one who became the victim of whoever this guy was.

The man tied his hands together in front, then cut Mason's feet free.

"We're going somewhere?" His head was a little clearer now, but not much. He was still at home.

"Walk." He hauled Mason to his feet.

"So you can kill me elsewhere?"

"I could kill you right now. Doesn't make much difference to me, she'll still access the Secret Service's computer system and get what's needed."

"So I'm leverage?" He wasn't sure if that was better, or worse, than being the weak link. His brain couldn't quite process the whole thing well enough to figure out an answer. What he needed to do was make a plan to get free from this guy.

The man pulled a gun. He pointed it at Mason, out of reach. Mason would get shot if he even tried to fight the guy. "Walk. Fast."

Mason took two steps down the hallway. Whatever happened, Rayna would be told he'd died. That thought almost gave him the will to ignore the risk and bat away that gun with his bound hands, before he then launched himself at the guy. His reactions were way too slow though. He'd get shot just for trying.

The gun jabbed in his back. Mason was walked to his own car, and the bank robber said, "Pop the back open."

It was an SUV. His SUV. Mason grabbed the handle on the back door and pulled it open. Was he going to get shot in his own car? "Why are you doing this to Talia?"

The man smirked. "You think I'm going to tell you?" He paused for half a second. "Get in." He leaned close. "Now."

They were in a hurry? That meant the longer he could stall this guy, the greater the chance of rescue...or getting shot. Or taken as a hostage.

Mason sat on the back bumper and started to scoot back using his hips. He held up his hands in front of him, as though being bound made the rest of him basically useless. He could play it like he wasn't thinking straight. "Give me a second."

"In a second you're gonna be dead."

"Then tell me what you want with Talia." His thoughts were clearing now.

But the gunman didn't say anything. He lifted that weapon and aimed it at Mason's chest. *No. Rayna. Talia.* Yes, in that split second he thought of those two women. His daughter, and a lady he'd met only today. One he'd wanted to help, and get to know better.

Mason sucked in a breath as those thoughts raced through his head.

The bank robber pulled the trigger.

A flash exploded in front of his face and Mason fell back inside his SUV.

The door slammed shut.

———

"Get out of my way!" Talia screamed in their faces.

Two Secret Service agents blocked her. One younger, maybe a rookie, the other middle aged—guys working late on their case. And *neither* wanted to let her through. Well, they might have guns, but she had attitude.

"He'll be dead before we get there!" She screamed the words in their faces. Appealing to their concern for a fellow agent could work. Assuming they looked past her being up in their space.

The younger one flinched, but neither moved.

"Ms. Matrice." Stanton kept calling her that. She wasn't sure he actually had anything to say. Maybe he would just keep saying that until *Mason was dead.* He stood behind her. If he touched her, they would learn what crazy looked like. Mason had been kidnapped. Tied to a chair. If she didn't do something, that bank robber was going to kill him. Didn't they understand that?

"Talia." Victoria's voice was all schoolmarm. "Take a step back."

She swung around to face her boss. Before she could scream something else at all of them, Victoria lifted one finger. "No."

Talia closed her mouth. Then she took a breath. "He's going to die."

They'd had to tell the Secret Service about the video. No other choice on that part. But the fact she was part of the bargain to save his life? No.

A man had beaten and tied up Mason. That was the priority here. Life.

So they hadn't told the Secret Service *why* Mason was targeted. Neither had they told them why she'd been the one who received the video. Their focus had to be Mason. Hers was going to be damage control.

But if it saved a man's life, who cared?

"Your job right now is to get that hacker out of my system," Stanton told her.

Oh, so now he needed her help? She was mad, but that actually helped her sound more convincing. Not like she was purposely stalling. "Is it more important than someone's life?"

"It is equally as much of a threat." Stanton folded his arms. "Unless you're prepared for the firestorm that will come after I file a report that says you did nothing about a breach in my system."

Talia hadn't exactly done nothing, considering she was the one who'd let the hacker in the system in the first place.

It was that, or let Mason die.

"I need to be there. To make sure he's okay." She sounded as scared as she felt. So at least she was being honest. Still, they were right that she had to get the bank robber out of their system. Or help their techs do exactly that.

She had to get the timing right, though. Allow him enough time in their system to do what he wanted, while also getting the agents to go to Mason as quickly as possible. As in, before the bank robber could kill him.

"Alvarez is at Mason's house." Victoria looked up from her phone. "He'll get Mason back in one piece."

A sick feeling rolled through her stomach like the rinse cycle. Even though she was in the middle of a huddle of four people, their closeness didn't help. Maybe even made it worse.

Victoria's expression didn't change. "Right now they need your help."

This was what they had to do...she had to stall to give the bank robber enough time. No matter that it felt like betrayal, it was the best play they could come up with. Fast enough to actually give them a shot at minimizing his access *and* getting Mason back.

"Talia."

She'd let him into their system, and now she had to get him out. This was how they'd arranged it. She lifted her chin. "Fine."

Just like the bank. Would she end up like Sarah Palmer, dead in her bathroom?

It had to look like she was a disgruntled employee. Victoria had been right there and heard every word of the threat against Mason's life—every word of what Talia was supposed to do for the hacker. About how she was supposed to get him access to the Secret Service's network, a secure, unhackable system. He hadn't said anything about her not keeping tabs on everything he did.

Now the Secret Service had to believe Victoria was the one who could keep Talia in check. That the director was their ally with the team. It was a delicate balance, a power play Talia didn't like, but to be honest—everything was about politics. Even the federal government was about who you had on your side, bringing the weight of their influence to the table.

She walked back to where her tablet sat on the conference table. Checked to make sure it was still recording the path he took through their system.

"We need him out of there." Stanton stood behind her, though she didn't think he spoke to her this time. It appeared the whole group had followed her back to the conference room.

She held her tablet to her front and squeezed through them,

not willing to make eye contact even with Victoria as she moved out of the room. She wanted to know Mason was all right.

She wanted to know she hadn't just let a hacker into a secure federal network for no reason.

Victoria hadn't even batted an eye about essentially negotiating with a terrorist, or giving in to their demands. Not when a life was at stake. They were on the same page about that, at least. She'd told Talia to do it on the way to the door, where she'd yelled for Welvern. And then she'd sent him to go get Mason.

Alvarez was there.

The team was on their way.

Talia got to the closest computer and sat down. She bypassed the whole login screen and went straight to the command window.

Lines of green text scrolled up the screen.

Talia typed. She pushed away all the worry and fear and looked for a brute force way to simply eject him from the system.

He'd bested her before.

Don't think about that right now.

Victoria's phone rang. Her voice was quiet when she said, "Bramlyn." A pause, then she sighed. "Copy that. Keep me posted."

Talia turned, her hands still tapping keys. She could go for a short time not looking, but eventually she'd mistype something.

Victoria saw her. "Alvarez got to the house. Mason was held there, but he's gone now. So is his SUV."

Assistant Director Stanton pulled out his phone. "This is an abduction. I'll have to notify the FBI."

"Welvern probably already called them."

"Still…" Stanton stepped away, on his phone.

"Get him out, Talia."

She turned back to the computer. "I'm trying."

Where was Mason?

10

U p in the computer lab it took an hour for Talia to manage to evict him from their system. A hard shutdown that was unavoidable. They'd rebooted their entire network and, as it had come back up, she uploaded a program that denied him access. But was it too much, or not enough? She could have used a different method. Would it have worked better? They were on the clock. If he'd gotten what he wanted from the Secret Service's system, did that mean he was now going to have Mason killed?

She couldn't help doubting herself.

Talia didn't know if the abductor was the hacker or not. She did know he was the bank robber. She'd heard his voice and saw his face on the video.

Her fingers drifted toward her tablet. She pulled her arm back. Watching that video again wasn't going to do her any good. She needed to focus on their network.

She leaned back in the chair and watched the network scan, reading the results as they filtered down the page. There were a couple of spots where they could use help closing a vulnerable part of their system. She'd include that in the final report, and their techs could do the work to implement her suggestions. Or they wouldn't. As hot as everyone was on data security these days, some people just didn't want to know. Or they couldn't be bothered to do the work to make things as secure as possible.

The government should be on the cutting edge. But the truth was, every time a private party invented some new technology or way of doing something, it put the government behind the curve. Always playing catch up.

"Did it work?"

She spun to Stanton. "Any word on Mason?"

He shook his head, standing straight. "Your friend Alvarez is heading the search along with Assistant Director Welvern. They say it won't take long."

"You were right to defer to him." She had total faith in her teammate. "He's the best."

Stanton didn't nod. "And the network?"

"We should know soon enough what he looked at."

They'd told the Secret Service that the threat on Mason was a different occurrence than the network breach. Not the truth—that her enemy had leveraged Mason's life on her giving him access from the inside.

As far as the Secret Service was concerned, there were two problems in the pipeline right now. That was the truth. They just didn't know it was Talia who connected them.

Later, when they knew all of it, she would have to answer to them. As would Victoria. It occurred to her that Victoria could hand her over. Feed her to the wolves, as it were. Talia had reasons why that wouldn't surprise her, even if the betrayal would sting.

"Keep me posted."

She nodded, and Stanton strode out. He'd done flybys every half hour or so. That was the fourth one she'd endured, as though she wouldn't alert him right away if they discovered precisely what the hacker had looked at.

Talia went back to her tablet and took a look at the program she'd set in motion after the hacker entered the system. Sure, the Secret Service network techs were looking at the same information. It would take them hours to comb through it, and they had to get everything else back up and running fully first.

Her phone buzzed. The sudden noise made her jump, and she almost dropped the tablet. With shaky fingers, she lifted the phone and turned it face up. Then pushed out an exhale. Just her mom.

COULDN'T SLEEP. WAS URGED TO PRAY FOR YOU.

Talia sent a text back.

PRAY FOR MASON.

Her mom's reply came almost as quickly. She was going to pray for both of them, despite having no clue who Mason was. Talia probably should pray as well.

Why hadn't she done that right away when the video came in? Then she might've gotten a better idea of what to do that didn't include allowing a hacker into the system. At the time, she hadn't been able to figure out a way to save Mason's life. Other than supervising everything the hacker did, and then kicking him out at the first opportunity.

She scrolled through lines of text on her tablet and fought back tears. Maybe she should just quit her job. Her whole life, even. Get offline, permanently. Too bad this was what she was good at. Too bad the hacker had poisoned everything good in her life—even this. Her work had meant everything to her, and now she didn't even want to do it because he'd twisted it into something horrible.

Mason's life.

Those girls.

The one who'd died. Whose identity her friends at the NSA were still attempting to discover.

Talia swiped a tear from her cheek. The FBI saved the rest when Victoria had saved her. The hacker had tried to sell her, but he hadn't succeeded. All those middle men had been rounded up. Maybe shot, probably just put in jail though. Shame. People who did that deserved to have the full weight of justice brought down upon them.

Now this? Mason's life was in danger. A man with a daughter.

The thought of the hacker doing to Mason's daughter what he'd done to Talia made her want to vomit into the trash can under the desk. She tossed the tablet on the desktop. Reading right now was pointless. She wanted to know Mason was all right.

"I got something!"

She turned to see a man with Indian coloring wearing a white lab coat rush over, face flushed.

"What is it?"

"I know what he accessed."

The half dozen people in the room all stopped what they were doing. She walked with the group to the middle of the lab, where a computer screen stretched across the desktop.

Talia waved at the screen. "Do you mind?"

His eyes widened. "It would be my honor."

Talia wasn't sure she would go that far. "Thanks." She swiped through his results. "You're right. You did find what he looked at."

He beamed.

It was a classified file.

"Do any of you have the clearance to get into this folder?"

They all shook their heads. Talia got her phone, so she could call Stanton back down. He likely had the password to access this file folder. Then they would know what the hacker had looked at.

Before she'd found his contact, the door whooshed open and Victoria strode in. "Alvarez got him."

Talia almost sagged to the floor. Mason was all right. The fear squeezing the life from her loosened and left her with no equilibrium. She knew what to do with terror choking her. Without it, there was nothing to hold onto. She grabbed her tablet, phone, and purse. "I'm coming with you. I want to see him."

"But—"

Talia motioned to all the Secret Service network techs. "These very capable people can hold down the fort here."

They all shifted, like a flock of birds fluffing their feathers. Talia strode as fast as she could to the door.

She wanted to see Mason for herself. If he was hurt, then all this would have been for nothing.

Again.

———

Mason handed Alvarez back his phone. "Thanks."

"She's good?"

He nodded, then realized how much doing that hurt. His ears still rang from his close proximity to the gun going off. The bullet had barely missed his head.

He sighed. "Rayna is safe at home with her mom." Mason grabbed the handkerchief Alvarez had given him and started to get up from the bumper of the back of his SUV.

"Not yet." Alvarez put pressure on Mason's shoulder until his legs buckled, and his butt landed back on the interior carpet. "Wait for the ambulance."

It pulled up a couple of minutes later. Parked beside them in the superstore lot where the bank robber had left the vehicle.

Mason let them prod and poke him even though he knew for a fact his nose wasn't broken. His wrists were red, the skin abraded, from being restrained. "Just put goop on them, and I'll be good."

"No can do, my man," the paramedic said. "Gotta get you all checked out by a doctor."

"I'm fine."

"You're not medically qualified to make that assessment." The paramedic shrugged. "Neither am I, so you're coming in with me. Your friend here can pick you up later."

Alvarez had stepped away and was on his phone.

Mason decided to tell the truth. "I've never seen that guy before in my life."

The paramedic frowned. "Huh."

Secret Service agents he worked alongside milled around. They'd been there with Alvarez when he pulled the back door of the SUV open and cut Mason free. As had a handful of FBI agents, and that guy Welvern. This had turned out to be a multi-agency operation. All for little old him?

Okay, so he wasn't little or old—unless you asked Rayna—but that wasn't the point. Mason had been kidnapped from his house. The bank robber had made a video call to Talia, where he'd told her to let him into the Secret Service's computer network.

The guy threatened Mason's life, and he'd seen Talia's reaction. The bank robber had laughed at the look on her face. Then he'd given her ten minutes to give them access before he killed Mason.

But he hadn't done it. He'd driven Mason to this parking lot and left him here.

Did that mean...

No. There was no way he'd actually gained access to their system this way. Talia and Victoria would never have complied with the demand. They'd never have given in to a threat.

After the bank robber got off the call, he'd gotten a notification of some kind. Then he'd tapped his phone for a few seconds. Contacting someone, or trying to hack the Secret Service from a cell phone? Mason didn't know. But they needed to find the guy so he could get the answer.

"Ready?"

Mason took the ice pack the guy handed him and got up. His head swam, and he had to grab for the paramedic.

"Didn't figure you'd want to get on a stretcher." The paramedic took some of his weight, until Mason could get his balance.

If he'd been under orders from someone, they hadn't felt the need to keep close tabs on him. Maybe he wasn't the one who'd wanted access to the Secret Service network and maybe it was the person in charge instead.

Mason didn't know.

Nor did he know what the hacker could want from their system. They weren't involved in witness protection, and they didn't have anything to do with the president's security. Not on their end. Someone with the necessary skill could use their system to get information about daily security words, protocol updates or to take charge of the nuclear football. But that was a stretch. This would be a pretty roundabout way of getting into that stuff.

Maybe they wanted to make the president vulnerable for some reason. Doing it like this—using Talia and putting his life at risk—could be a way of throwing everyone off the scent.

He sat on the stretcher inside the ambulance and laid down, blowing out a slow breath.

"Yeah, you'll have bruises tomorrow." The paramedic flashed a penlight in Mason's eye. "Did you hit your head?"

"No."

The guy shined that light in his other eye. When he was done, Mason shut his eyes. Orange light flashed behind his lids.

"Mason!"

He lifted his head and looked to see who it was. Talia raced toward him. Mason sat up. She climbed into the ambulance while the paramedic shifted out of her way. "Whoa there."

She stopped, bent over him.

Mason moved his legs. "Sit down."

"I want to hug you, but you don't look good." Her eyes flared. "Not that you don't look good. That's not it. I—"

"Talia." When she closed her mouth, he said, "I could use a hug."

Both of them shifted, she sat on the stretcher, and he wound his arms around her.

"Are you okay?" Her breath touched the skin of his neck above his collar.

Mason had to hold back the shiver and gave her a quick squeeze. "I will be."

"I can't believe he kidnapped you." Her voice hitched, and he knew it was more than that.

"He was waiting in my kitchen when I got home."

She leaned back but didn't meet his gaze with hers. Why did he think that was about shame more than not wanting to look at his injuries up close? "He could've killed you. Like he killed Sarah Palmer." She bit her lip.

The paramedic busied himself, shifting supplies around. Probably just giving them a semblance of privacy in which to have a conversation.

Mason set his hand on her shoulder. "Come with me to the hospital?"

She nodded. "I want to know what they say about your injuries."

"Good. We can compare notes, see how to catch this guy. We don't want him trying to access the Secret Service network for real."

"You don't have to worry about that. We kicked him out of the system. He can't get in again."

Mason leaned back a fraction. "Again? He got in?" There was no way... "You let him into the system."

Talia lifted her chin, her lips pressed into a thin line. It bothered him that she hadn't had the time or the inclination to refresh her lipstick. She'd been that worried about him? Or just too busy.

Letting the hacker into their system.

Her voice was steady when she said, "He would have killed you."

Like that made it right?

11

"Talia!"

She spun to find who had called her name and heard the door to the ambulance shut. The engine revved, and it pulled away. But she didn't turn back.

Mason was mad.

He'd heard that video call happen. Any one of his colleagues, upon hearing the whole thing and understanding what had been at stake, would agree with her choice.

"Get over here!" That was Alvarez.

Beside him, Welvern glanced over and frowned. "Bro, you have no skills with the ladies."

Talia got close to their huddle. "He claims he doesn't think of me like that, more like a sister. Whom he will apparently happily yell orders at. Across a crowded parking lot."

"Sounds like the title of a country song," Welvern said.

They both glanced at Alvarez.

"What? I'm supposed to know about country songs?"

Talia figured if anyone would, it'd be him.

Instead of continuing the conversation about country music, Alvarez motioned to the departing ambulance. "He okay?"

Talia winced. "I don't think he appreciated my efforts to uh...

buy him time." Both of them stared at her. "He'd rather have been killed?"

"Who are you trying to convince?" Alvarez shifted his slender hips and cocked one knee, which she figured was to take weight off an old injury. His boot tapped the concrete.

"Don't give me your night-school, self-study psychology, m'kay?" She put all her frustration into her attitude. "We need to find this guy, not stand around picking apart my methodology."

Welvern shook his head, but she saw that smile play at his mouth. "That's why we called you over. My people found surveillance footage where the bank robber parked the SUV—" He motioned to Mason's abandoned car, now a crime scene. "—and walked off in that direction." He shifted his hand to the west, between him and Alvarez.

"Where did he go?"

Welvern said, "They backtracked the footage, looking to see if he left a car close by."

"He had to have done that after he killed Sarah Palmer, right?"

Welvern nodded. "It didn't take long, since they only had to wind back a few hours. They found a man they think is him, parking a car over there earlier this afternoon."

"He had a getaway car waiting."

"And it was parked there until the camera went dark about an hour ago."

Satisfaction surged in her. "Make and model?"

"And license plate," Welvern said.

She could have kissed him.

Alvarez broke in. "So he had this all planned out?"

"Looks like it." Welvern glanced back to her. "We have a BOLO out now to all law enforcement in the area. I'm confident we'll get a hit on it soon enough."

Alvarez had spent the entire conversation studying her.

Talia was kind of sick of him pinning her with that disap-proving stare. She shot him a look right back. "What?"

"You really didn't think he would be mad?"

"That I let the hacker into their system?"

"You gave in," Alvarez said.

"He'd have rather died? I bought time for you to find him, and yes that meant giving a hacker access to their system. But whatever he looked at, or did, was monitored. And the first chance I got, I ejected him from it."

"Risky move," Alvarez said. "Given how good he's proven himself to be."

"It was a gamble. But his assumption that he's better than me is going to be his downfall." She hoped. "I accounted for things I wouldn't have otherwise thought of, to give him the least chance of slipping away undetected." She lifted her hands, then let them fall back to her sides. "It worked, didn't it?"

Alvarez said nothing.

She turned to Welvern. "We'll find him, right?"

He nodded. "Might take time, but we'll get him. No one can hide forever."

Alvarez made a grumbling noise.

"Something to say?"

"I was *already* looking for the hacker." He actually huffed. "The trail was running cold, and then he just walks into the bank this morning?"

"You're mad you didn't find him first." Talia studied her colleague. Her friend. "It's okay that you don't win every single time, you know? You don't have to be perfect."

"This conversation is about you messing up, not me."

Welvern started to argue. Talia waved away his concern and said, "Its fine."

Welvern was a new addition to the group. Though not part of the task force, he'd been working closely with them for a couple of months.

She glanced at Welvern. "Alvarez is going to double down on this surveillance thing. No doubt he'll be scouring the streets all night for that car."

"Darn straight." Alvarez wandered off, long, skinny legs eating up the parking lot.

"Interesting fellow." Welvern chuckled.

She smiled. "He's a good guy."

"Oh, I know that. I've met enough bad ones to recognize goodness when I see it." He stared at her, a pointed look on his face. As though she should read something into that which she otherwise wouldn't.

"It's too late in the day for subtext." She brushed hair back from her face. "We've got a man to find, and an agency with ruffled feathers to soothe."

She thought about all those computer techs at the Secret Service office. People who knew her reputation from the circles they ran in outside the federal government. Okay, they were nerd fans, and she'd been around long enough she'd made a name for herself.

Welvern winced. "I don't envy Victoria that job." As he spoke, he motioned for her to walk with him toward his car.

She strode alongside him and noticed him shorten his stride so she could keep up. Did he do that with Victoria? Did she notice? Maybe she did but didn't appreciate what it meant to have a considerate man in her life.

Kind of like Mason.

No, they hadn't spent enough time together for her to know for sure. He'd kept her safe during a tense situation at the bank that morning, though.

It seemed like days ago, not just hours. Now Mason was in the hospital, and she had to convince the Secret Service—and him—that she'd made the right call. That she had done the only thing she could've in order to save his life. Which hadn't worked for Niall, back when he'd chosen his family's safety over the team and working the case. But that whole thing worked out in the end, hadn't it? Everything was fine now, and he had Haley in his life as well as in their office.

Welvern stopped by the passenger door. "Was it him?" Any

humor in his expression was gone now. "Was it the hacker?"

Talia shrugged, though it was hard to lift her shoulders even that much with the weight that seemed to sit there. "I don't know."

"We'll find him."

She nodded, and got in. When he turned away she let the shudder come over her. The hacker had targeted her, and now he'd gone after Mason.

None of them were safe until he was in custody, or dead.

Welvern climbed into the car. Before he could turn the engine on, she turned to him. "I want a protective detail put on Mason's daughter and his ex-wife. I don't want them getting hurt."

He nodded, and shifted to pull his phone out of the front pocket of his pants. "Of course. I'll have a team sent over."

———

A LIGHT TAP sounded on the door. Mason looked up from his iPad, where he'd been writing up his report on everything that had happened.

Victoria Bramlyn came into his hospital room, and shut the door behind her. "How are you feeling?"

Mason shrugged one shoulder. "Fine."

But disappointed it hadn't been Talia coming to see him.

She stopped at the end of the bed. "You're still mad." She said it with no inflection in her voice, no emotion either way on the subject.

That initial frustration over the fact she'd actually gone ahead and allowed a hacker access to the Secret Service network had burned hot. Since then, the fire had calmed considerably. He was still unable to believe she'd given in to a ransom demand. But he could also see why she'd done it.

"I get it." He smoothed down the edge of the blanket, feeling at a disadvantage. "I'd have probably done the same thing in her place." Especially if it was Rayna who'd been threatened, or even his ex-wife. Then there was Talia. His feelings for her were as complex as his feelings over this. "I may have overreacted."

Victoria's lips twitched. "I'm thinking you should tell Talia that."

He would have, if she'd been to see him yet. It had been hours since the ambulance. They'd run tests, and even done a CT scan. Apart from a few bruises and abrasions, he was totally fine. Though, they'd insisted he stay overnight just to be sure.

He'd spoken to Rayna, for longer this time. She had a detail of FBI agents in the living room, and her mother was trying to grill them for information she could use when she taught her next workshop at the university.

Victoria waved to the chair. "Do you mind?"

He shook his head.

"If you could go over for me exactly what he said and did, I'd be grateful. A clear picture of who this person is will help the ongoing efforts of the task force."

He wondered what the real reasons were. After all, that was as political of an answer to anything as he'd ever heard.

When he nodded, she said, "It was the same man from the bank?"

"Yes." She already knew that. Maybe it was like a control question on a lie detector test. "He hit me from behind, and when I came around, I was tied to a chair."

"What kind of knots?"

Mason hesitated, mouth open. He lifted his hands and looked at the bandages. Underneath, not visible at the moment, were two rows of abrasions on each wrist. "Two half hitches."

She nodded. "And the bruises?" She motioned to his face with a flick of one index finger.

"Punches and slaps, mostly."

"Military?"

He shook his head. "Open palm strikes. Martial arts, maybe."

She nodded again, then said, "Accent?"

Mason shut his eyes for a second. He knew she'd heard the

man's voice over the video call, but that was distorted the way a phone call could be. Not the same thing as hearing it in person. "Pretty generic. Only…"

He thought, but couldn't put his finger on it.

Victoria said, "I got a Canadian vibe from his word choices."

Mason considered that. "Maybe."

"Okay. Any impression he was the one doing the hack, like he initiated a program from his phone?"

Mason had thought about this a lot over the past few hours. "Wouldn't he have to do something like that on a computer? Is it really just enough to run a program?"

"I've seen Talia do it from her tablet, but maybe that was a unique circumstance."

"I'd have thought he would need to respond to things that come up in real time."

She said, "The alternative would be to simply flag everything labeled with a certain keyword, and then pull all those files. Or copy them to his own server."

Did she know what the keyword was? Seemed to him that someone like Victoria Bramlyn would be in the know about information like that. Mason had to wonder what the hacker had been after, and whether it was about their operation last weekend. That was the biggest thing they had in the works right now.

Victoria let out a frustrated sound that was incredibly delicate.

"What is it?" Maybe she would confide in him, and he'd have a better idea of what on earth was going on. He'd landed in the middle of a Northwest Counter-Terrorism Task Force operation with no idea which way was up.

"I don't like any of this." Her hands curled into fists on her lap. "I can't fight an enemy I can't see. A faceless, nameless scumbag who almost succeeded in *destroying* Talia's life. And her career. *And* her sanity." She shook her head, her gaze distant as though her thoughts were far away.

Mason spoke very carefully. "What happened to her?"

It took Victoria a minute to answer. "A few weeks ago, we were hot on the trail of a suspect with serious computer skills. Even Talia was having a hard time piecing it all together. She was going through the database for the lab that was destroyed down in Oregon…"

She paused long enough for him to nod because Talia had mentioned that incident, then she continued, "He breached the security in our office. That place was supposed to have been impenetrable, and yet he got in. Sent a team of mercenaries to drag her out."

Given her tone, Mason figured she had watched the video and it had been literal dragging.

Victoria said, "They took her to a huge house in central Oregon, a place known to be a brothel."

Mason's gut tightened.

"Threw her in the basement, where the girls sleep. Left her there for hours while the sale went down on the dark web. Cost me two million to get her back, and there's no way he didn't know full well it was me buying her. He let it go through and kept me from using any method of tracing where the money went. Which gives me no way to figure out who he is." She paused, flashing gritted teeth. "When the FBI raided the house, they found her in the corner of the basement, shackled to a teenage girl. The girl was dead."

Mason shut his eyes for a second.

"She was also African American. And fifteen."

"That's why she reacted to Rayna like she did." He opened his eyes to see Victoria nod.

"Her therapist is providing me with weekly reports. So far she hasn't mentioned the girl Welvern wrote about in his report. The one whose identity she's asked the NSA to find out."

"Isn't there an issue of doctor/patient confidentiality at play there?"

Victoria didn't look the least bit offended by his question. "This is how my team works. Full disclosure. And I'm not looking for any new members right now, in case you were curious. The roster is full."

"Was I asking?"

Before she could respond to what had been a rhetorical question anyway, her phone buzzed. She pulled it from her coat pocket and looked at the screen. "She's here." Victoria stood and pulled her coat on. "Get her to relax. She needs to sleep."

Mason never got the chance to ask her what that was about before she slipped from the room. A minute later, another tap sounded on the door. "Come in."

The door opened a fraction, and Talia stuck her head in. "Hey." She looked nervous. Probably at the thought that he was still mad at her.

He shot her a small smile. "Come in." He waved toward the chair. "Please." While Victoria's words stuck in his mind. *Shackled to a teenage girl.*

Dead.

12

T alia awoke in the same chair she'd been sitting in the night before, talking to Mason. Sunlight streamed in the window, across his jeans-clad legs. He was upright in the bed, fully clothed with his shoes on. He sipped from a mug as he read a newspaper he'd spread across that rolling table.

She must have made a noise, because he turned to her. Soft eyes, and a slight smile. "Hey."

That voice. She'd fallen asleep listening to it. And for the first time in weeks, hadn't woken up in a cold sweat with nightmare images rushing through her head.

She shifted and realized a blanket had been laid over her. Then she heard her phone's low chime. She reached into her purse on the floor and pulled it out. The number on the screen was the task force office. "Matrice." Her voice sounded groggy from sleep.

"It's Haley," the caller said. "Did I wake you up?"

"It's fine." She cleared her throat. "What did you need?"

"I should have sent you an email. I'm sorry. I just wanted to make sure you were okay, as well as update you on the progression of the case."

Talia shifted in the chair, grabbed the blanket with one hand and balled it in her lap. "So, update me."

"As long as you're okay."

"Hon, I'm fine."

They both knew that wasn't true. Haley knew better than anyone else as to the state of play in Talia's head. The things she hadn't told anyone else—the nightmares, for one—but that Haley, as her roommate, hadn't failed to pick up on. Talia was pretty sure her new friend and roommate had told her boyfriend everything. Talia would have, had she been the one in that position. It had to be why NCIS Special Agent Niall O'Caran had been looking at her with so much pity lately.

It was hard to get away from those compassionate looks. They were all hyper protective of the people they cared about. The fact none of them had prevented her from being abducted made the tension in the office skyrocket. Thankfully, only Haley was there on a regular basis.

The rest of them worked cases in the field, but the former Navy petty officer was the office manager.

Haley sighed, loud enough Talia heard it through the phone line. Out the corner of her eye she could see Mason. Reading his paper like he wasn't listening to her side of the conversation.

Haley said, "Josh and Dakota hit a snag in their case. I ran the photo they sent me through your system, like you told me, but I didn't get anything back."

"And the next step?" She kept it vague, because Mason didn't need to know about *everything* she had access to.

Haley said, "Someone is there, and you can't talk much?"

"Did you run it through the secondary program?"

"Yes. Nothing there, either. Is there anything else we can do?"

"I can take a look." Though she'd need to be in the office to do that. Her tablet didn't get that deep in the weeds of what she could do. "Later, maybe."

"Thanks. Until they get another lead, they're pretty much

dead in the—" Haley stopped speaking halfway through the word. "Sorry. They've stalled out."

"It's fine. Anything else?"

"Couple things I'll send you. Nothing urgent." Haley chuckled for a second. "Dakota's wedding dress pictures."

"She tried some on?"

"Yep." Haley chuckled. "And she had the sales assistant take photos of her since we couldn't be there. Oh wait, sorry. Because she didn't *need us* to be there."

Talia laughed. "That woman."

"Right? But she still needs us to help her decide?" Haley said, "For the record, I'll totally take you when I go looking for a gown for *my* big day. We should drag Dakota along with us, just so we can make her suffer."

Talia's smile held. "Shouldn't be too long. Your boy is getting antsy."

"He's not the only one," Haley said, a smile in her voice. "Right now, I'm just glad Dakota is wearing a dress and not getting married in boots and jeans."

"And a jacket."

Both of them laughed. It felt good. Unfamiliar, but still good. Mason glanced over and studied her until she looked down at her lap. This conversation was nice and all, but there was an important question to ask. Especially since she hadn't had time to talk to Mason when she woke up.

Talia squeezed the hand in her lap into a fist, clutching the blanket tight in her grip. "Have you heard from Alvarez?"

Haley was quiet. Yes, Talia had sounded strained. Maybe the enjoyment would last longer once this guy had been caught. Or would they come up against another case, another bad guy? She probably needed a vacation. And she would take one, if she didn't think he'd just target her wherever she went.

Haley said, "He's on it. That's all I know right now."

Apparently that was all Talia was going to get, too. It did make her feel better. "Thanks." She ended the call.

Alvarez was good. Really good. It wouldn't be long before the bank robber was in custody. She wasn't going to get mad that he was still loose. She was just going to be grateful when he was caught. The team didn't respond well to someone getting mad that they were taking too long to get a result, and Alvarez was worst of all.

"Everything good?"

Talia looked at Mason and saw he'd folded the newspaper closed. She shrugged. She was okay, but that wasn't the same as being good.

The nurse came in, and Mason was given discharge papers. They wanted to wheel him down to the front door in a wheelchair, but when he hopped off the bed and lifted a backpack off the floor, the nurse quit trying to argue.

He glanced at Talia. "Ready to go?"

She nodded, and they made their way downstairs to where Welvern waited in the lobby. He said nothing, but handed Mason a set of keys. "Parked at the curb."

"He can't drive." She looked between the two men.

Welvern gave her a wave as he turned, then headed for the door. She shifted to face Mason and put her hand on her hip.

Before she could say anything, he set off for the side door— the pickup lane. "Come on." He leaned his back against the door and used his weight to push it open. "We can't leave a car unattended at the curb for long."

Talia followed him. He stopped right outside and waited for her, his gaze scanning the area. Protecting her from threats. "Do you think he's watching?"

Mason beeped the locks and pulled open the front passenger door for her. "Can't be too careful."

She stopped between the door and the frame. "Are you really okay to drive?"

His face was kind of swollen on the left cheekbone, and he had a decent black eye coming in. "Pull your legs in."

She did as he told her, not convinced that he was all right.

She just didn't want to argue about it. When he got in the driver's side, she shifted to face him. "Are you one of those alpha male guys who can't sit in the passenger seat while the woman drives?"

He turned on the engine and pulled out. "You mean guys who protect the woman they're with?"

"By needing to be in control of everything." Yes, she had a *tone.*

The corner of his lips twitched. He reached over and squeezed her hand. She didn't want to let go, but refusing to do so would be weird enough. He didn't need to know she was a total basket case.

She looked at her phone screen again.

Still nothing from Alvarez.

———

MASON KEPT his attention on the road in front and behind, watching for any car that might be following. Apart from the ones he already knew were there, of course.

Talia didn't need to be aware she had more than just him watching her back right now. And if he could manage it, she wasn't going to find out.

He took her directions and headed to her place—an apartment her coworkers had already told him she shared with their office manager. Haley Franks, the woman who was dating Niall the NCIS agent. The one Talia had been on the phone with.

Laughing. Smiling that beautiful smile of hers.

He reined his thoughts back in.

Welvern had tried to explain the relationship status of each task force member. He ended up sending Mason an email that laid out all their names and the agencies they worked for, along with who was dating who and who was engaged. It wound up looking like a family tree, with Victoria at the top. The matriarch presiding over all of them.

"So, what are we doing at my place?" she said as he pulled up in a visitor's spot.

Catching a bank robber.

He smiled at her. "You're taking a shower, or doing whatever to get ready for the day. Then I figure we'll be due for breakfast before I take you to the office."

"You don't need a shower?"

"I washed up at the hospital, after one of my coworkers brought me the change of clothes I keep in my locker."

She eyed him.

"Stanton told me I don't need to go into work until tomorrow. I figure that means the only way I'm going to stay updated on this case is to stick with you."

Those eyes on him narrowed.

"Assuming you're going to work today, and not take it off." He paused. "Though, if you want to make it a half day and then go see a matinee movie later, that might be fun. I haven't seen a movie during the day in forever."

Talia cracked the door and gathered up her purse, still giving him that look. When she turned away and climbed out, he breathed a sigh. Then realized she could be in the line of fire right now. He got out his side and trotted around the car, the way he would with any other protective detail.

Yes, he'd hoped to get on the detail that protected the President. However, that was back when he'd lived in Virginia. Now that being in Washington state meant being close to his family, he was reluctant to give that up. At least until Rayna went to college.

The fact Talia worked in this part of the country as well... Mason didn't want to get ahead of himself. Except, he did this with every relationship—considered all the possibilities and outcomes. Thinking about it was part of his process. But it was also what had kept him single for so long. He was generally reluctant to jump into a relationship if he already knew all the ways it could go wrong.

Mason led Talia to her front door, backpack over his shoulder.

She knew what he was doing but didn't call him out on it. If she had, he'd simply have told her that protecting her had become imperative. Kind of like the way she'd protect him by making the choice she had, letting the hacker into the Secret Service network.

Despite all the ways his mind could come up with for how a relationship could go wrong—most of which ended with one or both of them getting killed by the bank robber—it was all being overridden by his need to stick with her. To ensure her safety.

At least until this guy was caught.

Would they have a relationship involving coffee dates or dinners past that? He didn't know the answer, only God did. Mason trusted that God had brought her into his life for a reason. If it was only so he could protect her, then he would know it was for good reason. Were it to turn into something a whole lot more, Mason would praise God every day she was in his life.

His phone started to ring just as she let them into her apartment. Talia turned to him. He didn't pull the phone out.

She stared.

"You should go take your shower."

"O-kay." She shook her head as she walked down the hall, calling back, "Make yourself at home then, I guess."

He pulled out his phone, and the second she clicked the door shut, he looked at the screen. It was Welvern.

"Anderson."

"Everyone is in position," the FBI assistant director said.

"Any sign of him while we were on the road?"

"Nothing." Welvern sounded disgruntled about that.

"You really think he's going to make a move with both of us here in the apartment?"

"We publicized it pretty widely," Welvern said. "Anyone who is local law enforcement that knows anything about what happened at that bank knows exactly where you two are right now."

"You're counting on one of them blabbing to the wrong person, or being in league with him?"

"Or that he's dialed into one of our channels somehow."

Welvern sighed. "This whole thing is making Victoria crazy. She wants him brought in so badly she's about to blow. I had to talk her down from sitting with the sharp shooter across the street just so she can get a shot at taking him out. Alvarez is about to rip someone's head off."

Mason heard the shower turn on. "She doesn't know he's close."

"Maybe he broke off," Welvern said. "Could be he spotted one of us and ditched the idea."

"Or he's in Mexico, and we'll never see him again."

"Could be."

Mason said, "Not sure which I'd prefer at this point. But if he shows up, at least we'll get him. Then she won't have to worry he's still out there."

"Exactly." Welvern said, "Gotta go."

Mason hung up. He made coffee, because it was better than standing there waiting for something to happen.

While it percolated, he walked down the hall. His gun was snug in the back of his pants, ready, in case he had to pull it out. He slowed by the door to the bathroom where Talia had disappeared. If he could hear nothing, he'd assume she was good. Welvern had assured him that her apartment had been swept before he and Talia got there.

He wasn't too worried about—

"I can't do that, Dakota." Her muffled voice was audible through the door. "No, I don't want to stay. I don't want to be anywhere near Mason Anderson. You need to get me as far from him as possible—"

Mason took a step back. Hearing those words was like an audible blow.

"—or this very nice man, and his *daughter*, are going to wind up getting *killed*."

Before he could begin to process the fact she was scared for his life, and Rayna's, noise erupted from outside. The loud crunch of metal against metal. He raced to the living room window and pulled back the drapes to see outside.

A rusted-out, silver car had slammed into the back of the vehicle he'd parked in the visitor's spot.

Over a bullhorn, he heard someone say, "You are surrounded by federal agents. Step out of the vehicle with your hands up."

13

Talia tied the belt on her robe and stepped out of the bathroom into the hallway. "What was that? What's going on?"

Mason turned back from peering out the window. "Don't worry about it. Just take your shower."

"I'm done."

He frowned. "Already?"

She hadn't needed to wash her hair, and it wasn't the day for her to shave her legs, so it wasn't like washing off had taken long. Was she going to tell him that? No way. "I still need to get dressed." Like that wasn't obvious by the robe she was wearing. She'd secured her hair up for the shower, and it was still in the vinyl cap.

Bare feet. Not dressed. If her mother knew a man had seen Talia in this state, she'd have been horrified. Talia would've had to suffer—again—her hour-long lecture on what a "lady" should and shouldn't do. She could practically recite the speech verbatim at this point.

"Take your time." His smile wasn't quite honest.

Talia didn't turn and go back to the bathroom. She walked to where Mason stood, still clutching a fistful of window drapes. She peered past his shoulder and gaped at the scene outside. "What are all those federal agents doing in the parking lot?"

They looked to be surrounding a vehicle that had crashed into the car Mason drove her here in. Not his SUV, but the vehicle Welvern had loaned him.

Mason sighed. "They're arresting the hacker."

"Outside *my apartment?*" He was here? Fear rushed back, even after she'd worked so hard during her shower to push it aside and focus. Dakota was on her way. Talia didn't like the idea of Dakota being in danger, but between her gun, her fiancé and their dog, she didn't figure anything could get through. Mason, however, had no protection. Because he *was* the protection. He was fully deter-mined to stop any bullets fired at her.

Then where would his daughter be?

She couldn't even think about that.

Mason moved toward her, reaching out like he was going to comfort her.

She took a step back and shook her head. "You weren't plan-ning on telling me the hacker was outside my place, were you?"

He said nothing.

"I was the bait." Maybe they were both the bait, but she didn't waste time saying that. "They were lying in wait for him to show up so they could take him down."

"What do you want me to say?" His voice was soft, but not remorseful.

"How about, 'hey, Talia. We're going to arrest the bank robber while you're in the shower'." She probably looked like a crazy old washer woman, yelling at him in a bathrobe and a shower cap. He could deal, though.

The muscle in his jaw shifted.

"That's what I thought." She strode back to the bathroom and got dressed.

He'd seriously thought that being with her while she drew the bank robber's attention—and possibly his gunfire—was a good idea? She hated to think he didn't consider Rayna, or what would happen to her after he was gone. But seriously, hadn't he thought about that? The girl could wind up fatherless. All because Mason insisted on being the one to drive her here.

He should have gone home. She should've called Dakota hours ago. *God, I keep putting him at risk.* Tears gathered in her eyes. She couldn't be responsible for whether or not someone lived or died. Her heart couldn't handle that. Not now, and not ever again.

Talia slipped the dress over her head. She'd pulled it out of the "thin" side of her closet. Given how much weight she'd lost in the past few weeks, it was worth a try. The dress fell to her knees, no longer tight in the places it used to be. Looking at herself in the mirror, she had to admit she felt more confident than she had in weeks. Too bad the reason why.

All the better for Mason to watch her walk away.

She added enough makeup so she didn't look like she'd slept in a chair and spritzed herself with perfume. She slid her feet into a pair of nude Louboutin's and headed down the hall to the kitchen where she swiped her purse off the counter. She was halfway out the front door before Mason even turned around.

"Talia!"

She left the door open, though closing it in his face would have been satisfying. Talia trotted down the sidewalk to the crowd of federal agents. Welvern was there, but she didn't see Alvarez. The agents all seemed to be FBI.

In the center was a man with his back to her. Hands on his head, leaned over the hood of a car.

She didn't particularly want to study him so she allowed her gaze to move over him to Welvern. Just to prove that fear didn't have that much power over her.

The tablet in her purse chimed a few times. She hadn't looked at it since her shower. What was coming in now? News about the arrest, or something else?

She pulled it out. Victoria had a call coming in to her phone from the department at the NSA where Talia used to work, and

Niall needed to check his email because there was a DEA agent trying to contact him, and she was *mad*.

There were several other notifications, ones for her and not the team. Stanton still hadn't given the techs at the Secret Service permission to get that Prometheus file opened. Why was he taking so long? They all needed to know what the hacker had been trying to access.

Welvern got done talking to the agent he'd been speaking with.

"Hey." He turned at the sound of her voice. "Can you give me a ride to the office?"

"I'll take you."

Welvern glanced over her shoulder.

Talia twisted to see Mason behind her but ignored the unhappy look on his face. Why was he dragging this out? She turned back to Welvern, not prepared to respond to Mason's offer. "I'd like someone *else* to take me."

"I can do it." Welvern frowned, but his word was good. He would take her because she'd asked. "Just as soon as this guy is processed." Welvern showed her a cell phone and android tablet. "He had these in the car with him."

She shot Mason a pointed look. "Are these going to tell us what Prometheus is? Because at this rate we'll be waiting years for Stanton to get around to giving us access to the file the hacker got into."

They could hardly do damage control on the breach of information if they didn't know what it was about.

Mason's eyebrows rose. "Are you seriously trying to pick a fight with me right now, just because you're mad I didn't tell you these guys were following us?" He waved at the agents surrounding them.

The bank robber was patted down by an FBI agent, cuffs secured on his wrists.

"You think that's why I'm mad?"

Welvern said, "Dude, you didn't tell—?" He shifted before he could finish the question. All the agents moved. Spurred into action. Welvern yelled, "Everyone down!"

But it was too late.

Sniper rounds smacked huge holes in the hood of the closest car. Each round moved closer and closer in Talia's direction. The bank robber got hit. He and the agent holding him went down.

Talia couldn't move.

And then two hundred pounds of California redwood slammed into her and she was tackled to the ground.

———

"THAT ISN'T THE BANK ROBBER." It was the first thought to go through Mason's head. The moment they hit the ground, it came out of his mouth.

The shots continued.

Beneath him, Talia shifted. "No, it isn't him."

Mason figured she didn't need to see a dead guy. But before he could tell her to turn away, she shoved at him. "Get off me."

"Not until we're clear."

"You're not my bodyguard." She kept shoving. "Now get off."

The shots stopped. Still, he said, "Not yet." They weren't going anywhere until he knew for sure they were in the clear. "We've got two guys down over here," he called out to the personnel around him. "Someone get a headcount."

Welvern shifted and looked around. Mason saw the blood over his shoulder. The FBI assistant director tugged his right arm to lay it across his stomach and sat up behind the cover of the closest car. Then he keyed his radio. "Control, this is Welvern. I've got an agent and a suspect down." He paused a second, then added, "And I want all positions to sound off."

Talia's shoving got annoying, so Mason shifted off her. She tugged her purse across the asphalt and pulled out her phone. She tapped the screen, then held the home button down and held it close to her mouth. "Alvarez, you read me?"

She was using her phone like a walkie-talkie.

The phone screen lit up. "I copy. In pursuit of sniper. He's on the run on the north side of the complex, headed west." Alvarez's voice was breathy, like he was racing after someone just as he'd said.

Welvern nodded in Talia's direction, then called out, "All available agents to the north side, suspect is headed west on foot. US Marshal in pursuit."

Then the FBI assistant director's face flushed pale, and he laid back.

"Mark!"

Mason glanced over. Welvern had been hit?

Talia crouched and moved over to him, waddling on her heels, trying to stay low. She sank down beside him. Blood covered his side, low and close to his hip.

She turned back. "I need something to put on this wound." She looked at Mason, pleading with her expression. She needed his help.

Mason wanted to point out that a few minutes ago she'd been insistent on *not* needing his help. But Welvern was bleeding on the asphalt, so he didn't bring that up. Mason unbuttoned his shirt and handed it over. Underneath he had a T-shirt on, since his father had instilled in him the importance of an undershirt before every Sunday church service. Old habits were hard to break.

Like protecting a woman, even if that wasn't what she wanted. And why not? It was bizarre. As though she didn't want his help at all.

The ambulance arrived, and EMTs started treating the injured. There were three agents wounded, Welvern being the worst. One was dead, as was the man they'd arrested from the car. The man who hadn't been the bank robber.

Mason went through the guy's pockets and found his wallet. Tucked in the front of his jeans was a wad of folded twenties. Four, maybe five hundred bucks. An agent held out an evidence bag. Mason dropped it all inside.

The agent said, "You think he was paid to hit the car?" motioning to the wreck.

"Maybe."

Talia stood close by, where the EMTs were working on getting Welvern patched up. Her elbow was scratched, bad enough that blood dripped onto the pavement beside her foot. Mason pulled a handkerchief from his pocket, mentally thanking his father for instilling that in him as well. He moved to her side, going slow, but she jumped anyway. He touched the cloth to her elbow.

She sniffed.

"Sorry."

"It's okay."

Her voice was soft. He lifted his gaze. "You okay?" Even though they both knew she wasn't.

Her phone broke in before either of them could say anything else. Alvarez's voice. "Suspect is in custody." The marshal let out a frustrated grunt. "Don't even try it." He paused, long enough for Mason to realize he was wrestling with the suspect. "We're headed for the Secret Service office. Stanton called first dibs on questioning him."

Talia lifted her gaze, and one eyebrow.

Mason shrugged. "The bank connection, and the transfer to you, make it a financial crime. Which is the Secret Service's jurisdiction."

"I didn't even know you guys investigated stuff like that."

Most people didn't, which was the way they liked it. The FBI had their thing, and the Secret Service had theirs. Turf wars weren't fun for anyone, and rare, but adding in the Northwest Counter-Terrorism Task Force was certainly proving interesting.

Welvern was taken away, though not before he gave Mason a new set of keys and told him which car belonged to him. Talia called Victoria to tell her what had happened before Mason could even tell her that Victoria was here somewhere.

The boss told Talia that she was going to head to the hospital, then she'd go to the Secret Service office for an update. Everyone was looking to interrogate the bank robber, but that was going to be down to Stanton.

Talia said, "Do we know for sure the man Alvarez caught is the actual bank robber this time?"

"We'll know soon enough." He led her to where Welvern had told them he left his car. About half a mile away from the apartment.

"Being out here is giving me the willies." She even shuddered.

Mason wasn't sure she would accept it, but he slid his arm across her shoulders, giving her the chance to pull away.

Talia leaned into his side as they approached the car. "Thanks for driving me."

"I wasn't sure if you'd appreciate it."

She didn't say anything, just got in, probably because the answer to that was the fact she hadn't had anyone else here to do it.

Half an hour later, he had her all signed in through Secret Service security check-in. This could go badly if Stanton decided to throw his weight around about the breach. Mason intended to talk to him first thing. Get a read on where he was at with it.

He couldn't believe this was all related to a file on Prometheus. That couldn't mean anything good.

They took the elevator to his office. He glanced over as it rose. "How's your arm?"

She had the handkerchief balled in her hand and bent her elbow to see. "Stings."

"I'll find the first aid kit for you." The doors slid open, and he turned.

Stanton stood there. "Security said you were headed up." He glanced at Talia. "If you'd come with me, Ms. Matrice. I'd like to ask you a few questions."

She didn't exit the elevator. "For a chat between colleagues, or an interrogation?"

Mason had to hold the doors open.

Stanton said, "That will be entirely up to you, I think. But this department requires an explanation of why *you* let a hacker breach our system and obtain highly classified information."

She strode out, chin high. Stanton wasn't the type of guy to suffer a woman's attitude for long. Not a good characteristic, that lack of patience. He was old school. In this case, that meant a strong woman was unexpected, and he didn't consider it a positive trait. Mason had heard him say more than once that the female analyst from the second floor was "brash" just because her voice was louder than it needed to be.

Stanton said, "Let's head to the conference room."

"At least it's not a cell."

Mason followed them. "You aren't under arrest." He didn't really know what else to say. Should he tell his boss that he wanted to go with Talia? She likely didn't feel she needed him there. "Sir..."

Stanton said, "You have work to do, Agent Anderson."

Mason opened his mouth to ask what, but Stanton beat him to it. "I want Prometheus shored up."

Talia glanced between them. "This is bad, isn't it?"

Once they'd all laid their cards on the table—assuming Talia was granted clearance to know—then she would understand Stanton's issue. This was so much more than a breach of security. It was a leak of classified intelligence.

And the reason they'd set up that take down outside Talia's apartment.

"Yes," he told her. "This is very bad."

14

Two hours later, Talia lifted her head from the conference room table. Wasn't it lunchtime yet? She was actually hungry. This momentous occasion should probably be celebrated. "You don't think my skills would be better put to use trying to find out who this guy is?"

She was thinking entirely too much about a huge meatball sub.

Stanton sat back in his chair, his face completely impassive. "I think you should answer the question."

Talia sighed.

"After all," he said, "you haven't managed to ascertain his identity thus far. Despite allowing him access to our network."

Which was what Sarah Palmer had done with the bank. When she'd plugged a flash drive into her computer before leaving for the day…and was then murdered.

Did that mean Talia was next?

As it was, Welvern currently lay in a hospital bed in who-knew-what condition. No one had told her anything. She'd been in here with Stanton for hours now. Answering stupid questions over and over again. If she had more information to add, she would have offered it to him already.

Beyond the glass windows, Mason worked at his computer. Alvarez sat in a chair at an empty desk. Sipping coffee. She'd been counting, and he was up to his third cup. Waiting for what, she didn't know. The bank robber was in custody, and yet she was the one being interrogated.

Talia looked down at her hands. She'd canceled the standing appointment she had to get her nails done every two weeks. Why had she done that? She was enough of a mess without her nails making that completely obvious.

Stanton gave her a measured look. "What do you know about this person that you didn't know two days ago?"

She ignored the fact he'd assessed her and evidently found her lacking. "How about what he looks like?"

Not that it had helped, considering they hadn't found the bank robber in any database. Or online. Who in the world *didn't* have their picture on some site somewhere these days? He clearly had something to hide. Like his identity.

"He's just that good," she said. "But now he's in custody, because Alvarez caught him. So maybe you should go ask him all these questions."

"Am I bothering you, Ms. Matrice?"

He didn't want to know the answer to that.

Talia said, "Look, I'm sorry I saved Mason's life by allowing the hacker to have monitored access to your network. Now we have him in custody. Your agent is safe, and we know what he wanted considering the hacker went directly to a particular file and accessed it."

"My techs tell me you can't know for sure he purposely accessed the details of Prometheus," Stanton said. "There's no reason to believe he knew about it before Special Agent Anderson was abducted. Could be he simply found the most restricted file and figured there was something good in it, so he got into it assuming the contents would be juicy."

"He knew what he was looking for. And he knew it would take *me* to get it for him." She'd thought about this a lot over the last few hours. "The hacker knew that without someone inside to access the network and allow him in—just like he did at the bank with Sarah Palmer—there was no way he would be able to get the details of Prometheus."

"So I should applaud my people on a job well done?" He waved a hand, then let it drop back to his lap. "Because that means the only vulnerability to our security here…is you."

"I know." Always the weak link. She wanted to walk out the door. Go back to the task force office. Work on figuring out answers to the lingering questions. Too bad Stanton would probably have her arrested if she did that.

The hacker had targeted her. Did he know he would likely destroy her career in the process?

Out the corner of her eye, she saw Alvarez straighten. He set his cup down but didn't get up. Was the still-healing gunshot wound from a few weeks ago bothering him? Maybe he had pushed too hard today and now was in pain.

"If you would remain where you are," Stanton said.

She realized she had started to get up. See? Totally about to be arrested.

Before she could ask him what else he wanted to know, she spotted Victoria walking toward Alvarez. Talia's boss looked tired as well, but in tiny ways anyone who didn't know her really well wouldn't notice.

She spoke for a second with Alvarez, and he pointed toward the conference room. When Victoria looked over, Talia gave her a small wave. She didn't want it to seem like, *HELP ME.* But she did want to get rescued.

Victoria immediately strode over, not happy.

Behind her, Talia saw the curl of Alvarez's lips. Mason said something to him, and the marshal barked a laugh. That didn't entirely convince her. He was in pain.

Victoria twisted the handle and let herself into the conference room without invitation.

Stanton started to speak, but Talia cut him off. "Alvarez needs some Ibuprofen."

Victoria nodded. "He told me it's taking time to start working." They shared a look, then Talia's boss turned to Stanton. "This conversation is over. If you don't have what you need by now, you won't get it. File your report, and let's move on."

He stood. "I asked around about you. Got some interesting answers."

"This again?" Victoria didn't back down, but she also didn't show any attitude. Men saw emotions as a weakness. Especially federal agents like this guy. "You have your hacker, and my team is done here. Unless you require our unique brand of *assistance* with the Prometheus issue."

"What gave you the impression it's an issue?" Stanton paused. "And why are the two of you assuming I don't intend to arrest Ms. Matrice."

Talia was starting to feel awkward, watching them face off in front of her. She caught Alvarez's gaze through the window and made a face. He grinned. Talia pulled her phone from the floor beside her foot and sent him a text.

Is the bank robber being interviewed?

He tugged his phone out from his back pocket and sent her a reply.

That's Stanton's next job.

She nodded instead of sending a message back.

Alvarez sent her another text.

Is he going to arrest you?

She shook her head, then sent a text.

He'll try. I figure Victoria will argue him down to a formal reprimand.

That was the least of her worries right now. Victoria would cover her professionally, though this was so big there was a chance her boss wouldn't be able to do the kind of damage control that would keep Talia from getting fired from the NSA.

She figured if that did happen, Victoria would take her on as an independent contractor. After she fabricated an entirely new identity so no one knew the contractor was her.

Stanton was right up in Victoria's space now. "After that call to the Director of the Secret Service, I should call the President. See what he has to say about your task force."

Talia considered the idea that maybe she wanted out of the NSA, anyway. It wasn't like she needed to stay for the pay, considering the apps she'd designed and programs she'd written generated an income.

Then there was the last conversation with the director of the agency that still issued her paychecks. Like she was going to spy on Victoria for them.

Her boss said, "Maybe you should. Seems to me like you need all hands on deck to deal with the aftermath of this breach."

Talia didn't know what that meant. She'd been kept out of the loop on the fallout, not to mention on what Prometheus actually was.

She walked a fine line, but considering Victoria had asked for complete honesty before she would hire her, Talia had told her.

She'd told Victoria everything.

———

MASON PULLED the door open and stepped into the interrogation room where the bank robber had been situated.

"Finally." The guy made a wide gesture with his arm, the cuffs on his wrists clinking. "I've been waiting hours."

"Unfortunately for you." Mason dropped the file onto the table and pulled out the chair. "Given your recent choices, I'd expect your life will be on other people's timetables for some time to come. Judges. Attorneys. Prison guards, other inmates." He sat. "Your future is looking quite dim."

The man's eyes narrowed. "I'm sure we can make some kind of deal."

Mason leaned back in the chair. "That assumes you bring

something of weight to the table. Which means you'd have to have something to offer me."

He left the file closed on the table. They still had next to no idea who this guy was. Even after running his photo and fingerprints through every database known to man. Nor did they have a clue where he'd come from. But he didn't need to know that.

The bank robber studied him.

"So." Mason pulled a pen from his shirt pocket and waved it. "Whatcha got for me?"

"You have no idea who I am. Do you?" There was a glint of satisfaction in the man's eyes.

"You tied me to a chair and then proceeded to vent your frustration on me. All for the express purpose of persuading Talia to allow you access into the Secret Service's network. What more do I need to know? What name you've decided to go by for the benefit of our talk?" He shrugged.

When the guy said nothing, Mason asked, "Was it you who accessed the network, or are you under the employ of someone else?"

The man just sat there, his gaze on Mason. Older than him, maybe. Or he'd lived a hard life that put lines on his face. Time spent in the sun. A mercenary in some blazing hot foreign country?

Mason thought again about the conversation he'd had with Victoria at the hospital. This guy had been efficient in the way he punched and hit. Precise. He'd known how much damage he was going to do, and Mason was feeling every inch of it.

His thin lips spread into a knowing smile.

"Tell me what you know about Prometheus."

There was a slight hitch in his gaze, a moment of celebration he allowed to slip through.

Mason folded his arms, even though it hurt a couple of his bruises. "You know who we have in custody. Are you one of his men?" When the bank robber said nothing, Mason went on.

"Hoping to be in on the operation that gets him back out in the world, free to cause havoc again?"

The man started to chuckle.

"I see this was a waste of my time." Mason slid his chair back. "Clearly you don't know anything that could get you deal." He made a production out of pushing the chair in and gathering up the file. "Otherwise you'd have said something already."

He laughed the whole time Mason had been speaking. When Mason turned away, he quit, then said, "I know what he's going to do."

"Prometheus is in custody."

"Is he?" The man sat back in the chair, looking pretty smug. "When you realize the truth, I'll be here."

"Yes. You will." Mason let the door shut behind him and strode to the elevator, where he went up to his desk. Stanton was back in his office. Victoria now sat with Talia and Alvarez in the conference room.

Mason tapped his knuckles on the door of Stanton's office and then stepped in. He shut the door behind him.

"That bad?"

"Our man downstairs seems to think Prometheus has been severely compromised."

"Have you heard back from our people in place?"

Mason had been trying to contact their detail on Prometheus for the last few hours. The responses had been... He couldn't put his finger on it, but he'd been trying to get someone on the phone ever since the first email came in.

Stanton showed none of the worry coursing through Mason. In fact, the man looked stone cold. Because any problems could be blamed on the Northwest Counter-Terrorism Task Force?

Mason pulled out his phone. He didn't like the idea of throwing Victoria and her team under the bus. Prometheus was their thing. Despite Talia's part in the breach, it wasn't going to sit well with him if they were dragged into a war over whose fault it was if, or when, something happened.

Mason said, "No call backs yet. Just the same canned email."

Could something have happened?

"I'll call in as well. They should have responded to the request by now." Stanton clicked on his mouse. "We got an ID on our dead man with the money. Two stretches for B and E. Petty stuff, local."

"Hired to follow us and crash into the car so the guy downstairs could get the drop on us?" Had Talia been the target of those shots that had killed him and wounded Welvern?

"That's the consensus."

Mason thought for a moment. "I wish we knew what this bank robber guy knew about it, and how. Is this all just some plan from Prometheus—one of his guys trying to get him out? Maybe they hired a hacker with the skills to pull it off, and the bank robber is a foot soldier."

"And the hacker's history with the task force?" Stanton motioned to the windows in the direction of Talia and her friends.

Mason didn't have an answer for that. "Could just be coincidence that I was there at the bank when it happened."

"Or Ms. Matrice was right, and she was drawn into this for the express purpose of her giving him access to our system."

"Because he has a thing about targeting her."

Stanton shrugged. "She was just his guinea pig of choice, he could angle her to the bank. Get her on our radar. Get her dragged here to the office."

Mason tapped his foot on the floor. "The breach of our network was the plan. Getting her to the bank was just the first part." The hacker had made sure he was in position with Mason in time to make that video call. Whoever was behind it, this thing was heavily coordinated.

"She's been on his radar for a while, and he targeted her directly. I think since she got away from him before, he decided to use her for this. Whether that means he's related to Prometheus, or just a hired contractor, it got her pulled in."

Without that, they'd never have met.

Mason turned to look at them. Victoria sat close to Talia, her stance one of quiet conversation where they were possibly making a plan, or she was reassuring Talia. Alvarez sat off to the side, watching them and listening.

It was clear they were all close. The team seemed to be especially protective of Talia. Now that he knew she'd been abducted —and her experience so much worse than his—he understood how they felt. He didn't like the fact this guy seemed to have such an intense focus on her.

He wandered back to his desk but didn't know what to do next. He cleared out some emails and answered a couple of questions a junior agent had. It was almost time to clock out for the day. One he wasn't supposed to have been working anyway. He ran his hands down his face, feeling the swelling and wincing at the tenderness of the places he'd been hit.

So smug, that guy had been. Mason wanted to hit him back, but that wouldn't have been professional.

Stanton called out, "Anderson."

Mason turned and saw his boss stride over. "What is it?"

"No one is able to contact any of our agents at the safe house in person. We can't get anyone on the phone."

Mason's gut flipped over. That wasn't good. At all.

"What's this?" Victoria moved to stand with them. "You have a problem?"

"You know very well what this is," Stanton said. "And whatever the damage, it's on *your* team."

"Then perhaps you'd care to explain to me why you have a serious threat not in federal prison, but in protective custody?" Victoria folded her arms.

She knew about Prometheus?

"If this is going to land on my shoulders, I refuse to believe it's simply so the President can save face. There's more going on here, isn't there?"

15

They geared up and got on the road within fifteen minutes. Mason changed into tactical clothing, despite several side glances she saw him receive. She didn't blame them. He looked a mess from all the bruises and moved like he was stiff. She figured that didn't mean he was going to sit on the sidelines. Even Alvarez joined up with the team headed to the safe house where Prometheus had been located—after they'd confirmed his security clearance.

Talia watched while they had a quick briefing and then filed toward the door. Except Mason, who motioned for her to join him off to the side.

Considering Stanton and Victoria were still butting heads, she didn't mind letting them argue while she talked to Mason.

"What is it?"

Mason said, "Can you stay here until I get back? I'd rather you didn't go out on your own. At least not without protection."

Now he cared about her? Before he'd been content to have her be the bait to draw the bank robber out. She knew he didn't have time to argue about it, though. "I doubt Stanton will let me go anytime soon."

He made a face, communicating how he felt about that. It was nice to know he didn't consider her a threat. But that didn't mean the Secret Service were about to trust her with anything.

"Sir!" One of the agents on a desk stood and called out to Stanton. "Security said there are two agents headed up. Dakota Pierce, from Homeland Security Investigations and Josh Weber, DEA. They have a dog with them."

Stanton said, "Copy that."

Alvarez wandered past where Talia stood with Mason. "Hurricane Dakota just made landfall."

Talia smiled, then said, "Should you be going with them?"

"Ibuprofen kicked in."

"So you're fine now." She rolled her eyes. "You know it only masks the pain you're in. Which is your body trying to tell you that you're not a hundred percent."

"Of course I'm a hundred percent." Alvarez headed for the elevator.

"Yeah, sure." she called out. "Like the rest of us."

Alvarez shook his head and glanced back over his shoulder. "Anderson and I are just tagging along. The tactical guys are going to take point."

"And Josh. Take him with you." The second their DEA agent team member found out an operation was in the works, he was going to jump right in. Talia would be surprised if Dakota didn't try and get in on it as well, though she'd be torn between that and staying to protect Talia.

Mason said, "I've got to go." He took a step away from her. "You'll stay here?"

"I won't go anywhere without protection."

He frowned but nodded. He'd heard what she hadn't said, as much as what she had. Talia hadn't promised not to leave, she'd just promised not to be unsafe. She wasn't going to put her life at risk unnecessarily. If there was a problem, she might be able to help the Secret Service. Right? That could shore up her standing with them.

Not an opportunity she would allow to pass by.

The elevator opened. First out was Neema, who trotted into the office on her doggy paws like she came here every day. Her tail wagged as she moved to Talia, sniffed her leg and then made a beeline for Victoria.

"Love you, too," Talia said to the dog's back, a grin on her face. She spotted Mason, his gaze on hers. A soft expression in his eyes. "Are you a dog person?"

He said, "I think I am now."

Dakota said, "Talia!" Like they weren't both in the same room, as opposed to being across a football field from each other. She strode over, that take-charge stance rolling the sensation of being cared for through Talia's body. Her friends were here. Not all of them, but enough. She'd been friends with Dakota for years. Despite the fact Dakota didn't let many people past that tough outer shell. And she *definitely* didn't like it when Talia left a purple lip stain print on her forehead.

Josh stepped off the elevator behind her. Alvarez planted a hand on his chest. "Not so fast. We've got an op."

Dakota turned back to her coworker and her fiancé. "Without me?"

"Keep Neema with you," Josh said.

Dakota folded her arms. Mason stepped past her into the elevator with the other two men. "Hope it's boring and a complete waste of time."

Josh grinned. "Hope the coffee is awful."

The elevator doors slid shut. Dakota turned to flash Talia a grin. "He only *thinks* he's going to have fun without me."

Talia wanted to smile back, but what exactly was there to banter about? Nothing was right in her life. As opposed to Dakota, who was engaged and shopping for a wedding dress. Happy. Looking forward to the future with the man she loved.

She wasn't the target of a hacker. A crazy man up to who-knew-what.

Dakota blurred as she strode over. Talia realized it was because her eyes had filled with tears. Her friend put her arms around her, and Talia was gathered against her chest. "I know I look bad if you're hugging me."

Dakota's body shifted with a chuckle. "You look tired. You okay?"

"My life is a mess."

Dakota gave her a squeeze, then stepped back. "Happens to the best of us." There was a knowing look in her eyes. Talia didn't want to go there, though. She needed to keep this as light as Dakota and Josh had kept their goodbye.

Talia swiped at her eyes, brushing off the heaviness along with the tears. "Ain't that the truth?"

"You're such a good doggie."

Talia turned, and Dakota did as well. Victoria had crouched and now rubbed Neema's face while telling her she was such a good girl. Yes, she was a good girl.

Stanton looked baffled. "You need to get that dog out of here."

"She stays," Dakota told him, practically shouting it across the room.

Victoria straightened. Neema shifted, then sat beside her leg. Position claimed. "She's a federal dog, and she's part of my team." Stanton didn't look overly impressed by that. He started to argue, but Victoria cut him off. "Let's go sit in your office. You can tell me all about Prometheus."

Dakota tapped Talia's arm. When Talia glanced over, she saw Dakota tip her head to the side. While Victoria took Stanton's attention, the two of them wandered to the hallway.

"The bank robber guy is downstairs?"

Talia nodded, then directed Dakota to the stairwell. They headed down and checked in with a uniformed security guard at the desk. Hopefully they'd get information from the bank robber before their names were flagged and Stanton—or whoever showed up—hustled them out of the interrogation room.

Dakota said, "You want to go in first?"

Talia only needed a split second to think before she pulled the door open. The bank robber could know who their hacker was. Or, he could *be* the hacker. Either way, he had valuable information in his head and she needed to know what it was.

She strode in. "Time to talk."

Only that wasn't going to happen.

The bank robber sat in the chair. His head was cocked at an unnatural angle.

"That guy is dead."

Talia glanced at Dakota. "You think?"

———

As SOON AS Alvarez got off the phone, Mason said, "Well?"

"Mark Welvern just got out of surgery. They're expecting him to wake up in a few hours. No visitors until tomorrow night." Alvarez pocketed the phone.

Josh Weber was driving. Interesting guy. Mason had gotten to know him a little bit during the two-hour drive into central Washington. They'd told Mason that Dakota had been shot the same day as Alvarez, though her bullet had been in the thigh and not in the chest as the marshal's had been.

The Northwest Counter-Terrorism Task Force didn't lead quiet lives. That was for sure. They'd told Mason about the weekend when Dakota and Josh had met, and then a crazy story about their NCIS Special Agent, Niall, and their office manager, Haley. Something about a mind control app and contaminated water.

The whole thing was bizarre, but they'd tied it all together for him. The mind control thing was when Talia had been abducted from their office by mercenaries and nearly sold. It still turned his stomach, just thinking about it, and he hadn't lived it the way Talia had.

He was still putting the pieces together. One thing he had picked up on was the connection to this. "The money behind both investigations was the same?"

"Yep." Josh gripped the steering wheel. "Whoever funded the lab at that college. Cerium was the name." He shook his head. "We still haven't managed to figure out who it is."

"Because Talia should have?"

Josh shrugged. "She's the tech guru. But she's been...subdued lately. Taking that bank job was supposed to be a big step back toward normal."

"And now she's going to be twice as cautious." Alvarez, in the backseat, spoke without looking up from his phone. Evidently he was totally tuned in to their conversation. He was probably playing Candy Crush, or watching a dog video on YouTube.

Mason blew out a breath and shifted to look out the window. He wanted to fiddle with the radio, or adjust the heat...or download that game on his phone. Anything to cover how hearing about Talia and what she'd been through affected him. It was probably pointless, though. He doubted Josh or Alvarez missed the tension in him.

Could this really all be directly related to Prometheus? He could hardly believe someone had potentially hired a hacker—one with a grudge against Talia—all to compromise the protective detail of such a high-value target.

Locked down. A cushy prison, but a prison nonetheless.

Prometheus could never get out. Despite what Stanton had said, that couldn't be what happened. If he escaped, those loyal to him would rally. The Secret Service would have a serious mess on their hands.

The rest of the drive had been pretty quiet, so he'd broken the silence, asking Josh about his life before the team. Talking about the Marine Corps had led to a bunch of stories from the DEA agent's time in Iraq and Afghanistan. Mason had been to Iraq years ago, on a detail of agents sent with the Secretary of State at the time.

Four days of jet lag and sweating. Standing at attention for hours on end. Followed by a flight home that was all turbulence and nowhere to sleep.

The safe house, whose address he'd been forced to disclose to them despite its top-secret nature, was in the middle of nowhere. Not so isolated they couldn't get to it after a forty-five minute drive through a maze of dirt roads that snaked up a mountainside. Why people lived like that, he didn't know.

"So who is he?"

Mason twisted to look at Alvarez. His bruises sent sharp pains through his chest at the movement, but he ignored it. "What?"

"The guy y'all have locked up here?"

"You don't want to know." Mason had been given particular clearance because of that work in Iraq and the conversations he'd been privy to. It had stuck and meant that upon transferring to Washington state, he'd been "read in" on the operation. "And I'm not sure I can tell you, even given the circumstances."

"And if we end up hunting this guy, what then?"

Alvarez had a point, but Mason had to say, "I'll get it cleared from Stanton that you're authorized. Then I'll show you a picture. I highly doubt you'll ever be in the know on his name, or who he is."

"Whoa." Josh shook his head. "I thought Victoria was para-noid about need-to-know."

Alvarez leaned forward to stick his head between the front seats. "What's that supposed to mean?"

Josh said, "Didn't Niall tell you she had the whole office bugged in Portland?"

"So?" Alvarez huffed. "Didn't that mean we had surveillance footage of those men abducting Talia? We knew right away who it was."

Josh shrugged one shoulder. "She still could have told us. If she had, I could've gotten to the footage of Haley shooting Dakota before my fiancé could burn a copy and go home and watch it a hundred times."

Alvarez sat back.

Mason decided to ask, "Why would she want to watch herself get shot?"

"Haley was drugged," Josh said, like that helped Mason understand. "But she still wanted to see if there was anything she could've done differently."

"Wow."

"Yeah." Josh huffed a laugh, and shook his head. "That's Dakota for you."

"You're the one who put a ring on it."

Mason shifted to look at Alvarez.

"What?" The marshal glanced between Mason and Josh. "Isn't that what the kids say?"

"I don't know what to do with that." Josh glanced in his rearview for a second. "I'm going to just let it go, because that was way too bizarre."

"I can be hip with the lingo."

Josh laughed. "Sure you can."

The safe house was down a street that was essentially a blind corner off the dirt track they called a street. They were forced to make a U-turn and come at it from the opposite direction. Just to see the street Josh was supposed to turn down.

Two miles from the highway, as the crow flies, Josh pulled up in front of a single-story home. The kind that had two halves delivered on trucks and attached together on site.

Mason looked around, then looked at the house. "There should be a guard."

"Looks pretty quiet." Alvarez had his attention on the front door.

Two SUVs pulled up behind them and tactical agents piled out. Mason waited for them to take point, then got out to join the middle of the group. There was zero point in asserting his position. He wasn't a hundred percent, and neither was Alvarez.

"Front door is open." The lead guy picked up his pace.

Mason didn't like the look of this at all. "Be careful."

With every step, he felt the weight of everything sit heavier and heavier on his shoulders. There was a small possibility he wasn't up to doing this, so he let his pace slow to hang back. No point in being a liability. The difference between the team getting out of this with no problems, and an agent getting hurt.

The lead agent eased up to the front door. Gun ready. Team braced.

There should have been six agents on the property, two on the road, two in the house, and the other two on roving patrol. A small detail to guard such a huge issue. One that had plagued this administration and the previous two. It did niggle at him that the Secret Service was essentially paid to keep the government's dirty laundry out of sight.

But the fallout of everything coming to light would be far worse.

Already a young woman, the bank manager's assistant, had been killed. He could only pray that no one else was killed because of this.

The lead agent reached out and pushed the door open.

Two seconds of quiet. Followed by a click.

Before Mason could realize what it was, someone yelled, "Run!"

16

T alia was leaning against the wall in the hallway outside the interrogation room when Stanton marched off the elevator, followed by Victoria. She hadn't gotten anywhere near the body, and had no intention of doing so.

Inside the room, Dakota straightened. She'd been peering at the man's mouth from close up. She turned to the two of them. "Looks like poison, but I can't be sure. There's foam on his lips." The dark look on her face was likely a result of there being a dead guy in the room. And the fact she'd dealt recently with the victims of a version of VX gas.

Before Stanton could speak again, Dakota glanced at Victoria. "Neema?"

Victoria pointed at the door. "In the break room, asleep on the couch."

Dakota nodded.

"Two agents are on their way down. Both have experience in homicide investigations." The Secret Service Assistant Director stared at the dead man with a frown.

The security guard moved past Talia to stand in the doorway, blocking her view. The flash she'd seen of his face looked seriously guilty. She figured that was more about this happening while he wasn't watching than anything else.

"You really saw nothing?" Talia guessed he'd probably been on his phone instead of paying attention to his job.

"Nothing to see." He glanced back at her. "According to the screens, you all aren't in here and he's still sitting there." The security guard waved at the dead man.

Talia looked at the camera, high on the wall, then at the desk. Stanton followed her. "You're not authorized to touch any computer in this office—or operate any technology, for that matter."

She shot him a look, then turned to the screen. The footage of the cell where the bank robber had been held showed an image of him sitting in the same chair he now sat dead in. Only he was very much alive.

Stanton said, "Tell me you didn't allow the hacker access to our network again."

She wasn't going to respond to that. "Clearly the bank robber is not the hacker, given this has occurred."

"So a murderer came in before you and Special Agent Pierce came downstairs. Whoever it was killed the man in custody, messing with the security feed in order to do so." It wasn't a question. Was he giving her his opinion, or stating a theory?

Talia said, "Your network security technicians should be able to find out if this was the result of the…earlier breach."

It very well could be, and they would be able to tell. Someone had caused the video to loop. She'd been staring at it long enough that she could see, despite the fact the bank robber remained relatively still, the image was on a two minute or so repeat.

She turned to the security guard. "Who came down before us?"

He started to speak, but Stanton held up a hand. "Don't answer that. Save it for your report."

Seriously? She looked back at the feed. "Look at him. I think he knows he's being recorded. That the feed is looping."

Which meant the bank robber and the hacker had communicated. In the event the bank robber was here, he'd known what to do. Maybe.

"So he was murdered, or not?"

She motioned to the computer, which she hadn't actually touched yet. "May I?"

Beyond him, Dakota and Victoria were having a quiet conversation in the interrogation room. Two agents walked down the hall and went in carrying duffel bags. Evidence collection supplies. Not Talia's thing, but she understood the mechanics of it. How long before a coroner was summoned?

Talia didn't want to be here when the body was removed.

Stanton's lips thinned even more. "I'll be watching everything you do."

Sure, but would he understand what she was doing? Talia nodded, determined to maintain that professionalism she drew around her like a coat. "Mason's life was at stake. I do not put security above someone's life. I never have, and I doubt I ever will."

"And that's why you're part of my team," Victoria said from the doorway. "Not a rule-following, paper-pushing NSA analyst."

"It's not procedure." Stanton folded his arms.

Talia lifted her chin. "You'd have been prepared to allow Mason to be killed?"

"He knows what he signed on for."

She shook her head, seeing her feelings mirrored in the expression on Victoria's face. They felt the same way, and they both knew it.

Talia said, "His daughter didn't sign on for her father to get killed just to protect the Secret Service's butts. The stakes outweighed the cost."

The assistant director shook his head. Stanton wasn't going to be persuaded.

"May I *please* use this computer?" Just to prove she could be polite, as well as professional.

Stanton motioned to it with a nod.

Talia clicked the mouse at the corner of the screen, then typed into the window that popped up. She rewound the feed, and they watched in reverse.

She hit pause. "There."

Stanton took a step closer. Talia pressed play, and they watched the bank robber lift his left arm above his right shoulder, then bring his palm across his body at a diagonal angle to his hip on the left side.

"What was that?"

Talia pointed to the code in the window, scrolling as the feed played. "It was a signal the system recognized. A command code left behind in the network, just in case it was needed. The code initiated a program that proceeded to record the next two minutes of feed in this room. After that, it replayed those two minutes on a loop."

"He did this?" Stanton motioned to the dead man in the interrogation room.

Talia nodded. "He gave a signal. I'd hazard to guess that no one came in and killed him. There was nothing the security guard could have done." She straightened. "I think he killed himself."

The man flushed, stood off to the side. He obviously had no clue this had occurred right under his nose.

Talia typed on the keyboard. "The camera was still recording."

She found the footage underneath the loop. She had to fool the command code into thinking everything was still in working order. Then she played it. They watched as the bank robber pulled something from his cheek and swallowed it. Seconds later his body convulsed.

He went limp.

Talia had to tell Stanton the truth. "I'd need to check in order to know for sure, but I'm pretty certain the hacker left this when he accessed Prometheus. He probably knew it was possible the bank robber would be caught at some point. This gem was left behind in the system for just such an eventuality."

At least, she was mostly sure of that fact.

Stanton's gaze darkened.

"It isn't like *I* killed him." Why she'd felt the need to say that, Talia wasn't totally sure, but it was out now. "I was in the conference room with you."

Stanton pressed his lips together. He was about to say something when Dakota said, "Hang on, I'll put you on speaker. Everyone is here." She touched the screen of her phone and stepped out into the hall.

"...total chaos here." It was Josh.

Victoria moved close to the phone. "What happened?"

Talia's stomach churned at the thought of any of them injured. They were breaching the house where Prometheus— whoever it was—had been holed up. It should have just been a simple operation. Make sure everything was all right. Check in to confirm things were still good, that the hacker hadn't gotten to the house.

Josh said, "Everything is fine, no one got hurt. But—"

Someone cut him off. "Give me that phone." Mason coughed. Was he okay? Josh said no one was hurt, but why was Mason coughing? Something had to have happened.

Stanton said, "Anderson?"

"Yes, sir. Prometheus is code black."

"Copy that." Stanton spun around and raced for the elevator.

———

MASON MOVED to the head of the conference table. He smelled like smoke from the explosion that had ripped through the house. Stanton was on the phone in his office still. He paced back and forth the same as he'd been doing for the past hour.

Victoria, Alvarez, Talia, Dakota and Josh all sat around the table. Eyes on him. Even the dog was in a "down" position by the wall.

Josh and Alvarez smelled the same as Mason did, and Josh had a scraped-up elbow. Mason had thanked God out loud the moment he realized there had been no serious injuries.

Josh had said, "Amen."

Mason glanced at each of them in turn now. Good people. "As much as the Secret Service believes we can handle this problem, I'm of the belief that the more skilled agents we have on this, the better."

Victoria nodded her approval. She likely knew what he was about to say, but seemed content to allow him to talk.

Mason said, "Eleven months ago we took a man into custody. This man had been running an operation across several states. He recruited foot soldiers and was preparing an attack on Air Force One. I was read in when I transferred here because of my clearance level. I've confirmed with your respective agencies as to each of yours and was unsurprised to find your clearance suddenly at the same level."

He shot Talia a glance.

She lifted her hands. The picture of innocence. "It wasn't me."

He wanted to smile, but there was nothing amusing about what'd happened today. "We think the bomb that exploded in the house was a booby trap left behind for whoever came around. We've put in a call to an ATF response team to head the investigation, but essentially the damage is done."

Alvarez said, "Bodies?"

"All six of our agents that had been on the detail were found in the rubble, gunshot wounds sustained before the explosion. They were all executed."

No one moved or said anything. The loss of agents from any branch of law enforcement was a blow they all felt.

Mason pulled out a chair and sat.

"Who was it?" Dakota's tone was hard. From grief or impatience, he didn't know. Maybe both.

He grabbed the remote and clicked the screen behind him as he turned the chair to the side. "This is Ethan Yewell. He is the only child of the current Secretary of State and his late wife, though you won't find that information on any official record dug up from anywhere at any time. The man's identity has been comprehensively scrubbed from existence."

He took a breath. "Yewell is thirty-nine and has been in private hospitals most of his life. The list of disorders he suffers from is...extensive. Basically, he's an extremely persuasive sociopath, like the worst kind of cult leader wrapped up in a bow, making even Hitler look like the mail man. And you'd be right to consider my opinion not based on medical science."

"Great." Dakota leaned back in her chair. "I love it when they're psychos."

Josh squeezed her hand.

Across the table from them, Talia said, "Is he the hacker?"

Mason shook his head. "Until yesterday, he was in our custody. No contact with the outside world and no access to technology. Not even a television or radio. He was on total lockdown."

"But not in a federal prison?" Alvarez shot him a pointed look.

"Requests from the very top were passed down. We had to keep this quiet. We couldn't even risk witness protection within the prison system, and he couldn't be among general population. Solitary was deemed not an option."

Alvarez made a sound like a snort.

"It was not my decision to make."

The marshal leaned forward in his chair. "Yewell wouldn't have been broken out of federal prison. He'd still be there, and you wouldn't have dead agents and a big problem on your hands."

Mason lifted his hands. There was nothing he could've done about that. "The Secret Service is on high alert, and the FBI has been pulled in. Those on the search have been read in. But this has to stay under wraps until found. Then he will be locked down, and I've no doubt alternative measures will be taken."

"But y'all are just going to deal with the fallout?" Alvarez sat back in his chair.

Victoria waved her agent off. "Any idea what his plans are?"

"The President was due to visit Seattle next week. We'd moved Prometheus to a new location in preparation, but Browne wanted to go meet with him."

Alvarez made another sound.

Mason continued. "President Browne considered it worth his time to attempt to speak with Prometheus. See if he could reason with him."

Josh shook his head. "Too risky."

"Regardless, it's not going to happen now. If Browne was at risk, Prometheus would have held off and had his people break him out at a time when he could've killed the President and then escaped. But he cut out early." Mason shrugged. "Either way, it's moot now since the President called off the trip. He isn't coming anywhere near the Northwest until this situation is…resolved."

"Why is Yewell such a threat?" Dakota's frown pulled her Native American features in.

"Along with being mentally, uh…challenged." Someone snorted, but Mason ignored it. "Ethan Yewell is also extremely persuasive. He can basically talk anyone into doing anything. Prior to his arrest, Yewell was actively engaged in recruiting an army of his own in order to stage a coup. His plan was to first take over state government in Texas, after which he would have proceeded to Washington D.C."

Alvarez sighed and shook his head.

"He had four hundred men."

The marshal's brows rose. "How many are left now?"

"At least a hundred, maybe more. The takedown was a bloodbath due to the quality of intel we received. A man we had on the inside fed us back information we later learned was only a drop in the bucket of what was going on. He was arrested, along with dozens of Yewell's men. We've been running down more over the weeks since. And we managed to keep the whole thing from getting out to the media."

"How you did that is astounding." Victoria shook her head. "All this has been going on under everyone's noses?"

Mason nodded. "The administration wants it to stay that way."

Victoria's mouth worked side to side as she processed that information.

"Which is why I need all of your help to aid in bringing this guy in before he can meet up with what's left of his army."

Dakota said, "What about the ones you have in prison?"

"They're all on lockdown, and we're interviewing them one by one. But they're true believers. They're never going to give up his location, or his plans." Mason took a breath. This was bad, and he couldn't let his emotions get the better of him. That wasn't going to help the manhunt. Nor would it keep people from being hurt.

The threat was present and very real. This country was in danger.

"Domestic terrorism is what you guys fight against." He looked at each of them again. "I can say with some certainty that this is the toughest battle you'll ever face."

Alvarez got up and walked out.

"You'll call in!" Victoria yelled after him.

The marshal waved over his shoulder as he strode to the elevator.

Talia got up as well, gathered her purse and the electronics she'd placed on the table in front of her, and turned to the door.

She was leaving?

He stood. "We need your help."

It was all hands on deck and would be, until Yewell was brought in—again—and the threat neutralized.

Alvarez had left. If she went as well, he would lose the chance to get Victoria's whole team assisting the Secret Service on this.

"I know." She took a step toward the door.

"Where are you going?" Didn't she know staying, and helping, would literally save lives? He didn't want to sound desperate, but that was the truth. He was desperate. The Secret Service needed all their help.

And he needed Talia.

The woman who had risked her whole career to keep him alive.

She frowned, her gaze softening. "I've got an idea."

17

Talia pulled the network cable from their router and plugged it into the one for the accountant's office upstairs.

"What are we doing?"

She jumped, startled from figuring out if this was even going to work. Mason stood just outside the door in the hallway of the office building where the Northwest Counter-Terrorism Task Force had set up shop.

"Borrowing the Wi-Fi from upstairs so the hacker won't see us coming." There were about six additional steps in that process, but it was a good start.

"And this?" Mason looked behind her, at the racks of hardware.

"A network closet." She edged past him. "So when you report back to the Secret Service on exactly what we did here, you can tell them the CPA office upstairs pays for super-fast Wi-Fi so their partners can stream Netflix while they work."

She strode past him.

"Talia."

She glanced back, over her shoulder. "What?"

She could see the "what" all over his face. Mason didn't like being relegated to the sidelines because he still wasn't a hundred percent, considering his injuries. She didn't have time to explain enough for him to help her. He didn't like not being at his office in the middle of a major crisis. *And* he didn't like babysitting their task force—the assignment he'd been given by Stanton.

Meanwhile, his whole office back at the Secret Service were deeply engaged in hunting for Yewell and his men. Stopping a terrorist attack.

Talia had a new angle, one of her own.

If she could find the hacker, then maybe *he* would lead them to Yewell.

"Come on." She felt herself soften toward him, and decided to just go with it. Why not cut him some slack? They'd all had a rough couple of days. "I'll show you where the coffee pot is."

Mason took two steps and caught up with her as they headed back into the office. "You really think you can find this guy?"

"If I can't, that means he's nowhere to be found."

The open plan office had a wall of windows down one side, light streaming in over the killer view of downtown Seattle. Haley had told Victoria they needed blinds to cut down the glare on their computer screens.

No one had bought them.

No one wanted to cover up that view.

Though, Talia figured it was more about the fact she'd told them all she liked the light. After hours of being swallowed in the darkest of black, she needed to see it.

Haley looked over from her computer. "Done?"

"Yup." Talia strode to her desk, face-to-face with Haley's. Both of them sat at right angles to the door with Talia facing the window. "You should be able to log in now."

Niall wandered over and handed Mason a coffee mug. "You're really going after him?"

Talia got to work on her computer. "Yes."

Her co-worker moved to her. Out the corner of her eye she saw Niall sit one hip on the edge of her desk. "Honey."

She looked up. "Don't."

"We're just worried about you. That's all."

"Last time, I was alone." She didn't look past Niall, where Mason stood. She couldn't, or he would see the plain truth on her face. He'd see she didn't believe one word of what she was saying. The team already knew, but she couldn't let Mason see the one thing she couldn't let go of.

Talia was scared out of her mind.

Niall tried again. "Hon—"

"Don't."

"We know who that girl was."

Talia's fingers tripped on the keys. The screen blurred. She shut her eyes. They were going to do this now?

"I got an email this morning from one of your old team members at the NSA." Haley's voice was soft. "They ran her DNA through every database and got a match. They know who she was."

Was. Because the teen girl Talia had been trapped in that dark room with had been young. *God.* So young.

Talia shoved the memories away. "I need you to tell me that later." She glanced up at Niall and repeated herself. "I need you to tell me that later."

He said, "Okay, honey."

"Does your girlfriend know you call me honey?"

Haley giggled. "It was my idea. Anyway, he calls Siobhan that."

Niall's niece was about the same age as Rayna. "Okay."

He squeezed her shoulder. "Okay."

"Dinner's here!" Dakota strode in, the dog trotting close to her side. Josh followed her, carrying an open cardboard box. The smell of barbecue floated in with them.

Talia's stomach rumbled.

Haley giggled again.

"We have work to do." Talia pinned her co-worker, roommate and friend with a look.

"I'll get you both some food." Niall wandered off.

The heaviness that had been sitting on her shoulders for weeks was eased by the fact all of them were there together. And they all knew it. Despite that, the fear lay dormant underneath. A great beast waiting to rear its head and strike.

They'd moved the office from Portland to Seattle. She didn't have to work in the place she'd been kidnapped from. Talia had constructed her own firewalled office in their Portland location, in a storage closet. She'd turned it into a fully-loaded haven for her to work, complete with security measures that included a retinal scan. She'd also blasted her music as loud as she wanted. Without any of them asking if she was *done yet.*

Now she liked this much better.

Haley was going to help. Niall was going to feed her. Mason was going to... She looked over. Stand there staring at her?

A tiny smile curled his lips. She said, "You look awful, you know."

The words came out before she could stop them. It was true, considering his face was a mess of bruises. She imagined his ribs didn't look much better. But thinking about his bare chest wasn't going to help her get any work done.

Mason's lips widened into a smile. A *very* nice smile. He placed a palm on the desk and leaned down so his face was close to hers.

Was he going to...

Kiss her?

She sucked in a breath, her mind racing as she tried to figure out whether she wanted him to or not.

His eyes smiled. "Water or lemonade?"

Talia tried to hide her disappointment. "Water is fine."

Mason leaned in the last two inches and touched his lips to hers. "Okay."

Then he was gone, striding across the room like he hadn't just rocked her entire world. No, she wasn't oblivious to the fact there were serious sparks between them. They just hadn't had the chance to have a regular conversation or even do something normal, like go to coffee. Let alone actually talk about it.

Talia got back to work, ignoring the smirk on Haley's face. Though she had to say, "Now you know what the rest of us saw when you met Niall."

"I didn't meet you until later."

"Surveillance video. From the lab."

Haley's jaw dropped. "I went crazy."

"Yeah, but I kept the footage of you sneaking into the ward where they kept him, and then him nearly beaning you with that pipe." Talia kept her gaze on the computer. "I'm going to play it at your wedding."

"What?"

Talia shrugged. "It was a nice hug. I'll get the still image framed; it'll be your favorite photo."

Haley tipped her head back and laughed.

Talia grinned at the team, who all turned back from the barbecue. She was about to say something when her phone buzzed. She looked at the screen. "Victoria just landed in DC."

The director was having a meeting with the Secretary of State, Aaron Yewell. A *chat* that was essentially going to be a pleasant interrogation. Victoria was determined to find out if he knew where his son Ethan might be or what he was intending to do.

Dakota lowered the corn bread muffin from her mouth before she could take a bite. "If it hadn't saved our lives more than once, it would worry me that you monitor all our communications and have a lock on our GPS locations every second of every day."

Mason actually looked impressed, but Talia couldn't let that affect her.

She said, "When you stop getting kidnapped, I'll stop keeping tabs on you."

"Okay, but…" Dakota shrugged. "Maybe not, though. Yeah?"

"Agreed." Josh kissed his fiancé on the forehead.

Talia turned back to her computer.

Haley said, "The anonymizer is all set and ready to go."

———

EVERYONE HAD the food they needed. Even the dog got a plate of chicken pieces and raw carrot sticks. Mason took a seat at what looked like an empty desk, but for the computer. Either the person who sat here had no personal items at work, or it was unoccupied. He wanted to be close enough to hear what Talia and her coworker—apparently Niall's girlfriend—were doing.

"You guys do this often?"

Josh glanced over. "Dinner?"

It was Niall who answered. "Couple of times a month, when we need to be on standby."

"What about Alvarez?"

Niall said, "Talia?"

She tensed a second. Agitated that he'd disturbed her? Then she looked at her tablet and swiped the screen. "He's a hundred miles from here."

"Doing what?"

She glanced over at Niall, tightness lining her face. "Maybe you should call and ask him?"

"Maybe I will." He fired back.

Dakota pulled out her phone, sat on the office couch beside Josh. The dog was eyeing her plate. "I'll do it."

Talia turned back to her computer, more tension in her shoulders than had been there before. Mason figured Niall realized he'd been bothering her. Niall said, "So what's that anonymous thing you guys are doing?"

Before Talia could answer, Haley said, "It's a way to move about the dark web without this hacker figuring out it's us."

Us. Because Haley knew how Talia felt about being alone.

Niall opened his mouth to say something else.

Mason spoke before he could. "An anonymizer masks your IP address, so someone trying to locate you can't see what computer you're accessing the internet from."

Talia turned around, wide eyed.

"I assume you used a series of proxies?"

"Yes." It was like he'd asked her to dinner. That was the level of happiness on her face.

"So the hacker, if he's looking for Talia, will have his eyes on the IP addresses this office uses. Because he wants to know what she's up to. That's why she connected to the CPA office's internet connection. She's using their network, so anyone who does figure it out and comes looking for her—or us—will literally go upstairs first because they'll think she's up there." He paused. "Then, for added security, Talia and Haley will use a series of servers set up on the dark web to further cover their tracks. They'll be able to snoop around and look for evidence of the hacker. And Yewell. Virtually undetected."

"Hopefully we'll get a hit on something." Haley glanced at Niall. "The anonymizer is like that thing we set up to trap those people who held Talia."

Mason saw her stiffen, but she managed to cover it. Mostly.

Niall said, "With the virus thing?"

She nodded. "The anonymizer masked who we were. Then when people logged onto that server on the dark web, a virus Talia wrote, injected with a traceable code, made everything they did visible to us. We sent that to the FBI, and they brought down the whole ring with our evidence."

Dakota got off the phone. "Alvarez set up a meet with some of Yewell's guys. He's trying to get in on what they're doing, using an undercover persona he's had for a while. If he can get with their group, he'll let us know where Yewell is. Or any other intel he finds out."

Mason was impressed. "Wow."

Dakota shrugged. "He's good. But Talia is better."

Talia said, "Different skillset."

"Maybe." Dakota made a face. "But when he went up against those townies in Malvern County, he got his bell rung."

Mason had no idea what they were talking about.

Dakota continued, "And when the hacker tried to implicate

you by putting that bank money in your account, you sent it right back."

"Then I'm glad you're not the one who does everyone's yearly evaluations."

"You know I'd give you a bonus anytime."

Talia chuckled, but they all heard the edge in her voice. How she'd forced herself to sound relaxed, though she was far from it.

"Especially if you can find this guy," Dakota said. "I'm in the mood to watch Neema take a bite out of government cover-up." She leaned toward the dog and petted her face. "Yes, I am. But I don't think it will taste good. Not like barbecue. But I'll get you a steak."

Nearly everyone laughed at her. Enough that Mason couldn't distinguish the sounds.

"You love that dog." Niall shook his head.

Josh pinned him with a stare. "And that's a bad thing?"

Niall lifted both hands, but it was Haley who said, "We're going to get two kitties." She tapped on her screen, unable to see Josh's look of horror behind her. "I'll show you a picture."

"Later." Talia snapped her fingers. "Look at this."

Mason got up to look over her shoulder. Haley stared at her own screen. "I see it. Is that him?"

"I think so."

Niall wiped his mouth with a napkin. "Care to share with the rest of the class?"

Mason shot him a look, then noticed Josh and Dakota had done the same.

"What?" Niall said. "There's been way too much kidnapping lately. To be honest, I don't want either of them going anywhere near this guy." He waved at Talia and Haley. "Not if they could get hurt."

Talia turned in her chair and looked at the NCIS agent. "I'm not worried about the worst that could happen. Because the worst *already* happened." Her words were measured. Steady.

Mason set his hand on her shoulder.

Talia kept her attention on Niall. "Dakota was kidnapped. Josh got shot. You got kidnapped. Haley got *brainwashed*. Dakota got shot. So did Alvarez. And I got kidnapped."

Mason's whole body went solid. These people had lived some crazy times.

Dakota said, "It's been a busy couple of months."

Mason coughed. "Months?"

She nodded, but it was Talia who said, "Until we get this guy, we can't assume things will be fine. Because they probably won't. But I have something going for me—something that he doesn't."

A muscle in Niall's jaw clenched. "What's that?"

"You guys, and Victoria." Talia took a breath. "I know you're worried. I'm scared out of my mind that he's going to grab me again." He heard the tremor in her voice, but she continued, "That's why we're *all* going."

Mason angled his body toward her. "Where?"

She looked up. "I know where he is. I know where he was when he hacked the bank and the Secret Service office, and it looks like he's still there."

"You're not coming." Niall shook his head.

"Last time I nearly got sold by sex traffickers, I was alone in the office."

Niall stood. "I can see how that—"

Talia grabbed her purse and stood.

"—might make you think twice about…" His words trailed off. "Talia."

She looked at Mason. "Ready?"

He stood. "You're not going anywhere without me, and neither will you be staying here alone. Or with Haley." He leaned to the side and said to her, "No offense."

The other woman grinned. "You think I'm gonna miss the fun?"

Niall let out a frustrated sound. "Doesn't anyone listen to me? This place is secure."

"Nowhere is secure." Talia settled her purse on her shoulder. "That's why I'm staying with you guys while you bring him in."

"Deal." Dakota stood and brushed off the legs of her skinny pants. "Pretty sure I'm never leaving you behind in the office by yourself...say, *ever*."

A smile played on Josh's lips.

Haley kissed Niall's cheek. "Sorry." Then she pulled on her jacket. "We do this as a team, so we can have each other's backs. Isn't that what you wanted, for all of us to work together?"

He shook his head. "Not when it puts you guys in danger."

"Maybe you could work out your own issues later." Mason pulled out his car keys. "Because right now we have a hacker to bring in."

Talia looked at him. And the way she did, he couldn't not lean down and plant a soft kiss on her forehead. "Make sure you bring your stun gun."

18

Talia was tucked in the third row with Haley. She'd rather have sat beside Mason, but Neema had climbed up on the seat and rode the middle row between the captain's chairs with both front paws on the center console between Josh and Dakota.

She shifted in the seat and tugged on the edges of the bullet proof vest they'd strapped on her. "Why are these so uncomfortable?"

Haley glanced over with a smile. Mason shifted in his seat, twisting so she could see his face. "You leave that on."

"But we're not even there yet." The house where the hacker had breached the Secret Service office from was still forty miles up the road.

Mason glanced at the rest of the occupants of the van. "How many of you have been in a car chase?"

All of them raised their hands.

"How many of those ended with the car flipped over?"

Only one hand lowered. Niall's.

Haley said, "My brakes were cut. I slammed into a house. But when it was a car chase, I was in the trunk, and it did flip over."

Dakota shifted in her seat. "Josh's truck got exploded with a grenade. But we were standing right by it."

"Okay, I get it." Talia huffed.

Up in the driver's seat, she thought Josh might have muttered, "I miss that truck."

Dakota reached over and squeezed his knee.

Mason glanced at her again. "I'm not saying we're going to get ambushed."

Niall didn't look up from his phone. "We probably will be, though."

"What I'm saying, and I think everyone in this car will agree, is that your life is under our protection. And we don't take that lightly."

"I know." She blew out a breath. "Too bad Stanton still thinks I betrayed your agency. I had a great idea of what to get him for Secret Santa."

Mason cocked his head to the side. "You give good Christmas presents?"

Niall said, "Dude." Like that was all the explanation he needed to give.

Dakota waved a hand. "You have no idea. Just wait."

Talia stared at Mason, a smile tugging at her lips. "Just wait."

He gave her a tiny nod, a whole lot of promise wrapped up in that one action. He intended to still be here, and part of her life, when Christmas rolled around in a few months. And maybe more Christmases to come.

He said, "I love Christmas. Rayna bakes these cookies, and they have a layer of caramel on top that's covered by a layer of chocolate." He made a humming noise for a second. "They're so good."

It was like getting hit with a bucket of ice water.

Mason saw it. Of course he saw it. Talia reached in her purse and dragged out her phone.

"Everything okay?"

She nodded without looking up. "I'll just feel better when he's behind bars."

No one said anything, but she could feel their attention on her.

They were going to feel how they were going to feel. There wasn't anything she could do about that. Not until this thing was done.

Talia read the Bible verse her mom had sent her. Of course it was all about being surrounded, protected. She prayed through it, thanking God for the people here in the car with her. God had given her the best of the best, placing them right here with her when she needed them.

Not when the hacker had hired mercenaries to kidnap and torment her. She didn't blame them for not being there in that moment. God had a plan in mind, and His will had been done. It had hurt. It was hard now, trying to move on. But whatever God was doing, Talia knew it would be the right thing in the end.

Maybe all this was needed in order to bring the hacker down.

Maybe there had been no other way.

She didn't want to make a bargain with God but there was no way she could handle it if something happened to Mason's daughter. And yeah, she'd never even spoken to the girl. But that didn't mean Talia wanted to be responsible—even indirectly—for Rayna getting hurt or winding up fatherless. Talia knew what it felt like to grow up without a dad. She didn't want Rayna to feel that missing part of her life, too.

Talia found Victoria had landed in DC. She tapped to call the director and put the phone on speaker.

"Director Bramlyn."

"It's me," Talia said. "You're on speaker. Everyone's here."

"Have you heard anything about Welvern? How did the surgery go?"

"I'll call and find out," Dakota called from the front seat.

"Keep me posted. I'm just about to head into a meeting with the Secretary of State."

"Be nice, yeah?" Talia said. "We don't need him on our bad side."

"Perhaps he should be concerned about being on *my* bad side."

"I'm just saying—"

"I know." Victoria was quiet for a second. "Now tell me what you all are up to."

Talia told her about the hacker using the house they were going to as a base, from which he had hacked the Secret Service network. "The funny thing is, I actually looked at the listing for this house. It's a smart house, and it's for sale."

None of the rest of them thought it was funny. Not before when she'd told them, and not now.

"So, this is a trap then." Victoria's voice didn't betray one ounce of emotion.

"Probably," Talia admitted. "But right now this is the only lead we have. He's been there. I accessed the security system, and we got footage of him entering. He wore a hood, but I'm sure it was him. Maybe he saw me looking at it and decided to get in there first. Maybe he left me a present."

"Yeah, like a bomb," Niall said, loud enough for Victoria to hear.

"I don't want to hear later, on the news, that my entire team was blown up." Victoria huffed. "Can you imagine living with Alvarez after that? It'll be a nightmare."

Talia wanted to smile.

Victoria said, "How will going to this house get us Yewell?"

"It may not," Mason answered her. "But it's an angle my team isn't exploring."

"The hacker touched the keypad to get in." This was the part Talia was most excited about. "We can get his fingerprint." She had a program on her tablet that could run it straight away. They'd have an answer as to who he was within a few hours. How could Victoria argue with that?

"Be careful." Victoria muttered a few more words under her breath.

Haley leaned over to the phone. "We will."

"You know we'll take care of her." Dakota called out from the front passenger seat. "And we'll get this guy."

"Mmm." Victoria's emotions finally began to bleed through

her tone. "I've got to go." She sounded like she was getting choked up.

The line went dead.

Talia had never in her life heard Victoria sound like that. It was kind of unnerving, if she was being honest with herself.

"Do you ever figure she goes to a quiet place alone and just cries?" Haley said. "Like, she literally despairs over what will happen to us next."

Talia said, "No way. She's like the Iron Lady."

Dakota glanced back at Talia. Her expression claimed she didn't exactly agree with Talia's statement. And maybe that was right.

Maybe Talia was wrong.

Haley said, "You think running his fingerprint will get us an ID?"

"It has to."

"But that would mean somewhere along the line, he made a mistake."

"I'm counting on that." Talia nodded. "We already know he's good. I'm counting on him also being human. No one is immune from making mistakes."

Talia just prayed they weren't making one by coming here.

———

MASON CURLED his hand into a fist. It was that or reach for her, to help her out of the car. Talia climbed out and took a look at the area around them. Trees. Dirt.

"How far is it?"

He pointed west. "Half a mile that way."

Dakota strode over. "Here." She handed Talia a pair of beat-up sneakers and a balled-up bundle he figured were socks.

Talia shot her a look.

"Because you'd rather ruin your shoes tromping through the woods?"

Someone snorted. Mason didn't turn around to look and see who. Talia huffed out a breath and took the shoes. She sat on the edge of the open rear door of the SUV and took off her heels.

"For the record, I prefer those." Mason pointed to the shoes she tucked behind her.

"Me too." She shot Dakota a look and separated the socks.

She might be bantering with him, but she was still shut down. The way she had been since he mentioned his daughter. The second he'd said Rayna's name, talking about her cookies, Talia had pulled in on herself.

Mason figured she'd suffered terrible tragedy, but life should be celebrated. She was allowing fear to swallow her and keep her from enjoying life.

He wanted to know what she was like when the weight of this hacker's continued evasion of law enforcement didn't sit on her shoulders. When they'd caught Yewell once again, and she was between cases. He didn't believe she'd never have another worry after the two men were caught. Life didn't work that way. The next case would surface, and she would be back on the job. But it would be a whole lot less personal.

He wanted to know what the sound of her laugh was like. Not the pseudo-humor she expressed now. That was subdued, muted. He wanted to know what her full-out, overwhelmed-to-the-point-of-tears laughter sounded like.

"Ready?"

Mason glanced over his shoulder at Josh. He nodded. The DEA agent attached to the team had snapped a leash on his dog—not that she needed it. The animal leaned against his leg, ears pricked. Looking like she needed the barest encouragement to set off running.

Hunting.

"Dakota and I will circle around to the south, come up on the back door."

Mason nodded. "Keep it low and quiet."

Josh didn't need to be told that. He nodded his assent anyway, and the three of them set off. Mason waited for Talia to stand. "Good?"

She clutched her purse to her side. "Yes."

The team had argued that she didn't need something in her hands, but no one had a backpack she could use, so the argument was short lived. She needed her tablet and phone, as well as a few other things. No one could debate that fact with her. It was a smart house. She wanted to connect to the server and copy all the data on it.

See what the hacker had left behind.

She worried the edge of her lip. "He's going to see us. Doesn't matter how quiet we are."

"Josh and Dakota know what they're doing."

"I know."

Mason squeezed her shoulder. It was nice she cared about them. This team had a deep connection with each other, one he couldn't say he had with his colleagues at the Secret Service. Before meeting this task force, he'd considered them friends, as well as co-workers. Now he knew it was superficial. This team was more like a family in comparison.

They followed Niall, with Haley bringing up the rear. Only Talia didn't carry a weapon. If he'd had a helmet, the kind armed-response teams wore, he would have strapped it on her. All he could do now was pray for protection and favor as they walked through the woods to the smart house.

If the hacker still had any kind of connection to the house, he would see them coming. Talia was right about that. There likely wasn't a way to keep their entry from him.

Still, they had to try to get the information from the server.

Talia looked at her tablet as she walked. Mason held her elbow so she didn't trip. She said, "There aren't any signals going to the house that I can see."

He let go of her so she didn't think he thought she couldn't walk without falling. Some of the things Rayna had told him about how a woman's mind worked were just baffling. "And you said there's nothing on the power grid?"

"If anything is on inside that house, it's not connected to the local power company."

"So that would mean a battery or a generator, right?" Haley walked behind them. "Or solar power. Something not drawing power you can see."

Talia said, "There's also no Wi-Fi signal."

"Could be he cleared out?" When she nodded, Mason went on. "Maybe he did what he needed to, packed up, and left nothing behind him."

Talia tipped her head to the side for a second. "I think I would prefer that even if it did make this a waste of time."

Ahead of them, Niall slowed at the tree line. Beyond him sat a low, one-story house that looked like something out of a futuristic movie. Lots of glass. Clean lines that moved to a point at the front of the house so that it had a wall of windows at the south end, where the sun shone down as it moved overhead.

For Sale sign in the yard.

"I really liked this house." Talia sighed. "I'm not buying it now."

Mason wasn't sure she'd like his bachelor town house either. "I've been thinking about moving as well. You'll have to show me what you've found. Maybe we can go look at a few together?"

Niall spun around. "We need to focus right now, not be setting up a date."

"Right." It sounded more like a "sorry" should have been said. But it wasn't like he'd intended to just ask her out right now. He knew it should wait until later. "Let's go."

He led the way to the house, watching all angles for movement. Then he studied the house. "I don't see cameras. Or security lights."

"It's all tied to the system. The one that's getting no power right now." Talia's voice was behind him. "Did he leave already?"

Mason was going to meet any threat to her, head on.

They stopped at the front door, and she drew a portable battery pack from her purse. It looked like one of those phone chargers Rayna bought him for when he went on airplanes. She popped a panel from the siding by the door lock and plugged in the power source. Within a minute, she'd gained access. The front door slid aside, moving into the frame of the wall like a single elevator door.

"How do realtor's get in, if you had to hack the lock?"

She stowed the battery pack in her purse. "I didn't hack it. I used the access code I got from the realtor's computer system. The power is turned on when someone is coming to look at the house."

Mason wasn't sure he exactly understood but she'd stepped inside, so he followed to make sure she didn't get surprised by someone hiding inside. Then he turned to Haley. "Stay with her."

The former navy petty officer nodded.

He and Niall cleared the house. Stale air, bare floors and walls. A layer of dust on the kitchen counters. He moved back to the front door. "No sign anyone's been here in weeks."

Talia frowned. "But he was here."

"Maybe." Mason shrugged. "Ready to get to work?"

She moved past him, saying nothing, and headed for the network closet. Niall and Haley had a low conversation by the front door, with the NCIS agent doing most of the talking. His girlfriend shot him a look that made him smile.

Mason turned to watch Talia, knowing they'd keep an eye out but also give them privacy. Talia plugged a micro SD cable from her tablet into a port on the rack in front of her. She tapped and swiped the screen.

"I should be able to connect. Then it won't take long to copy everything." She shivered. "I'm ready to get out of here. This place is kind of creepy."

"Does the server have power going to it?" He glanced at the display. None of the lights were on.

"I'm just about to fire it up."

And why did that make him nervous? She glanced at him. "Thanks for coming with me."

Before he could nod, the server behind her lit up and began to whir.

She glanced at it. "Why is…"

The front door slid shut.

Haley pressed the button beside the door. "It's not opening." She turned to them, wide eyed. "We're locked in."

19

"Hold this." Talia handed Mason the tablet now running a program that would copy everything.

"Did you turn the power back on?"

She didn't glance back. "No, I didn't. That happened all by itself." The front door was shut. "The panel to open it is outside."

Niall shifted beside her. "Isn't there a way to access it from in here?"

The wall beside the front door was at right angles. "Inside this wall."

"I'll figure out what's on the other side."

She nodded. "The garage, I think."

He wandered off, long strides taking him to the garage door fast.

"The copy is complete."

She glanced at Mason. "Pull the cord." Then she had an idea. "Wait." She strode over.

"Waiting." When she neared him, he handed over the tablet.

Haley crossed the room behind her. "I'll search for an alternate exit."

Talia swiped the screen of the tablet. She looked for a part of

166 | LISA PHILLIPS

the program she could access through the server. A way to open the door.

"No way to get into the garage," Niall said. "I'm going to look for something to make a hole in the wall." But he didn't move away just yet. "Did you know we might not be able to get out if the door shut?"

"I left it open."

Mason shifted. "Why don't you go find a crowbar, or something?"

Niall shot him a look, but wandered off.

"Is he always like that?"

Talia shrugged. "He doesn't like being trapped. Or drugged."

Mason frowned.

"Long story." She kept looking at the tablet. Mason moved to the window and placed both hands against it. Fingers splayed.

She glanced over and said, "It's tempered glass." Then went back to her tablet screen.

There had to be a way to access house controls even without Wi-Fi. The house had an internal network that had nothing to do with an internet connection. Though it was possible to activate that function and control the house...remotely.

"No. There wasn't a connection when we got here. There wasn't even power to the house, there's no way he..."

Mason walked back over. "You didn't shut the door, right?"

"No."

"Is it possible—"

"Don't say it."

He set a hand on her shoulder. "We knew this was a possibility. You said yourself when you were on the phone with Victoria that you agreed with her, and this could be a trap. We all came anyway."

"We should have made the others wait outside."

If something happened to them because the hacker had targeted her, Talia didn't know what she would do.

"You don't even know for sure this is him." Mason squeezed

her shoulder, then let his hand drop. "Could be some function timed out, and the door shut on its own. To keep out the cold so the house isn't powerless with the front door open. You don't know that he's accessing the house."

"He isn't." She shifted the tablet so he could see the screen, just not slow enough he'd see it as an invitation to take the thing. Or read everything on the display. "There's no connection coming in, or going out. Nothing. He isn't—"

Niall strode back in. "No crowbars."

Haley was right behind him. "And no other way out of…" Her voice trailed off as her attention was snagged by something.

On the other side of the living room window, Dakota walked across the grass. Haley rushed to the window. She waved, trying to get Dakota's attention. Neema trotted out from behind a bush and caught up to the Homeland agent. Dakota reached down and patted the dog's head.

Haley banged on the glass. "Dakota!"

The homeland agent continued walking.

Haley banged harder.

Josh brought up the rear. He passed in front of the window behind Dakota and their dog. Haley banged on the glass. Niall moved to her side and did the same.

Josh glanced over at the window. He frowned and moved closer. Talia saw him glance aside and call out to Dakota.

"I can't hear what he said." Haley glanced at Niall.

"Me either." Worry bled through his tone. "The glass is totally soundproof."

"And there's no window to open."

Josh took a step toward the glass. Haley and Niall started up again, banging fists on the glass. It was loud enough to threaten Talia with a headache. Josh didn't seem to even hear it.

They got louder, banging hard enough she was sure the glass would break.

"He can't hear them." Talia wanted to clasp Mason's hand.

Niall and Haley kept banging, trying to get Josh's attention.

She watched him lean close to the glass. Use both hands to shield his eyes from light outside as he peered in with his nose to the window.

"He can't see in." The words slipped from her mouth.

"Is there a way to turn on the lights in here, somehow? Try to make it so he can see us?"

She looked at the tablet. "I didn't power up the server." But if she did that now, would she have more control over the mechanisms? She got the power bank out and plugged it in one handed. She used her tablet to ask the system to open the door.

UNABLE TO COMPLY.

She tried the windows, a command to get any of them to open. When that didn't work, she tried to get the system to roll up the garage door.

UNABLE TO COMPLY.

She bit back the urge to mutter a curse. "It's not working. I have no control."

"So who does?"

No one needed to answer that question. Talia choked down the regret at having brought all her friends here. She should have forced them to stay back. Left the office before they knew she was gone. This was her fight.

Mason walked over to the front door.

What if one of them got hurt? She didn't want that happening. It would be her fault. And worse, she would probably have to watch them get hurt. Maybe even die.

Tears blurred the screen of her tablet.

A loud crash made her start. She looked up to find Mason shaking out his hand, a hole in the drywall beside the door. He'd punched a hole in the wall?

Mason lifted his foot next and used the sole of his shoe to kick the hole in the wall. He made a bigger opening. Set his foot down. Coughed.

Something snagged in Talia's throat. She had to cough as well. Had the dust gotten all the way over to her already?

Niall and Haley quit banging on the window.

"It's no use." Haley sounded so defeated.

Talia looked back at the tablet while Mason pulled chunks of drywall away. She needed to finish up here so she could connect to the front door lock mechanism the same way she had outside.

Nothing else she tried worked.

Talia yanked the cord out, too frustrated to worry if she'd broken it or not. She had a spare in her purse.

Gathering up her things, she strode to the front door.

Mason had his head practically inside the hole he'd made in the wall.

"Can you see it?" She had to cough again to get all the words out.

He pulled back. "Maybe."

She had the cord all ready, prepared to get out of here as quickly as possible. Being locked in with no way out was beyond freaky.

Niall wandered to the middle of the room and looked at a vent high on the wall that ended where the front entry gave way to the open plan living area.

"Guys. We have a problem." Then he sniffed. "There's something coming out of the vent. And it doesn't smell too good."

———

"Give me that plug."

She handed the end of the cord over. Mason didn't waste time sticking his head back in the wall to guide the plug to the rear of the panel. Maybe this would work, or maybe not. But they were all coughing now. Whatever was being pumped through the vent was going to build up until they passed out...or worse. This hacker guy had to be controlling it all still. Or he'd set layers of failsafes. She was at his mercy.

All their lives in danger.

"Got it." He pulled his head out.

"Thanks." Talia's voice was a whisper, but he couldn't allow emotion to slow him down right now.

Mason moved to the door he figured led to the garage, on the other side of the wall he'd just made a hole in. He lifted his foot and kicked at the door beside the handle. Much tougher material than the wall. Fire door? Maybe. Kind of felt like it was metal.

He lowered his foot. No damage.

Mason knocked on it with his knuckles. Sure sounded like it was solid. He touched his ear to the door and listened. "I think I can hear a rumble on the other side." But he didn't know what it was.

Niall wandered over. "Like what?"

Mason shrugged. If he knew, he'd have said.

"Uh-oh."

Mason looked at Talia first—still working on her tablet—before he looked to see what Haley was talking about. The former navy non-commissioned officer took a step back. Beyond the glass, Dakota had her gun out. She pointed it at the glass of the window.

Niall yelled, "Down!"

Haley dived to the floor and hit the tile with a grunt.

Two bullet holes splintered the outside of the glass. Tiny cracks splayed out, not more than three or four inches from the point of impact. The rounds had both embedded in the glass. Mason walked to the window while Niall helped Haley off the floor.

Dakota holstered her weapon, pretty much ignoring whatever Josh was saying to her.

Mason stared at the bullets up close. The impact had been localized to the area around where they hit. No damage to the window any wider than his hand span. What on earth was this window made out of?

He had to cough.

"Any progress on getting that door open?"

Talia shook her head and let out a frustrated sound. "I hate you right now."

Mason didn't know if she was referring to the tablet, or the hacker he figured was responsible for trapping them in here.

Haley was by the vent again. "I think it's like carbon monoxide. Like the toxic fumes from car exhaust."

"That means we don't have long before we're going to have serious problems." Niall put his arm around her. "Let's go check all the doors and windows again. Maybe there's a panic room, or another exit we haven't found."

Talia said, "Master bedroom closet. It was on some of the plans I looked at, but not others. It might be there. So don't get your hopes up."

"Got it," Niall called back to her as they made their way down the hall.

Dakota and Josh had moved away from the window outside. Where had they gone? The last he'd seen of them, it appeared they'd figured out that something was wrong.

Mason moved toward Talia, pulling out his phone. "Something is blocking my cell signal."

She nodded. "I figured as much. He's giving us no way to call out."

"While he suffocates us with engine fumes."

Were Josh and Dakota able to make a call? Maybe they could get local emergency services here. Hopefully in enough time to get a door open before the worst happened.

"I'm trying to get us out." There was a bite to her tone.

Mason frowned. "I know that. It wasn't a criticism. We're all on edge. Scared, if we're willing to admit that to ourselves."

Talia looked up at him. "Sorry."

"Don't be. We can figure this out together. Or Niall and Haley will find another exit."

"But I'm the one who gets this stuff done. They're all counting on me."

"So let's puzzle it out. Okay?" When she nodded, he continued, "You said there was no signal from outside the house, right?"

"Yes."

"So what does that leave?"

"The door was closed by something that didn't require a signal from an external source." She tapped the screen. "The diagnostic says a command was entered to close the door."

"And the vents?"

"Same."

He had to wonder about that. "So someone on the premises entered a signal?"

Talia blinked. "That means he's here."

Wasn't that a horrible thought? Mason wanted to bring this guy in. How could they do that, even if he was here? They'd have to get out first. Or get to where he was.

"Guys!" Niall's shout rang through the house. "Get in here!"

Talia disconnected her tablet. He swiped up her purse and handed it to her as they raced down the hall to the bedroom.

"This could be a way out." Haley held a sliding door open—a panel in the wall. She waved them to it.

Mason let Talia go through first, then followed. There were steps down. The air smelled clearer, though, and he sucked in a few lungfuls of clean oxygen before breathing out a relieved breath.

Niall called out from up ahead. "There's a tunnel."

"Is it a way out?" Mason asked, his voice ringing in the small space.

"I think so."

Mason's foot splashed water on the ground. Haley clicked on the flashlight on her gun and shone it around the tunnel as they moved. He did the same, illuminating a walkway of breeze block on either side of him. Giant concrete blocks stuck together with cement. Barely wide enough for him to put both elbows out to the sides. He'd graze the skin for sure.

Behind him, the door to the bedroom closet slid closed.

"This better be the way out."

No one replied to his frustrated comment.

"Here." Niall stopped up ahead.

Mason heard Haley and Talia come to a stop. He did the same, shining his flashlight around so he could stand close to Talia. He set a hand on her back to reassure her that they were here with her.

Still, her breathing came fast.

Too fast.

He realized then that he'd reacted to her fear even before becoming aware she was feeling it. Now she was heading rapidly toward a panic attack.

Niall climbed a ladder and pushed at a manhole cover above his head. Mason looked at his phone. Still no signal, even though they were no longer in the house.

Niall grunted with each shove. "It's moving." Slowly, though. Mason didn't like this. He looked around while he tried to figure out where the niggling originated. That sensation pricking the skin on the back of his neck. The one that made him want to tell Niall to hurry it up.

This was taking too long.

Talia gasped. She shifted and looked down the tunnel in front of them. "Niall, you need to hurry up."

Mason moved to climb the ladder beside him. He lifted one hand and helped push against the manhole cover.

"What is it?" Niall grunted.

Mason just pushed at the metal ring, praying it would come all the way loose.

Haley pleaded, "Hurry. Please."

Talia was the one who answered his question.

"There's water rushing toward us."

Mason braced his weight and pushed with both hands. "Come on. Open."

20

T he roar of the water grew louder.

"You need to hurry up." Talia crowded close to Haley, stood by the men's legs as they fought to get the manhole cover open.

A crack of light spilled down onto them.

He was trying to kill them. The hacker who had targeted her —and probably lured them all here, though they *had* come of their own volition—was now attempting to murder all of her friends. Anger roiled through her with the thought that they were going to die here. The hacker would win, and there would be nothing she could do about it.

If they'd stayed in the house, would it have triggered another issue? Maybe he accounted for them leaving this way. Their movement had changed the situation from death by carbon monoxide poisoning to death by drowning? A series of presents left behind in the house computer network.

Triggered by her showing up.

The two men pushed the manhole cover aside. Bright sunlight flooded the tunnel. Talia raised her hand to shield her eyes from the intense glare.

Niall said, "Haley, come here."

Mason jumped off the ladder as Niall tugged Haley up beside him. "Go." Niall shoved at her, forcing her to climb faster. Then he followed her up.

Mason waved Talia to the ladder. "Come on."

She moved forward. "What about you?"

"I'll be right behind you."

The water roared so loud she almost didn't hear him. Clutching her purse against her body, Talia climbed the stairs. Water sprayed at her. The rungs slicked.

Her foot slipped. She started to fall and grasped at the ladder with her fingers. Her leg banged a lower rung.

Talia cried out. Mason's body crowded her. Held her close to the ladder. "Go," he ordered loudly in her ear.

Talia hauled herself up. Niall and Haley both grasped her arms. They helped her out of the hole, fumbling and awkward. Her body pumped with adrenaline. Cold air buffeted her and she whimpered as she crawled out of the way so Mason could get out.

The rush of water was deafening. So loud she couldn't hear what Haley was saying.

It moved past her, down the tunnel. Mason's cry disappeared with the water.

Talia screamed. She dove back to the opening. The sight of nothing below her but water stole her breath. Like a river rushing through the tunnel. "Mason!"

He wasn't there. He wasn't below her.

He hadn't made it.

She screamed his name again.

"Talia." Niall touched her shoulder.

"No." She shoved his hand away. Leaned down and peered into the tunnel. Where was he? Where had he been swept to? The closed door to the closet, maybe. Had his big, thick body been slammed against it by the force of the water? Thousands of pounds of pressure throwing him against that solid surface.

She whimpered. "Mason!"

His hand appeared on the ladder, the knuckles pale as he

squeezed to hold on for dear life. Then his head emerged. He sucked in a breath. Water streamed down his face.

"Help me." She screamed the words at him, but Niall and Haley knew what she meant.

The two of them landed on their knees on either side of her. Together, the three of them pulled him out. Water swirled around his body as they helped him onto the grass.

Mason lay back. His chest heaved with each breath.

Talia whimpered.

Mason reached for her, but she was already moving toward him. He gathered her in his arms until she was held against the wet of the bullet proof vest he wore. One hand around her waist kept her tight against him while the other moved up the back of her neck, his fingers tangling in her damp hair.

Their cheeks touched.

She could feel his warm breath on her skin. Both of them were soaked through, trying to control the realization that he had almost died. She was just so relieved. Gone were the thoughts of what would have happened to his daughter.

"What would I have done?"

His face angled slightly, and she felt his lips move against the shell of her ear. "Talia." Her name was a groan from his lips.

She held on tight.

"Uh…" Dakota's voice had an edge of laughter. "You guys okay?"

Talia became aware that she and Mason were in a clinch, lying on the grass. All four team members stood around them. Neema wandered over and sniffed at Talia's hair.

Instead of embarrassment, pure relief washed over her. "Hi, dog."

Talia shifted her hand to push off the ground. She'd practically crawled on top of Mason. In a *skirt*. Goodness, what her mother would have said if she'd seen this. She shuddered to think of it. She tried to gracefully move away, but his arms were still around her.

For a second, she wondered if Mason was going to let her go. But he did.

Talia wasn't sure which she preferred. Okay, she knew what she wanted, and what her mother would approve of. But the team waited.

Mason sat up. He helped her to stand when he was the one who'd nearly drowned. More embarrassment. How was she ever going to live this down? He'd nearly been swept away, and she was the shaky one. Her legs almost buckled.

Haley reached out for her other arm. Talia shot her a smile. "Thanks." The two of them steadied her. "I'm okay."

Mason huffed out a long breath as he sat up, still on the ground. "Phew."

She shot him a look. "That's all you have to say? *Phew?*" Talia planted her hands on her hips. "You nearly died. I thought you *were* dead."

He climbed to his feet and brushed off his body as he moved. Then patted his chest, his pockets.

"Are you really okay?" She didn't want him to suddenly pass out. They'd have to carry that redwood body back to the car. Or to an ambulance.

Mason shifted his soft gaze to her. "I'm good, Talia." His chest expanded as he sucked in air, then blew out a long breath. He ran one hand down his face with a groan.

"He's not okay." She turned to Dakota. "We should get an ambulance. One of those helicopter ambulances."

Dakota's lips twitched. "He said he's good."

"I think I know where he is."

Everyone turned to Mason.

Talia said, "What? How?"

Fear raced through her with the idea of coming face to face with the hacker. Still, she would like the answer to those questions. The fact he thought the hacker was *here* hit her with a dose of reality like a slap in the face.

Dakota, Josh, Haley and Niall all took a step toward where she stood with Mason. One step, and the team huddled around them. Around her. Cocooning her in a little pocket of safety. Determined that nothing would happen to her.

"Guys…" She wasn't sure what she wanted to say.

"We know." Dakota shifted to Mason. "Where?"

"In the garage."

"But—" Talia realized they'd all started moving.

Haley patted her back. "Come on."

Apparently she had no choice. So Talia moved with them.

As they went, Mason reached out and snagged her hand. He held it in his stronger, bigger one, though his was very cold. Someone needed a hot cup of coffee. She could use a mocha with whipped cream.

"The garage?"

He glanced over. "There's a car in there, right? That's what I'm thinking was pumping carbon monoxide into the HVAC."

Did that mean the hacker was in there, though?

"He would have to be close, in order to switch plans when he realized we were in the tunnel."

"True." But she didn't want to believe it. Fear niggled the back of her neck as they approached the door.

Dakota and Josh glanced at each other, apparently not needing words in order to communicate. They both crouched, got a grip on the bottom of the garage door, and forced it up. Niall went to the middle and helped.

"Careful." She had to say it.

If he was in there, they could get hurt. Killed.

Mason pulled her to his side, gun drawn. Her entire body was tense. She felt like she was going to snap from the force of it.

Niall stared into the garage. "Bingo."

———

MASON SHIFTED TO LOOK INSIDE. A vintage Mustang had been parked in the garage. If the make and model were significant in some way, he didn't know. But this car, in this condition, would be hard to come by.

He moved along the side while the others carefully did the same, spread around the garage. He glanced back. Talia stood at the mouth of the garage, with Haley. Waiting for someone to give her the okay to enter? He had his gun out, but the thing was probably so waterlogged—like his phone—that he figured it wouldn't work. He certainly couldn't fire it without taking it apart to see what the damage to the inside was.

Mason moved to the back bumper. The engine was running. "There's a hose back here. Stretches up to the HVAC." The hacker had planned to kill them all along, leaving the engine running for when they got here? That didn't exactly sound efficient.

Maybe it had been hooked into the house. Mason was leaning toward the idea that their presence here had initiated all this.

Josh studied the hose. "You guys really couldn't get out?"

"Nope." Mason rubbed at the buttons over his chest with the flat of his hand. He'd thought for sure he would be swept away. Slammed by the force of the water against the door to the closet. Or it would have broken the door open and shoved him back inside. He'd have been gassed.

Either way, dead.

"He's not in here." Josh turned in a circle as he looked around.

He should call Rayna. Not that she knew he'd been in danger, but it was good to check in. Let her know he was all right.

One of these guys would probably let him borrow a phone.

It was on the tip of his tongue to ask when he remembered how Talia had frozen up the last time he'd mentioned his daughter. He could wait and call Rayna later to say hi. Right now he didn't want Talia pulling away and shutting down. Not considering he'd actually managed to get somewhere with her. And it had taken almost dying for it to happen.

He didn't think she had a problem with Rayna. More like the concept of him having a child—and that child potentially being fatherless because of a bad guy who saw Talia as a threat. She wanted no collateral damage. Didn't want the people she cared about to be hurt. Even a teen she didn't know.

Whatever was between him and Talia, Mason didn't want to lose the ground he'd gained. Before, he hadn't been sure if it was more than attraction. It was certainly more than that on his part, even with the craziness of all that had happened to him since he'd met her. Now he knew she actually cared about him. And not in an "I'm glad you didn't die" kind of way. It was more than that.

Eventually things would calm down. They would catch this guy, and he could take the time for Talia to get to know Rayna. It would be good.

He just needed to have patience.

"Talia." Dakota straightened. "There's a computer in the front seat. I think it's running a program." She waved over her colleague and pulled on the door handle. "One sec."

Talia slowed.

"Just checking." Dakota opened the door slowly. She looked between the frame and the door. "Neema, hier."

The dog trotted over. Mason heard a couple of sniffs, and then the dog wandered to Josh looking bored.

Dakota waved Talia over. "It's clear. We've been doing explosives training."

Mason did the same as she'd done on her side and opened the passenger door slowly. He didn't see any wires, so he planted his butt in the front seat and grabbed the latch of the glove box. It spilled open. He caught the tumble of papers and started to go through them.

Talia lifted the laptop from the front seat and sat down. She pulled the lever and shifted the seat all the way back to get the computer between her and the steering wheel.

As she typed on the keys, he rifled through old insurance slips and the registration. Receipts. A couple of pizza coupons from a national chain. He found a letter—someone's life insurance company wanted the details for an additional contact person they could add to their files.

Mason handed it to Niall. "Run the name and address?"

The NCIS agent nodded.

"My phone is probably kaput." He wanted to be mad, but it just wasn't there. It would be a hassle to get a new one. Fact was, though, Mason could be dead. He wasn't. He was still here.

The thought was like a rush. Enough his fingers itched to touch Talia's face and kiss her. Not with her team watching, so maybe later.

He wanted to, though.

To distract himself, he turned to her. "Anything on that?"

She clicked half a dozen more keys, and then hit enter.

The car engine turned off.

"I'm guessing, yes."

She looked up, a smile on her face. "I just need another second." She spoke louder, presumably so the rest could hear. "Then we can take this with us."

She wanted to get out of here. That was fine by him, he felt the same. Except did she think the hacker would draw them out to kill them, only to lead them right back to him when they survived?

The way he targeted Talia and the people she cared about, this fell under the column titled, "Cruel and Unusual Punishment." Mason didn't know if she could continue to hold it together. Anyone in her position would have buckled under the pressure by now.

Talia seemed okay. Maybe she was still running on adrenaline. Or she was as glad as he was that they were all alive. They'd beaten him. Again.

"You think you can find him?"

Her mouth shifted as she thought about his question. "I hope so. I mean, what else do we have?"

Mason nodded, conceding along with her. "Hacking the hacker?"

"After what he did, I was scared to even get on a computer. Hiding seemed like a much better idea. Now…"

He waited, but she said nothing. Mason touched her shoulder. "What?"

"I'm angry." She shook her head, not looking at him. "You nearly died. I'm so angry I could scream. We *have* to get this guy."

"We will. We're not going to stop until we do."

She gritted her teeth together, then said, "Good."

He wanted to say more, but the screen flashed. Mason watched as the window she was typing in flashed. The screen shifted.

Flickered.

"What…"

He pulled his hand from her shoulder. "You didn't do that?"

"No, I—" The screen changed again. A live feed. A camera, complete with a circle on it, like a scope. Like sniper sights.

At the end of the view, they watched Alvarez climb out the back of a car and walk toward two other men. Shake hands.

Talia typed. Then slammed her index finger down on the enter key, hard enough he winced, worrying she would break it. Maybe she needed to. Would it make things worse?

"What is he going to do?" Mason's gut clenched at the idea Talia would have to watch a trigger get pulled and her teammate go down.

Text flashed across the bottom of the screen.

SHOULD HE LIVE OR DIE?

The words scrolled, then were replaced by a single word.

CHOOSE.

21

Nothing else worked, so Talia typed a reply.

I'M NOT PLAYING YOUR GAME.

Then she got on her phone and sent a message to her former team over at the NSA. Could they trace the signal coming to this computer—this location? If they were able to figure out where Alvarez was, by zeroing in on the landscape around him, then someone could go to him. Before he was taken out by a rifle.

In her head, she could almost hear the hacker's laughter. Amused at her futile attempts to find him and get Alvarez out of danger. She texted the marshal to alert him to the danger. One word:

CROSSHAIRS.

Dakota crouched in the doorway. "Can I?"

"Why?"

"So I can hand this guy the piece of my mind I've wanted to give him for weeks."

Talia clenched her jaw. Dakota wanted to shoulder it, as well as vent her frustration. The team was around her. Mason was here. She wasn't alone, trapped.

She sucked in a breath. "I got it."

She typed.

ENOUGH. I'M DONE. DO WHAT YOU WILL, I'M NOT GOING TO BE PART OF IT ANYMORE.

His reply came straight away.

SPOIL SPORT.

Talia shut the laptop. If he was going to kill Alvarez, she didn't want to watch it happen. She'd warned her friend. The NSA were going to have to do whatever they could. She had to stand her ground. She couldn't bend to his will anymore.

"Let's go." She moved so fast she almost knocked Dakota on her butt. But her friend was agile. Talia took the laptop out of the garage. She wanted to throw the thing on the ground, but resisted the allure.

She dialed Victoria as she walked and handed the laptop off to Haley.

"Uh...thanks?" Her roommate held it.

The phone was answered mid-ring, "Director Bramlyn."

"Get somewhere you can talk." Talia stopped. She dipped her head and used her free arm to squeeze the back of her neck. Tears threatened to choke her, but she swallowed them back and cleared her throat.

"What is it?" Victoria's voice echoed like she was in a hallway.

"Alvarez needs cover. He was in the hacker's crosshairs." She had to stop and take a breath to push back the sparks at the edges of her vision. Passing out would not be helpful.

"You think I let him go unprotected?"

Dakota tapped Talia on the shoulder. "What's she saying?"

Talia turned. The whole team watched her. Great, an audience for her breakdown. He thought he was tormenting her, putting people in danger? This was worse. Their concern, and the fact they weren't off bringing in bad guys right now. Rounding up evil. No, they were taking care of her.

That wasn't how their team was supposed to work.

Talia did the support stuff. Not the parts where she was in the middle of everything, the center of attention.

"Put me on speaker."

Talia lowered the phone and tapped the button. "Go ahead."

"Everyone is there?"

Haley called out, "Yes."

"And Special Agent Anderson?"

"Yes, ma'am."

Victoria chuckled. "You make your mama proud."

Josh snorted. Talia wanted to smile, but she couldn't. "Alvarez."

Another one of her teammates was in danger. Well, given the cases they took, it was probably true that they were always in danger. It was how their line of work went. No social media presence. Living quietly. Being careful. Safe.

She'd done so much to help them in this, never thinking it would be her turn next. That they would be here, determined to keep her safe. But she still had to do that for Alvarez. As much as he knew the life he lived was not a safe one, she wasn't going to stand around and do nothing.

"As I was about to say to you, Talia, I made a call a few hours ago. Welvern has a friend. He's been a help in the past and has private investigator papers. His skills are in the neighborhood of contract undercover work for the FBI."

"Hours ago?"

"Alvarez has protection, and the guy is already in play."

Talia said, "We need that guy's number. So we can warn him.

"I'll send him a text." Victoria paused. "Okay, done. Our marshal shut off his work phone. He has the burner you gave him, and that's all." She went quiet again for a few seconds. "Drew says they're both good."

"Oh." So Alvarez hadn't even gotten her message? "He's okay?" She could text the other cell, though. She could mask her information and get him secure communication. She'd be able to let him know again if his life was in imminent danger.

"There's nothing to worry about, Talia. He's good."

Talia blew out a long breath. There was plenty to worry

about. "I'll keep you posted if my old team finds this hacker's whereabouts." Because it apparently wasn't here.

"Good." Victoria paused. "You guys all right?"

"Yes."

A couple of the others chimed in. Mason said, "Yes, ma'am."

Victoria's voice came through the phone speaker again. "The hacker is just trying to get you riled up. You know that, right?"

Talia figured that question was for her. "It's working. And we're *still* two steps behind, the same way we've been this entire time."

A hand touched her shoulder. She knew without looking that it was Mason, so she reached up and squeezed his fingers. The urge to run was strong.

People she loved kept getting caught in the crossfire. She could hardly stand to think about watching Mason get washed away again. Right there behind her one second, helping her out, and then he was gone. Whooshed out of sight by a rush of water.

She swallowed down the lump in her throat.

Victoria said, "I'll light a fire under the NSA director. He owes me a favor."

Who didn't? Talia certainly couldn't repay her for everything she'd done. "Okay."

"We *are* going to find him."

Talia bit her lip. Her vision blurred as tears filled her eyes. Victoria didn't know that. Since the bank, she had assumed they would get him. Eventually. Soon. Now. None of those things had happened so far.

Maybe they weren't going to catch him at all. He would continue tormenting Talia for years to come. Until he had destroyed her career, the people she cared about...everything.

Gone.

Talia hung up on her. She couldn't talk about this anymore. Not if she wanted to keep from screaming out her frustration at all of them. Given Victoria was the one who had rescued her from the worst day of her life, that wasn't exactly a showing of grateful thanks. Not that her boss would regret having done it. But still, Talia didn't want her to have to deal with that.

None of them were supposed to.

"Talia—"

She shook her head, already moving away. She figured they all saw it on her face. That urge she had to just up and run. Get as far away from them as fast as she could.

If he was going to keep coming after her—and wasn't it just delay tactics to keep them busy?—then maybe he should find her alone when he did. The rest of the team could get back to work.

In fact, that was a great idea.

Talia spun around to face them all. She lifted her chin. "You guys should go."

"We only brought one car." Dakota stuck her hand on her hip. Beside her, the dog shifted into a sit and leaned against her leg.

"That's not what I mean, and you know it."

Mason glanced between them. "I'll stay with you."

"No—"

Before she could finish, he cut her off.

———

"You really think any of us are going to let you go off by yourself?"

"I'm not a child." The pain in her eyes was stark. Plain for any of them to see. "It's not like I want to be by myself. But it's safer."

He tugged her away from the others.

Dakota saw his intention and jerked her thumb in the direction of the trail. "We'll see you guys at the car." In her gaze was a direct order for him to make sure Talia got there, whole and hearty.

Mason gave her a tight nod and wandered a couple of steps to the side with Talia. He was drenched, head to foot and shivering from the cold, but he still didn't want to be anywhere else except here. Talking to Talia. Helping her through this.

She looked down and surveyed the state of him.

"I probably look like a sorry sight."

The corner of her mouth shifted. Not quite a smile, but he took it for the victory it was.

"I'm not going to tell you that everything will be fine. Not when I don't know that for sure."

She bit her lip.

"But I'll be with you. Even if that means you and me, together, while the team goes and does their thing."

He just couldn't bear to think what might happen to her if she went off on her own. Probably exactly what she was worried would happen to him, considering he'd been abducted. But that guy was dead now. The threat was still real, though. This hacker definitely had something going on, and Prometheus was loose.

"You'd really do that?" She looked up at him.

"I don't want you out there, alone, swinging in the breeze."

"Neither do I." She started to say something else, but evidently thought better of it.

"But..?"

She sighed. "I don't want anyone else getting hurt because of me. It's too much. Too—" She ran her fingers through the hair on the sides of her face and grasped handfuls.

"Talia." He had to shake her out of her own world. This mess she felt like she was drowning in.

Mason dragged her toward him and slid his arms loosely around her. "You're not doing this alone."

"And if something happens to Rayna? What then?"

He'd been right. This was about her fear for his daughter. "Rayna might be fine, or she could get hurt tomorrow in a way she'd never recover. But I still have to live my life—even though the possibility is literally in my mind every single day. That's what parenting is. It can't paralyze me with worry over what might happen to her. I have to *live* now." A tear fell from her eye and tracked its way down her cheek. He swiped it with his thumb. "Please don't turn out to *not* be the woman I thought you were."

"What does that mean?"

"Stick with me," he implored her. "I know you've gone through so much."

Whispered words spilled from her lips. "I thought you were dead."

Mason leaned his forehead against hers and shut his eyes. "I know. For a second there I thought I was as well."

"He's never going to quit." She sucked in a breath that hitched in the middle. "He'll keep coming and coming, giving me the runaround until I loose my mind. It's never going to end."

This guy had to have some sick obsession with her. Mixed up with a furious need to compete with her in the realm of network security. They'd been wrapped in a battle since he'd met her in the bank, and before.

Talia said, "Your hands are freezing."

He let go of her face. "Sorry." Had she heard what he was saying? Mason needed her to understand. To be the kind of woman he could trust to not leave when things got intense. The need to know whether she would or not was driving this passion in him. He could almost understand this guy, in a weird way. Mason wanted something from her, and he was going to stick around until he got it.

The two were not the same, at all. But he had to admit that he did understand the hacker's persistence.

Talia snagged his hand and held it with hers. "It's okay."

"Promise me something?"

He watched her lips form the word. "What?"

"Talk to me first. Because if you go, I want to go with you." He'd say they should do it right now, only they'd all shown up here in one car. "I just need you to talk to me."

"That's all? Just communication?"

He nodded, and her expression softened. She liked that. A fact which warmed his freezing body from the inside. "We should catch up with the others."

"First…" She shifted closer to him. "There's just one thing."

Talia set her hands on his shoulders. She lifted up and pressed her lips to his. All thought escaped his mind for a few seconds, but he had the wherewithal to not pull her against his freezing wet body. She didn't need to show back up to her teammates with her clothes soaked all down the front. They'd know exactly what happened.

But he pulled her close enough. Tilted his head to the side and stayed there for a minute. When he could feel it wane, he leaned back. Opened his eyes. "Wow."

Talia giggled.

"That was nice, too." Before she needed to ask, he said, "Hearing you laugh."

"We should go. They'll wonder what we've been up to."

Mason rubbed at his lips with the back of his hand. When he lowered his arm, he saw purple lip color on his skin, "I doubt it."

She reapplied as they walked, then stowed the makeup tube back in her purse. "Maybe I should just leave my devices out here."

"My phone probably won't recover, given how waterlogged it is."

"We could both get new phones. I could try and catch him from a new source." Her voice had a thread of exhaustion running through it.

Mason squeezed her hand. "It's not just you. It's all of us, and your old team at the NSA. Right?" When she nodded, he continued, "I know it feels like it's aimed at only you. But we're all standing here, trying to shield you. We aren't going to let anything happen to you. Not like what happened before."

A shadow crossed her gaze. "I hope so."

They neared the SUV, door open. The team probably all buckled in. Mason slid his arm around her and kissed her temple. He'd made enough promises. It probably wouldn't be good to make any more and not be able to keep them. He didn't know what would happen, but he trusted that God had both of them—and everyone they cared about—in His hands.

Mason caught a muffled sound.

He twisted around and saw two men holding Haley, one with a hand over her mouth. He drew his gun and spun to see where the rest of the team were. He had to get Talia behind him.

Then he saw Niall lying on the grass, face down, blood in his hair. Gun discarded a few feet away. Was he dead, or just out cold?

Talia let out a sound, full of fear.

Mason shifted both of them so that he faced what was coming first. Always. He looked at the man walking toward him and lifted his chin. "Whatever you're doing, it's over. You're done."

The man grinned. "I'm just getting started."

22

S he didn't want to look at him, but she did. Younger than her —probably late twenties. Slender. Scars on his cheeks that she assumed were from acne he'd had as a teen. Talia wanted to see some evidence of evil in his expression. A menace, or ill will toward pretty much everyone. Not just her. She didn't want him to have singled her out, but he had.

All she saw on his face was…nothing. Maybe an edge of frustration, but that was all.

"Where are Dakota and Josh?" Why wasn't the dog barking? Chaos should have erupted. Instead, it seemed like they'd been hit hard and fast. No time to react. Now Niall was on the ground, out cold. Haley was about to take down the guy who held her. And Mason.

He shifted in front of her. Steady. Solid. Unmovable. Her shield, and a gift from God—she thanked Him again. She had to lean to look around him in order to see the hacker. She motioned with a glance at Haley. "Have your guys let her go."

The skin around his eyes flexed. It took a minute, but the hacker finally spoke. "Very well. As a show of good faith." He motioned to Haley with a flick of two fingers.

The men holding her released their grip. Haley scrambled to

crouch beside Niall. She touched his back, and the back of his head. She didn't flip him over. Whatever she saw there in his condition only made her more anxious.

"What do you want?" The quicker they got to that, the quicker Haley could call for medical help for Niall.

The hacker sniffed. "Just you."

"After what you did to me?"

Mason's body stiffened further. Like he hadn't already been completely tense. "That isn't going to happen."

"Don't worry." The hacker shrugged. "You'll get paid this time. We both will."

Her stomach flipped over. She wanted to be sick, but it had been so long since she'd eaten that she figured all she had were dry heaves.

"Let's go."

Mason shook his head.

Talia didn't want to. Too bad she had to face the fact they weren't going to get out of this in one piece—along with whatever Niall's injuries were—if she didn't move this along. Dakota and Josh could be crouched in the bushes. They might jump out at any second and take these guys out.

Then again, they might not.

Otherwise, wouldn't they have already done it?

The hacker motioned to the guys who'd been holding Haley. "Let's go."

Both moved. Guns held in a loose grip, they skirted the hacker and came right for her. She knew what was going to happen right before it did. Mason was exactly that kind of man. So it didn't surprise her in the least when he grabbed the first one's gun, swiped out with his other arm to punch the guy in the head, and at the same time kicked at the second man.

Talia swung her purse and batted the second guy's gun to the side. Yes, that made it aim across her body and she could've been shot in the stomach. But the first bullet shot right between them. The second flew past her right side.

She swung the purse again.

The guy lifted his hand, slapping the purse away from his head, then grabbed for her.

Mason's guy was on his knees. The man rallied quickly and launched up. Tackled Mason in the stomach. They both went down, a tangle of limbs and grunts.

Mason cried out.

"No!" Her guy grabbed her around the middle and lifted her off her feet. Breath forced from her lungs in one gush.

He strode past the hacker, still holding her off the ground. Talia kicked out and slammed borrowed running shoes into his shins. She should've never worn them. She could have done far more damage with her heels.

The man grunted, but appeared to find her attempts to get him to let her go amusing because his whole chest shook with the force of his humor.

Talia screamed out her frustration.

"Shut up." The hacker was right behind them. And apparently still frustrated.

"No. I won't."

The man let go, and she crumpled to the ground. He grabbed her elbow and hauled her to her feet. She snapped her head around to look at Mason.

The man he'd been fighting had the upper hand. Mason kicked at the guy as he brought his gun around. Two shots blasted. She saw a flash of teeth edged in blood, and then Mason kicked again. The gunman's weapon swung to the side. Mason punched him in the head, then dove on top of him.

A hand grabbed her bicep, hard enough she winced. The hacker dragged her around. "It's not like I *want* to do this. I have no choice."

"No choice but to hurt my friends?" She shook her head. "There's no way I'm going to believe that. Not ever."

A dull thud drew her attention, in time to see Mason fall back on the grass. The other man pushed out heavy breaths from the exertion of the fight, his chest expanding and contracting rapidly.

Talia bit down on the inside of her lip as the hacker dragged her toward a path. She looked again, but Mason was out of view. On the far side of the SUV, two more gunmen stood over Dakota and Josh. Both were out cold. Beside them, Neema lay panting.

"What—"

"Get moving, or we'll be late."

She struggled against his grip. Were they dead? She didn't even know. Neema didn't look good. Haley whimpered, still crouched over Niall as though she needed to protect him.

The two men standing over by her friends started toward them. One called out, "Let's go, Batts," over the SUV.

He was going to walk right by Haley.

Talia strained against his grip, determined to break his hold. The man came into view. He'd hurt Mason. "Don't you touch her!"

He closed in on Haley, who braced.

"No!"

The man lunged, but it was only a fake. He laughed out loud while Talia screamed. The others joined in with his humor as the hacker dragged her to their van.

"Maybe one of us should stay behind. To hurt them if she doesn't cooperate," one suggested.

Talia speared him with a death glare. "That's the *only* thing that will guarantee I do *nothing*. Try me." She wanted to cross her arms over her chest, so they'd know she meant business, but could only do it loosely. "You hurt them, and whatever you think is going to happen will never get done."

The hacker winced.

"Not that you'd understand caring about other people." She was on a roll now, so she figured, why stop? "Because you care about nothing but yourself."

"Come on, now. You don't know that's true."

"Your friends here just hurt a dog."

"Not my friends."

"All of you are beyond help." She huffed out a breath. "Hurting a dog? Not to mention whatever you did to the others? It's unconscionable."

"Can you shut her up?" one of the men asked.

She got right up in the hacker's face. On tip toes, and everything. Just so he wouldn't miss one word. "If any of them is hurt in a way they don't recover, Victoria is going to kill you."

The blow came out of nowhere.

Pain exploded in her head, and everything went black.

———

MASON BLINKED AGAINST THE SKY. He could hear someone—a woman—talking on a phone. Asking for help. Medical emergency.

He sat up.

The world swam around him, and he nearly heaved on the grass. He sucked in a few lungfuls of air and stood up. No time to feel sorry for himself. It wasn't just that, but he had no time to even think about all his injuries either. Let alone feel them.

Talia was gone.

That man. The man who had *sold her* on the black market had her again. He'd promised her that wasn't going to happen, as much as he would be able to prevent it.

He'd fought, but he couldn't stop it.

God, help her.

She had to be so scared. He needed to get her back in order to fix that. Standing here, wallowing in his failure, wasn't going to help.

Mason stopped beside Haley, the phone now discarded beside her. "Is help on the way?"

"Yes. Can you check on Dakota and Josh? I don't want to leave him."

"How bad is it?"

"I don't know." Tears filled her eyes. "They hit him so hard."

Concussion. Traumatic brain injury maybe? Mason squeezed her shoulder. "Just hang on." He moved around the SUV to where she'd indicated. Josh was in the process of sitting up.

The DEA agent glanced around, like he was trying to figure out where he was.

"Hey."

Josh reached for his gun.

"Easy." Mason knelt by the dog and laid his hand on her chest.

"They stunned her. Like they stunned all of us." Josh crawled to Dakota and patted his fiancé on the cheek. "Wake up sleepy-head, time to work."

She sucked in a breath. She sat up in one movement and almost knocked Josh aside.

Josh lifted his hands. "Whoa."

"Where are they?"

"Gone." Mason stood. Injuries here were minimal and aid was coming for Niall.

"Talia?"

"I'll find her."

Mason grabbed Niall's weapon and took off in the direction the heavy traffic of boot prints led. He prayed as he sprinted along the path. That she would be okay. That Niall wouldn't be hurt in a way he might not recover.

That this man would be brought to justice.

Prometheus would be found.

If God chose to use this gun to do that, well it was fine by Mason. That was his job. If it happened another way, that was fine too.

The trees parted, and he was at the road. No sign of a vehicle, just rutted dirt where one had peeled away quickly.

She was gone.

"Nothing?"

He spun around.

"Dude." Dakota strode past him and looked both ways. The highway was empty. "She had her purse?"

"Yes?"

"That an answer, or a question?" She pulled out her phone and jabbed at the screen, then put it to her ear. After a few seconds, she said, "Code Purple." Then paused. "Wasn't me. Mason was the one who was with her. The one who was supposed to be protecting her." She shot him a look. As though he hadn't been able to tell how she felt about that.

"Can we find her?"

She ignored his question and pressed her lips together, then shifted and said into the phone, "Okay. Copy that." Dakota hung up and stowed the phone before she walked past him with that long-legged stride of hers.

Mason followed. "Victoria?"

"Heads up." She called back over her shoulder. "She's pissed."

"She isn't the only one." Victoria didn't have a monopoly on caring for Talia, even if they were close and she'd known her longer. Mason was motivated to find her. "I want to help get her back."

"Good." Dakota walked at a fast clip back to the group.

Josh stood. "Paramedics are coming in a chopper. They're two minutes out."

"Good."

Was that all Dakota intended to say? Mason needed more than that. He needed assurances...and a working phone. But he didn't figure they'd be too hot on him making demands all of a sudden.

He tapped his hands against his legs. Thought. Prayed. Thought some more. His people were all looking for Yewell. If Victoria had gotten Talia back once, she could do it again. Right? Mason didn't want to wait that long. He didn't want to have to be here doing nothing while someone else saved her.

That wasn't how this was going to go down. At least not if he had anything to say about it.

He snapped his fingers. "Give me your phone."

Dakota looked at him. Josh shifted. Only Haley didn't react, aside from Niall who was still unconscious.

"Talia has a way to locate you all, right?"

Dakota nodded. "It's built in, or something."

"Unlock it and hand it over."

A helicopter flew overhead, drowning out her words. But the look on her face was clear. Don't rock the boat. Don't get in our way.

She thought he'd sit back, maybe take direction from their team? She didn't know him, then. Didn't know he was all in, not on the sidelines.

She held out the phone. "Victoria is going to find her."

"Good." Mason took it from her. "I'll be helping."

He tapped the screen and moved through to one of the only apps Dakota had on her phone. Seemed like she didn't use it all that much, which helped him narrow it down. The app kind of seemed homemade. Basic text functions. Something that acted like a walkie-talkie.

The settings indicated Dakota shared her GPS location with the admin. Mason worked his mouth side to side. "If I can…"

He found a way to access the admin side. Dakota's phone flashed. The screen turned black, and green text scrolled down the screen. He waited.

"Huh." She looked over his shoulder. "You know how to do that stuff?"

"Not like it's hard." It just needed to be going a whole lot faster for his liking.

"My talents run in a different direction."

"I'm sure they do." Mason took a few steps away from the group. Tried not to get mad that she insisted on talking to him when he was attempting to concentrate. He scrolled through the app and worked to get it to backtrack and show him the admin side.

"Anything?"

He ignored that, but glanced over at the EMTs now lifting Niall onto a stretcher. Mason turned to Haley. "You should go with him."

She nodded and hurried after them.

Josh strode over. Neema looked at him as he moved, but didn't get up from where she laid with her belly to the grass. Eyes still a little glassy from the effects of having been hit with a stun gun.

Dakota shifted even closer. "Anything?"

He typed on the screen and backtraced his way to Talia's device. "I think I got it."

A map flashed on screen. The wide circle was centered over the highway—and several miles around it. The dot sped away from where Mason stood. Could be she was being whisked away in a vehicle, or she was in the woods. The GPS location, that thin circle, started to contract as it loaded a more precise location.

"Is that her?"

He didn't answer the question. "Let's load up and go after her."

"Copy that." Dakota strode toward the SUV and pulled the door open. Josh called Neema, and the animal lumbered to the vehicle. He helped her inside.

"She okay?" Mason's attention was half on the phone, half on the others as he strode over and climbed in the front passenger seat.

Josh got in the driver's side. "She'll be okay once she shakes it off." He turned on the engine. "Where to?"

Mason looked down at the phone screen.

The circle tightened, then shifted to the east. Stopped.

"Dude."

Mason shook his head. "I think they tossed her purse onto the side of the highway." He looked back at Dakota. "She's gone."

23

Talia was squished between the hacker and one of the gunmen in the middle row of seats. She didn't even have room to move her elbows, but she glanced back. Tried to spot her purse on the side of the road. When she couldn't see it, she turned around again.

Nausea rolled through her, and she tried to pray. All she could think were broken phrases. Mixtures of pleading and scripture phrases came to mind. Pieces. Like her life, a collection of dissonant fragments she hadn't been able to put together since her captivity in that basement.

"Where are we going?" The question fell from her lips, despite the fact the man who sat in the front passenger seat had told her to keep quiet.

The hacker glanced at her. "Does it matter? Do what you're told, and you might keep this from getting even worse."

Like she was going to believe that? No way. The minute she was no longer useful, Talia figured, they would kill her. Toss her out on the side of the road like her purse. Discarded. Or she would be sold again.

Who cared what they did to her? She wasn't going to do any job.

Questions rolled through her mind like a shopping list. Why her? What was the job? He hadn't answered her as to where they were going. Turned out it mattered to her very much.

"Who was that guy, the bank robber?" He'd known her name. And while in Secret Service custody, he'd killed himself.

The hacker shrugged.

She turned to him and hissed, "How would you feel, dying with no answers and a whole bunch of questions?"

His gaze came to hers. "Like I said, keep your mouth shut."

"Or I'll end up like that guy, dead in an interrogation room? Was he some kind of collateral damage, dying for the cause?"

His mouth shifted. "You think I want to be here?"

"I think you owe me an explanation. After all, you practically destroyed my life." In some ways, he'd succeeded. It wasn't until she'd met Mason that the idea of being safe had become a possibility again.

Now all that had shattered. Like an illusion.

The hacker winced. He felt bad?

"Gonna apologize to me?" Rhetorical. It was more like a taunt. The edge of bitterness in his tone, even in just the few things he had said to her, made her want to stop, but what good would that do?

"That wasn't my doing."

"So who was behind it? You're just the hired help and it was who…Cerium?" That had been the name on the wall at the lab, at the college where Niall's life had been turned upside down. Niall had learned that Cerium was the money behind the research. Could the same person have hired this hacker to be part of his work? Maybe she'd gotten too close, and so they'd made her "disappear." Or they'd tried to.

"So you know more than I thought." He shrugged. "Am I supposed to be impressed?"

"Who is it?"

He shook his head. "I don't even know. All I know is I got

orders, and then they stopped. Pretty sure I got fired, considering it seems I've been contracted out to this Yewell guy now."

"The son of the Secretary of State."

The gunman on her other side shifted.

She didn't look to see what his issue was with her knowing that, or the fact she stated it out loud. "Why target me?"

"You can do this. It'll take both of us."

"And when I'm done, they'll kill me."

"Or you could make a deal," he suggested. "Keep working."

"I already have a job I like. Or I did, until you ruined that as well. Now I've got to get my reputation back. If Stanton doesn't make it so Victoria has to fire me. Because of *you.*"

He made a face like he didn't care either way what happened to her professionally. "I saw your work. He wanted you gone." The hacker paused. "I didn't want to get rid of you in that deal, but he hired those guys. I had no choice." He swallowed. "I didn't like it. I…have a sister. But there was nothing I could do."

"And the bank money transfer? That smart house setup?"

"New boss. New job." He lifted one shoulder, considerably less animated now. In fact, he almost looked forlorn. Because he'd been fired? Far worse than that had been done to her. Did she complain?

Okay, yes. She had. She'd pretty much buried her face in the sand. Retreated to lick her wounds. All those expressions that meant she'd pulled away from the team to live in a place of fear. Not in the knowledge that God had held her in His hands the whole time. That He'd sent rescue.

That He had saved her from fear and filled her with His perfect love.

"You think I'm going to feel sorry for you?" She tried to make her tone sound hard. Inside, she was shaking. And beginning to feel the first stirrings of empathy. No. She couldn't feel sorry for him.

No way.

Not after what he'd done to her.

God, help me.

Hearing it had been someone else's idea didn't make her feel better. It made her feel worse. This guy, she'd have been able to get over her fear of him. Take him down, and he would never be able to do anything else to her.

Now there was someone else? Whoever pointed Niall toward Cerium had set them on the right track.

Knowing that wasn't going to help her here. It wouldn't get her out of this, if they were "working" for Yewell now. The son of the Secretary of State had a plan. He had to. Now she was, apparently, part of that plan. Because the hacker had known she was capable? Not the kind of referral she was interested in.

She figured that whole thing about the smart house was all to draw her out. Just like the whole bank assignment, the money transfer, and the bank robber had all been to get her to the Secret Service office. She'd been targeted. But not for any of the reasons she'd thought. All along, ever since the bank, it had been about Yewell's plan.

She turned to the hacker then. "What are we going to do?"

It had to be a hack. One that would take both of their combined skills to pull off. Which didn't give her any ideas on what it might be.

He actually shuddered. "You don't want to know."

Except that she did, which was why she'd asked. Talia wasn't interested in being shoved aside or placated.

Before Talia could ask again, the guy in the passenger seat twisted around. "Shut up. Both of you." His gaze moved to the hacker. Didn't hold the guy in high esteem.

The hacker shifted. It had seemed before like he called the shots here. When he'd been commanding gunmen to hold her team at bay so he could take her. Threatening their lives to force her cooperation. Not now, though. He was almost on her level at this point. Someone they needed, but who didn't matter more than gum on the bottom of a shoe.

And wherever they were going, the team had no way to track her.

No way to find her.

———

MASON STOOD in front of Stanton's desk. Beside him, Dakota had her arms folded. Victoria was on speaker on his boss's phone. Josh had made the decision to get Neema checked out by a vet, just to be safe and make sure there was no lasting damage from her getting stunned.

Sitting in the chair on the other side of Dakota was the shrink who'd met with Yewell during his "incarceration" in a Secret Service safe house. The only person still alive who'd had any contact with him recently.

Stanton leaned back in his chair. "So it'll be fast, then? He's working his plan."

"He's had several plans in the past. It's just a case of which one makes the most sense *now*." The woman had gray hair pulled back into a tight bun that pulled at the skin of her forehead.

How Yewell had taken her seriously, Mason didn't know. But evidently he had. Enough she'd gotten a handle on the man's state of mind.

"Great." Mason squeezed the back of his neck, then let his hand drop to his side again. "So we have no idea what he'll do." He shrugged. "The President called off his visit. What if Yewell goes to ground? We'll never find him."

Her gaze shifted, and she eyed him over the rims of her glasses, her pointy nose angled down. "Given how angry he is, I feel that is unlikely. He wants to make a statement. It will be both notable *and* the action that causes the most amount of damage."

"And his network of soldiers?" Stanton folded his hands on his desk.

"Loyal subjects of their king. He has their allegiance, and they will be ready to die for him at a moment's notice. After all, that's what they rescued him for."

Mason tried to figure out what they were going to do about a guy who had a savior complex *and* his own private army. The Secret Service didn't know where he was, or what he was going to do. Was Alvarez really going to be able to get them actionable intelligence?

Stanton thanked the doctor, and she scurried out. Dakota shot Mason a look that told him all he needed to know about how she viewed shrinks. "Don't put much stock in psycho-therapy?"

"Psychos don't need therapy." She shrugged. "And it's not my job to give it to them. It's my job to hunt them down and *put* them down." Dakota turned to Stanton. "How does us being here get Talia back?"

Mason wanted to know the answer to that same question. They'd been called back here to the office. With no other leads, they'd had to answer that call.

Dakota said, "We have no idea what Yewell is going to do, and you all have no idea where he is."

Mason had been about to say that, maybe not in exact terms. He was kind of glad she'd done it first, though. Aches and pains from the bank robber's attack on him were perking up again. He needed pain meds—maybe an ice pack—and then he needed to get on the search for Talia.

"It's all connected." He slumped into one of the chairs and motioned for Dakota to do the same. "The hacker who took Talia is working for Yewell, right?"

"You're theorizing. You have no evidence. If you did, maybe you'd know where he took her."

She was really worried about her friend. Mason wanted to reach out and squeeze her hand, but doubted she would accept his small attempt at comfort. "True."

It grated on him that they'd essentially come up with nothing, and neither had the Secret Service. No one had seen Yewell.

Stanton's phone rang. He answered it, his face quickly blanching. "You cannot be serious." He gaped. "Hold on." The assistant director hit a button and replaced the handset. "You're on speaker with Agent Anderson and Special Agent Pierce."

On the phone, Victoria said, "I'm afraid I'm being perfectly serious. I wouldn't kid about something like this. In fact, the Secretary of State suggested I ride with him on the plane back to Seattle."

Stanton looked like he wanted to throw up. "He's really going ahead with it."

"He's going to do the rally in the President's place."

Dakota glanced at Mason, and they shared a look. Mason felt his brows lift. "You can't be serious," before he realized that was exactly what his boss had said.

"He can't think taking the President's place at this rally will be a good idea." Dakota waved a hand in the direction of the phone. "He's putting himself and all his people in danger by coming here. Not to mention those planning to attend."

"I tried to convince him to cancel the whole thing."

Dakota leaned forward, closer to the phone. "I thought they already had."

"I explained the threat, he asked me why I thought I needed to *explain the threat.* Considering it's his son, I guess that was valid. But he's clearly not thinking straight. There's no way this is going to go well. Evidently he's well aware, and still considers it accept-able to do exactly as you said." Victoria sighed, out of breath as though she'd been walking quickly. "Unless he thinks his son will make the approach before the rally and he can deal with it—or we will—so no one else is under threat."

"If he is thinking that, he needs to tell us," Mason said. "That way we can make preparations."

Dakota nodded. "And apparently the son is *angry.* According to the shrink."

"She's probably right." Victoria sighed, loud enough they all heard it. "He's going to do something. If we can't figure out precisely what it is, then the Secretary of State isn't going to change his plans. He said the rally is too important to miss."

"People's lives are too important," Mason said. But they were still constrained by the powers that be. If the administration said jump, they jumped.

Dakota shook her head. "There's no way his son will pass up the opportunity to make a statement. The Secretary is trying to draw him out. On purpose."

"As soon as he lands," Stanton put in, "I'll sit him down and make him tell me all of it. I can't in good conscience allow him to put all those people in danger. Maybe I can change his mind."

Victoria said, "You may not have a choice but to keep him safe. He's been ordering around his staff, getting emails out to everyone. He wants full protection, and if that means getting military personnel in to help with security, then he wants it done."

Stanton blew out a breath. "I'm expected to coordinate all that in the middle of a manhunt? Or does he not care that we apprehend his son without loss of life?"

"That would be the goal." Victoria paused. "Keep me apprised." She hung up.

Dakota sat back in her chair and blew out a breath. "He can't seriously think this is a good idea."

Stanton turned back to his computer. "I suggest the two of you find a lead as to what he's up to. Fast. If you don't want to be dragged into security detail for a political rally."

Dakota was up and out of the chair before Mason could even formulate a response.

Mason said, "Pierce. One more thing."

She turned back, already at the door. "Make it fast." Evidently she had somewhere to be.

"What about Alvarez? Have any of you heard from him?" Last they'd known, he was inside with Yewell and had an undercover guy with him. Whether he was safe, or not, they had no idea.

"I'll find out."

Mason nodded, and she left. Then he turned back to Stanton. "I need to be on the hunt for Talia, try to find a way to locate where she was taken. That will lead me to Yewell." It was a stretch, but he was pretty sure he was right.

The idea of her being back in that nightmare situation was like a rock in his stomach.

Stanton glanced over, the same frown on his face he'd had when he stared at his computer. "Then you'd better make it fast. You've been retasked."

"Sir?"

"It's all hands on deck, Mason. The rally starts at six tonight, and you will be there."

"Sir—"

"That's an order. What you do between now and five p.m. when you're to report to the stadium, is up to you."

That meant he had some time left to find her.

Three hours, to be exact.

24

A hand pressed on Talia's shoulder. Her legs folded, and she landed hard on the metal chair.

"Get to work." The gruff gunman moved away.

She glanced at his back, then looked at the hacker, who sat at a desk beside her. "What is this place?"

It looked like an office that had been cleared of people after a natural disaster. Desks and papers. Overturned chairs. Ceiling tiles hung down, askew. The copier they'd passed in the corner alcove had an OUT OF ORDER sign taped to the top.

The only thing that was new were the two computers on neighboring desks. Network cables running to a router.

The hacker shook his mouse.

Talia wondered what would happen if she did nothing.

A rustle behind her preceded a man leaning down over her. Hot breath moved against her cheek and her whole body froze. "Get to work."

She bit the inside of her cheek.

He moved away, and she breathed. Jiggled the mouse. The screen flashed to life, and she got a look at the portal they were supposed to hack. Remote access to satellites wasn't going to work. Talk about obvious that it was being hijacked from the outside.

They had to secure the connection as they went. Make it look like they were getting in…from within.

Like that was actually easy.

"You want the satellite. I'll take the stadium?"

She looked at the hacker. Looked back at the computer. Didn't answer him.

Talia typed some, poking around to get the lay of the land. This wasn't going to be easy at all. But if it had been, the hacker would have done it himself.

Question was, did he need her for real, or just to take focus off him and spite her by dragging her into all this?

She couldn't figure out the answer, but the mental image where she grasped the back of his neck and slammed his face against the keyboard in order to induce him to tell her the answer was incredibly satisfying.

That in itself was disturbing to her. She'd never been a violent person before. Now there was this…cold rage she couldn't shake. Was that better than being numb? She wasn't sure.

"Talia."

"What?" The word was barely audible. She didn't have the wherewithal to make it louder.

"Satellite, or stadium?"

She cleared her throat. "We should do the satellite first. One of us gets in, the other follows, closing doors as we go. Covering our tracks."

He nodded. "You get in, I'll bring up the rear."

"Fine."

If the hacker was occupied, and the gunmen thought she was working with him—cooperating—then she could figure out a way to contact Victoria and the rest of the team. Alvarez was supposed to be on the inside of Yewell's operation right now. Was he okay? She wanted to see him with her own eyes, but allowing him time to track the man down and take him out was better.

Yewell needed to be out of play. Off the streets before he did whatever damage he intended to have broadcasted across the world via communications satellites. Cellphones. Online. Like it was easy to literally hijack every server. She didn't even want to know how they were going to accomplish all that.

"Well? Are we in?"

Talia jerked around in her chair. The man who'd strode into the office, third floor, skyline view, was good looking in a banker-out-to-lunch kind of way. Button-down shirt. Tailored slacks and shined black shoes. He'd fixed his hair with gel. Evidently there was time to clean up before a terrorist attack. He should tell that to all the other bad guys the team took down. Her friends would probably prefer to take down clean-shaven suspects instead.

She shifted her attention beyond him and watched for Alvarez to come in.

"Time to daydream means we've neglected to explain the consequences of your failure."

No one else came in.

She turned back to her computer.

"Ah, good. I'd hate to have to bring the repercussions down on my men here."

Talia started typing. Did it matter what? They probably had no clue what she was doing, and she had no intention of talking to them.

"The plan is in place."

She had no idea if he was talking to her, or not. Was this Yewell? Across from her, the hacker sat completely straight. As though he expected to be hit from behind. This guy needed to say whatever he wanted to say and then get out of here, so she could send her team a message.

"That's good, boss." One of the gunmen spoke.

Talia worked the problem in front of her. She tried to place her trust in God's hand and her team. She could string this along, make it take longer, but for what? Yewell would probably have her killed anyway.

Out the corner of her eye, she saw him move to the hacker.

"As soon as the plane lands, I want updates on my father's location until he arrives at the stadium."

This guy was Yewell.

"Yes, sir." His voice shook.

Yewell squeezed his shoulder, hard enough the hacker winced. She'd known he was afraid of the man, but this was more like terror. Had he seen what he could do? Or what he was prepared to order his friends to do?

She braced for him to move to her next, but he didn't. She'd been through the worst experience of her life and come out of it intact. Not necessarily whole, but healthy at least. Working to get her life back. Would this time be worse?

She didn't want to believe that was even possible, but supposed it could be. *Lord...no.* She couldn't handle that. He wouldn't ask that of her, would He?

The NSA had found out the girl's identity. Haley had told her that, back at the office. Why hadn't she let Haley tell her all of it? Talia wished she'd asked.

"It's just a matter of time."

She squeezed her eyes shut. *He was right behind her.* Talia couldn't let Yewell know how afraid she was of him or what he might do to her. He didn't care enough about her to be interested or make some move specifically directed at her, unless he saw she was terrified. That would energize him, right? Those psychotic tendencies would enjoy the chance to play with her.

It wasn't worth the risk. He couldn't know how terrified she was.

"Then my father will die, and all his little sycophants can do nothing but watch the flames as they join him." He chuckled. "It's a short trip to hell, and one way." She heard him move away, then say, "Make sure nothing goes wrong."

"Yes, sir." One of the gunmen spoke again.

She glanced over at his back as he moved into the hallway and out of sight. Talia let go of the breath she'd been holding. Her head swam. She felt like throwing up.

A man moved over and stood close to her back. The barrel of a gun slid into her vision from the side. He pressed it against her cheek. "You heard the man. Get your work done. Or your pretty face has a bullet hole in it."

"O-okay."

"Good."

She bit her lip so hard blood touched her tongue. Talia gave herself a second to just breathe and pray. Her mom was probably doing overtime in her prayer closet. She always seemed to know when Talia needed to be interceded for.

If she'd ever needed it in her life, it was now.

———

THE SECRETARY of State was on the ground. His plane had landed, and he was on his way. The announcement had come over the comms, alerting all security for the event. Including all the Secret Service stationed at every entrance.

Lead on the operation was a Secret Service assistant director Mason had never met before. One who'd assigned him to search any bags being brought in. Everyone that entered had to pass through a scanner.

The guy had rubbed him the wrong way from the first second. Now he stalked around, eyeing all the local agents as though they were beneath the group from DC. The assistant director stopped and lifted his wrist to his mouth. "Let's speed this up. The event is about to start soon."

And Talia was still who-knew-where.

Three hours, and he hadn't been able to find one sign of her.

Mason motioned the next person up to his checkpoint. He waved a wand in the interior sections of her huge purse. Bursting wallet, loose papers and used tissues. "Thank you."

She hurried inside, eager to be at the rally.

Mason half expected a call to come that the Secretary of State's convoy had been ambushed, and there was carnage on the highway. Security wasn't as tight as if the President had come, but it was still sky high. Everything had been in place for the Commander In Chief's visit. Why not just utilize all the personnel available and keep everyone safe?

Maybe that was why the assistant director acted like this was a poor use of his time. Probably only wanted to protect the President. Anything or anyone else was beneath him.

A Secret Service agent passed by Mason, handler to a dog. Sniffing for bombs? Mason wanted to know if anything suspicious had been found. That was the most logical assumption for what Yewell had planned for his father, if he wasn't going with an ambush on the highway.

Maybe that wasn't splashy enough. Maybe he wanted maximum carnage.

The dog moved on.

Next guy to step up at Mason's line was mid-twenties and wore a big, bulky jacket. If he had to pick out of a lineup who was most likely to be a threat, it was this guy. Then the jacket flapped open. Mason flinched. Across the T-shirt were huge letters emblazoned with the current President's election race slogan.

The man grinned. "Today is gonna be awesome!" He waved his arms, and Mason got a nose full of body spray. The guy smelled like a teenage boy going to his first co-ed party.

Mason forced his body to relax, and smiled. Too tense, he was like a hair trigger. Or a bomb about to go off. Seeing danger everywhere it wasn't.

Mason waved the man through, and the next person stepped up. After a while they blurred together, and he was seeing gestures. Watching for tension, or the look in someone's eye. A different tactic, but no less effective.

His phone rang. Dakota's name flashed on the screen of his smart watch.

He motioned to the agent with him. "I'll be back in a second."

Mason had to skirt around a couple of people so the assistant director didn't see him. He'd get written up for leaving his post, but Stanton could clear it. They knew what was going on. The Northwest Counter-Terrorism Task Force were looking for Talia and the hacker, and they'd made it clear they *only* communicated through Mason.

Just another reason for the assistant director—maybe both of them—to be mad at him.

Mason wandered down the breezeway. "Anderson."

"No sign of her, so far."

He sighed, too disappointed to form the words.

"We're still looking."

"Okay." Only the thought that they wouldn't stop looking until they *had* found her reassured him.

Dakota said something, but he couldn't make it out. He looked around and took a few steps while he listened. Tried to hear.

A green army jacket had been discarded on the floor, by the wall. Kind of like that guy's jacket. The man who'd smelled like teenager.

"Wha...ness."

"What? You're breaking up." He looked at the screen of his phone, but he had full bars. "Dakota?"

She said something else. A handful of garbled, broken words.

"I can't hear you." Maybe it was all the concrete surrounding him. He walked to an exit and stepped out into the daylight. Still full bars. "Can you hear me?"

"Yes. That's way better."

"For me, too." He watched the crowd and looked for suspicious people. It was hard to shake the tendency to protect. To spot the inconsistencies and find the threat in play under the surface. "Weird. What were you saying?"

"She hasn't contacted any of us so far. And now we can't get ahold of Alvarez—even on the number Victoria had for him."

Clearly she'd been assuming Talia would reach out. They relied on the NSA analyst probably more than they should. Counted on her considerable technological skills to save the day where their guns and brute force couldn't.

"So we still have nothing?"

"If you didn't find anything on your end, no." Her voice had a distinct tone. She didn't like the fact he put all the responsibility on her to figure this out.

"Sorry. I just don't have a good feeling." He sighed. "And I'm stuck here working for the foreseeable future."

"I don't have a good feeling either. She should've found a way to contact us by now. I mean, what is she doing anyway? Talia is better than this. But since she got…you know…it's like she's been off her game or something."

"Which is completely understandable," he reminded her. "Considering what happened."

"But not helpful right now."

"I'll take that up with the hacker when I get my hands on him."

Dakota sighed.

"Keep me posted." He had to get back to his station before someone noticed his absence. Protection came first, even when he'd rather be anywhere else than here right now.

Mason hung up. For the first time, he realized he'd rather not be doing his job. He would much rather be out looking for Talia. He found he cared about her safety more than these thousands of people pouring into the stadium to see a man intent on putting them all at risk. The Secretary of State should never have come. And he definitely shouldn't have kept the event on the schedule.

For everyone's safety, he should have called the whole thing off.

Mason had the niggling urge to pull the fire alarm and get all these people out of here. But if Yewell—the son—saw mass exodus of the stadium on some surveillance, then he might bump up the timeline and do now what they might've been able to stop later.

They needed time.

"Dad!" Rayna skirted between two people. She bounded over,

all teenage enthusiasm—and wasn't that an oxymoron—and long legs she hadn't quite gotten used to yet.

Trailing behind was her mother, his ex-wife. Stella.

"You're here." He wasn't sure how he felt about that. Cold moved through him, a slow-moving dread that she was here. In danger. Both of them were. They'd get caught up in what happened today.

"We're here!" She hugged him while her mother stayed a couple of steps away, a polite smile for him. "We knew you'd be working, so we came to get a peek at the Secret Service agent in action."

Mason couldn't register her words. They were here. He shook his head. "You need to leave. Now."

25

T alia wanted to throw the keyboard on the floor, but none of them could know she was frustrated. The message she'd tried to get out to her team had failed. She'd worked so hard to send it in the background of what she was "supposed" to be doing so that no one noticed. All for nothing.

The hacker glanced over.

She didn't want to talk to him anyway. This was all his fault. And while she supposed forgiveness should be her goal here, there was no way Talia was ready for that. Absolutely no way. She was far too intent on nursing her anger to deal with the aftermath right now. She wouldn't survive this by going soft. She had to stay strong, the way Dakota had when she'd been abducted. The way Niall had when he'd nearly been experimented on.

She had to be more like her teammates, and less like herself.

Allowing peace to come in and calm her wasn't going to give her that edge she needed right now to stay alive.

"I'm in."

She glanced at the hacker and saw he'd turned to look back behind them, at the gunmen who hovered around. They made her neck itch the way they just stood there and watched. It was unnerving how they could be so still. So quiet. She felt like she was going crazy trying to figure a way out of this.

A way to call for help.

To incapacitate a room full of armed men, and not herself in the process. Okay, so there were only four of them, but it might as well have been a hundred for all she could do to physically subdue them. They'd take her down for simply getting out of the chair.

The gunman strode over. "We're ready."

She saw the twitch in the hacker's jaw. That wasn't what he'd accomplished. His body stiffened in disagreement as the armed man approached. "Well, not exactly. I'm in the satellite. I can broadcast the signal from the stadium to wherever I want."

"How is that not ready?"

Talia leaned back in her chair. "We can send the signal out. But we also need the servers on the other end to see the signal and play it over whatever they're broadcasting. We're piggy-backing networks all over the world. This is going to take time."

"Then I suggest the two of you quit taking breaks and get back to it." He palmed a handgun. "Otherwise you're going to have to figure out how to hack while you're bleeding."

Talia turned away from the look in his eyes. She'd seen it before and had no interest in being a party to sentiment like that. Not here. Not now, when Victoria didn't know where she was because Talia hadn't been able to get the message sent out.

She'd failed.

The only upside was that the team was hopefully busy taking down Yewell. Safeguarding all the people he'd said his father was going to entertain at the stadium. Assuming that was where the attack was going to take place.

If Yewell hated his father so much for effectively turning him in, then he should just kill his father. One man. Why he needed to involve the thousands at the stadium, she didn't know. They were there exercising their right to meet in support of a government that would work in their interests. It was what good citizens did.

Not to mention why they had federal law enforcement in the first place, to safeguard people and their interests.

Yewell needed to be found. Before he could hurt anyone.

"How far are you on your part?"

She glanced over at the hacker, then back at her computer.

"We need to work together."

"I don't need to be *together* with you on anything." She didn't have any interest in hearing him. Or talking to him. Why would she?

That call to forgive touched her mind again. The gentle urging of the Holy Spirit. Maybe He should try a two-by-four instead. Probably more effective at getting her to turn and start walking in the right direction. Otherwise she was going to stick with this path until she was out of danger and had the head space to seek out peace, or forgiveness. It would be much easier to try and forgive him if the hacker was in jail...preferably miles away from her. Where she'd never have to see him. Ever again.

"Sir!" A man strode in, holding a laptop. He was dressed much like the gunmen, but his tactical vest was unzipped and he wore glasses.

"What is it?" The gunman evidently merely tolerated the man's presence on his team.

Talia watched him stride past her, at which point he shot her a frowny face. She shrugged like, "What?" not willing to allow the opportunity to stand up to someone passing by. Even if the communication was all nonverbal.

The man stopped behind her. She could hear the rapid puff of his breath as he exhaled. Overexerted from that quick walk in here. He needed to get a gym membership. Or a dog to take on walks.

"One of them tried to send out a communication. I almost didn't find it, because whichever one of them did it is really good."

That narrowed it down. Talia nearly rolled her eyes, but

refrained. They didn't need to be aware of her opinion of this newcomer. Or the hacker.

She could feel more than see the hacker's attention on her from the very corner of her eye. She lifted her chin and kept typing. As though this interruption meant nothing, and she was determined to get on with the job.

Like she didn't know full well they were going to kill her as soon as this was done.

"Which one?" The gunman's barked question made the muscles at the back of her shoulders tense.

"I don't know. I can't tell the difference between their two computers." He sighed. "It has to be that way to get the job done."

And yet this guy couldn't do the "job"? Or was he just insurance to make sure they'd done it correctly? Someone on the inside, keeping tabs. No one had said anything about that to her. Though, that subterfuge was likely the point.

Someone walked toward them, heavy feet encased in thick-soled boots. She tensed with each step.

"It was me."

Talia's head whipped around to the hacker. What was he…

"I'm the one who tried to get a signal out." He looked convincingly guilty, but lifted his chin to face the armed man. "My employer needs to know that this is unacceptable treatment."

The gunman lifted his nine mil and shot the hacker in the thigh. The sound was like a firework going off beside her ear.

Talia squeezed her eyes shut and listened to him scream.

Those boots moved closer to her. The barrel of a gun pressed against her skirt, just above her knee. "Problem?"

"No." She didn't know what else to say. They were going to have to do this, right? It wasn't like she had any other choice.

"The two of you will get this done. Or I'll be forced to get creative."

Bile rose in her throat.

"Understand?"

She nodded.

He moved away. "Is the signal ready?"

"Yes," the laptop guy said. "The charges are all in place."

Talia bit her lip.

Help wasn't coming.

———

"You can't be here."

Rayna frowned. "But I thought—"

"I know." Mason did. He knew exactly why she'd come, she didn't need to tell him. He touched her shoulders. "I know. And thank you." It was a combination of support and the opportunity to watch her dad at his "cool" job. He kissed her forehead. "But it's not safe here."

His ex-wife took a step forward. Stella was dressed like she was going to work—slim skirt and blouse, covered by a suit jacket. Those fifteen pounds she should have kept instead of losing, along with the hard edge of her hair cut along her chin, didn't appeal to him. He much preferred Talia's curves, though they did dress quite similarly.

Somehow when Talia did it, it seemed more natural and less like a uniform. Like armor.

Her eyes looked like she was frowning, but her brow didn't wrinkle. "What's going on?"

Mason motioned off to the side with a dip of his head and tugged on Rayna's elbow. He led them away, glancing over at the assistant director from DC as he moved. No one had noticed his absence yet.

Mason spotted a jacket, folded under the table where a Secret Service agent stood. The female agent searched a woman's purse. The army-green jacket was close to her feet. Just like the one he'd seen on that man who'd come through his line.

Just like the one abandoned by the wall in the breezeway.

Entirely too much of a coincidence to not be worth noting. He'd need to tell the assistant director about it.

"What's going on, Dad?"

He stopped when they were far enough off to the side. "It's not safe for the two of you to be here."

Nor was it safe for any of these people. The whole thing should've been called off. But the Secretary of State didn't acquiesce to lowly Secret Service agents. It was only their job to protect him, not convince him that the danger for him to even be in the state was far too high.

Not worth the risk.

"You guys should go home. Stay off the streets, as far from here as you can."

A man walking past slowed. "Is there something going on?" He looked down, noting Mason's badge on his belt. "Is there some kind of threat?"

Mason shook his head. It was at the back of his mind to just yell at the top of his lungs. Tell all these people that the Secretary of State's son was out for blood. And they could all get caught in the crossfire.

"I'm talking to my family right now." Hopefully his tone clearly indicated this man was interrupting them. And that this was none of his business.

Mason could make some kind of announcement. Or get it broadcasted over the emergency system. Like an Amber alert that went to everyone's phone—a warning to clear the area.

But what could he do to warn people that wouldn't result in mass panic? That was the problem. He didn't want people getting trampled.

Yewell could attack his father's convoy on the freeway, which had been completely shut down for his journey from the airport to the stadium. These people could be safer congregated here than they would be by dispersing and making their way home. Who knew what the answer was? Mason needed to pray for wisdom, something he did while his ex-wife currently utilized her psychotherapist skills to assess his expression and conclude what the problem was.

She turned to Rayna. "He's probably right. There are so many people here, it's going to be a mad crush. And for what? To hear a bunch of bureaucratic jargon that's supposed to energize us into mindlessly following whatever the government says they want to do next?"

Rayna spun around to her mother. "Don't think I don't know you're taking his side."

"It's not about—"

She held up a slender hand, then turned to Mason. "We came. We saw. It's not like we even bought tickets." She shot her mother a look. "So now we're going to go, and you can tell me later why you're being weird. Deal?"

Relief rushed through him. "Deal." He planted a kiss on her forehead. "You're a smart girl."

"You can also tell me later where Talia is."

His ex-wife opened her mouth.

"Later." She tugged on her mother's arm while she assessed his gaze with a daughter's attention to detail. She hadn't missed a thing. Though she had been angry at him for not being glad to see her.

Mason mouthed, *Love you.*

Rayna blew him a kiss, and she and her mother turned to walk away.

"That guy." The man who'd stopped by them pointed at him now, in a conversation with a huddle of people. "He said we're in danger being here. He told his family to leave."

"Agent Anderson!" The assistant director called out.

In the nick of time.

He jogged over to the lead agent. "Yes, sir?"

"Return to your assigned post, Agent Anderson. I'll be mentioning you in my report."

"Sir." He motioned to the jacket under the desk. "I keep

seeing these jackets, left around the area. That's the third one. Same type and color, discarded."

"And this is reason for you to take a break for personal reasons when all other agents are doing their jobs?"

This wasn't going well. "Sir, I believe—"

The assistant director cut him off. "Back to your post, Agent Armstr—" His phone rang. He started to turn away as he answered it. "Assistant Director Carnes."

Mason moved back toward his post.

"Agent Anderson!"

He turned back, trying to keep the utter surprise from his face. "Sir?"

"You've been retasked, by order of..." He shifted the phone back to his mouth. "What did you say your name was?" His eyebrows crumpled together. "Thanks." He hung up. "Director Bramlyn. State Department. She said you'll know what it's about."

He nodded. "I really think you need to look into these jackets, sir."

"Don't tell me how to do my job." He motioned with a flick of his fingers. "Now run along to your special assignment." He said that like it was a dirty word.

Mason turned away and sent Victoria a text about the jackets as he walked. She could get the director of the Secret Service to put pressure on Carnes to look into the jackets. And why not? It really wasn't worth ignoring what could be a potential threat just for the sake of throwing his weight around.

As soon as the text sent, he called Dakota.

"Special Agent Pierce."

"It's Mason. What's going on?" He headed for the street and started walking.

"No, go the other way."

"What's that?"

She said, "Turn around. Silver compact. No comments, it's a rental."

He did as she'd instructed and saw a silver car pull out of traffic and stop close to him. Mason pulled open the front passenger door and got in, hanging up as he sat down. "What's going on?" They hadn't answered his question yet.

"Alvarez called." Dakota pulled back out into the slow moving traffic. "He knows where Talia is being held."

Mason blew out a deep sigh of relief he had no idea he'd been holding since Talia was taken. "Any movement on Yewell?" Surely if Alvarez had called in about Talia, he'd also informed them about their target, right?

"He's working on it. Says he's close to a takedown." In the driver's seat, Dakota glanced at him. "Josh went to assist. Our job is Talia."

"Copy that."

26

S he wasn't going to be able to keep up this ruse for much
longer. Her computer was accessing servers all over the
world, stringing them into her sequencer using a virus that was
programmed to work extremely slowly. Wouldn't want to have
them all link to it simultaneously and overload it. Or finish before
her rescue got here.

She almost smiled to herself. Almost.

Talia's mind insisted on reminding her that it was possible help
was *not* coming. She shoved aside that thought and started to sing
in her head. A hymn about being in a battle.

She pictured standing up. She would pick up the chair she'd
been sitting on and swing it around like a professional wrestler—
just with more clothes on.

The skirt would probably get in the way. And she wouldn't be
able to kick anyone in the shins with her heels, considering she
was still wearing Dakota's running shoes.

If they were going to rescue her, they needed to bring her
pumps.

"You've gotta focus."

She glanced aside at the hacker. His teeth were clenched. Pale
faced. Sweating. Should she be sorry he'd gotten shot? He'd tech-

nically done it to protect her, so maybe. The last thing she wanted was to feel any empathy for him. She needed to focus her energy on getting out of there.

His blood had collected in a pool under the chair, making a puddle on the tile floor. Why had he done that anyway? He shouldn't have said it was him who'd sent the transmission. Although, she wouldn't have owned up to it.

Better him than her?

No. That was a level of callous she didn't like, even after everything he'd done.

Then there was what he'd done to Niall. Was her teammate even okay? He could be dead now. Haley could be alone somewhere, devastated that she was going to have to face life without the man she loved.

Talia didn't even know.

Anger surged in her at all this man had cost her. The pain he'd dragged her into and caused for her friends. He deserved no sympathy at all.

She typed on the keyboard, even though the virus she'd programmed didn't require her input. It was running. Doing its thing, worming its way through the internet. Attaching servers together, and connecting them back to the satellite. When it was done...which quite frankly would take hours—a fact she was proud of, thank you very much—*then* she'd have to figure out the next part.

Right now she was just waiting for it to do its thing.

Waiting for...

Rescue.

"What was that?" Laptop guy stood up. He'd been sitting at her two o'clock position for half an hour, staring with beady eyes that made her want to squirm. He got up and moved to the front door.

Talia couldn't help the smile that curled her lips. A gunshot. She listened, everything in her reaching to hear it again.

Pop. Pop.

She wanted to laugh. Now they were done for.

One of the gunmen went to the door, along with their tech person—laptop guy. Two remained. She glanced back over her shoulder, where both had their attention on the door to the hall. Guns ready.

Pop.

The hacker rolled his chair away, and she heard his clothes shift. Talia grasped the edges of her keyboard in a tight grip as she turned back.

A gun went off, close this time. The burst of three shots that put the hacker on his back. Gasping, as though trying to figure out what had just happened.

She stood, kicked at the chair so it rolled toward the man. Pretty fast, actually. When he glanced at it, she yanked on the keyboard in a sharp and hard movement that broke the cord—or pulled it out of where it had been plugged in.

She threw it at the man.

He lifted his gun and his other arm. Movements awkward as the chair hit his legs and the keyboard slammed into his face.

And then she ran.

Fireworks echoed behind her. She crossed the room. Hide under a desk? No. He would see her. She went to the EXIT door at the end and shoved against the handle.

A bullet slammed into the door right by her head.

Talia squeaked and ducked through the door. Whether her friends were in the other hallway or not, there would be gunmen between them if she went that way. But if she fled down here to safety, they could find her. The gunman who'd remained behind wouldn't be able to use her as leverage. She didn't want to be a hostage any more than she had to be. And definitely didn't want him to press a gun against her temple to get her teammates to stand down.

Talia knew he'd be right behind her in a second. She tried the first door. A bathroom. Didn't matter that it was the men's. She ran to the farthest stall, shut the door and crouched with her feet on either side of the seat.

Her breath sounded like gasps.

She held it, then exhaled slowly. Trying to get it to calm and quiet. If she gave herself away, he would—

The door handle squeaked. She held completely still while the door creaked open.

Boots on the tile.

Talia made an O-shape with her lips and blew out a long, slow breath. Her heart thumped beneath her chest. She was afraid to move, or she'd slip and fall off the seat. Fall into the bowl. She shut off those thoughts, since in her head it played out like a comedy skit. Or a scene from a Heather Woodhaven novel.

Metal clanged metal. Then the sound continued, a long eerie note.

She gritted her teeth.

The sound drew closer. As though he ran the barrel of the weapon along the metal doors. It skipped. The frame. A door slammed open. Then the next.

He was coming closer.

Her stomach clenched, a muscle spasm that threatened to deposit food she hadn't even eaten on the tile in front of the toilet. *God, help me.* Her teammates were here. They would find her. Whether that happened before this guy discovered her was the question. The answer to which meant either life or death for her.

She bit her lip so hard, she tasted blood. Was this the end? Dying in a stinky men's room, minutes from being rescued.

Maybe she should call out for help. If they were close, that would let them know where she was. Would this guy shoot her before they could run inside the bathroom? Talia wasn't sure she would be willing to risk it. They always told her to hold fast and wait for them to show up.

She didn't appreciate always feeling like the loose end of the group. But this was the path God had called her to walk.

The one that led to Mason.

Boots appeared at the bottom of the door.

Talia sucked in a breath, and then held it. He shifted. Staring at the door? Would he kick it in, or just shoot her?

She crouched as small as she could and prayed he couldn't see her around the cracks in the door. Which of course, completely futile. America could send a man to the moon, but they couldn't make stall doors that didn't have gaps between the door and the—

A thunderous voice called out, "Hey!"

Talia wobbled and fell to the floor.

———

THE GUNMAN SPUN TO HIM. Mason fired twice. Both hit the guy, one to the chest and one to the neck as he fell.

Talia let out a kind of squeak, and he saw her scramble to her feet and pull the door open an inch.

"It's clear."

She poked her head out. "Is he gone?"

Mason waved at the dead man, crumpled on the floor. The faint sound of gunfire back in the office, or the stairwell, drew his attention. "I think Dakota might need help."

"She's here, too?"

He nodded. Was she just going to stand there, or was she going to come over and hug him? Talia moved past him, to the sink. *Of course.* She pumped out some soap and washed her hands. When she grabbed for a paper towel and found none, she shook out her hands.

"Okay?" He didn't care that he'd been flicked with water.

She slid her arms around his middle and gave him a small, but tight, squeeze. "Let's go."

When she moved first to the door, he touched her shoulder. "Hold up. I go first."

She eyed his weapon. "Right."

Mason tried to assess the situation in the hallway and keep her safe but not get caught up with the swirl of thoughts in his head. Was she not okay? Is that why she'd been quiet so far? One hug and off to help her friends. Nothing more to be said right now. Maybe she couldn't say anything because her time with the hacker and Yewell's people had been too traumatic.

He felt her fingers curl into his belt at the back. Good. She was tracking with him, and he didn't need to glance back to see if she was still there.

They moved into the main office. Dakota was crouched over a body. "The hacker just died."

Talia said nothing, but her fingers flexed. Still curled into his belt.

"He said 'Cerium.'" Dakota stood, a frown on her flushed face and hair coming free of her ponytail. "I feel like I should know what that is, but I can't remember." She looked over at Talia. "You okay?"

"Yes." Her voice was small and heartbreaking. "It's the name on Niall's lab. The money behind those experiments that hurt so many people."

"Oh, yeah."

Dakota flicked her gaze to him, and Mason gave her a small nod. He'd heard it as well. Talia wasn't okay. They'd need to deal with that—and he would do so gladly, if it helped her—but couldn't until Yewell was caught and everyone at the stadium had been caught. Until they were all out of danger.

Talia let go of his belt and moved around him.

He held still. Did she need distracting from what she could see and what had just happened? "Does all that stuff with Niall's lab play in with Yewell?"

"Probably not." She went to a computer. "I think Cerium is the person behind what the hacker was doing. He said his 'employer' sent him to work for Yewell, like he got fired or something."

Dakota had her phone out. "Did he say anything about selling you?"

"He felt bad about it. Said he was ordered to do it."

Mason gritted his molars together. Dakota was a wildcard. He figured she could say anything at any given point. Talia was probably used to the twenty questions, and expecting it. Mason was going to keep his thoughts to himself until he knew Talia was ready to hear them.

It didn't matter how he felt about all this. What mattered was that she work her way to feeling safe, getting her peace back.

"If he wasn't dead, I'd kick him." She looked like she'd spit on him as well. She lifted her phone to her ear. "Hey, it's me." Dakota walked away, and Talia watched her move. The ghost of a smile on her lips.

Mason walked over and sat in the chair beside Talia. The screen of the computer at the desk came to life. He peered at it. "Satellite broadcast?"

"I'm going to halt the program."

"We need to figure out who he was," Dakota said into her phone. "I'll find out if Talia knows and get that information to you. If the NSA can get anything from security cameras or surface street surveillance around this building, then we might be able to find where he's gone."

"What about the guy with the laptop?" Talia's fingers kept moving on the keyboard even though she wasn't looking at the screen.

Mason didn't want to tell her, but he had to. "He got away."

Talia lifted her fingers. She looked at the screen for a couple of seconds and then pressed the enter key. "He was the one making sure we did what we were supposed to do."

"If he could confirm all that, why didn't he just do the job in the first place?"

She shrugged at his question. "I had the same thought. Could be we knew more than he does, so he needed our help. He can probably put all the pieces together now and get it done. We were far enough along."

"You're shutting it down?"

She nodded.

"Okay," Dakota said into her phone. "Copy that." She hung up and slid the cell phone into the back pocket of her jeans.

"Yewell?"

Dakota shook her head. "Victoria said they have no idea where he is. The Secretary of State is just about to go on stage at the rally, and so far it's been quiet like you wouldn't believe."

That wasn't normal. There should've at least been something. Mason thought for a second. "And the jackets?"

Dakota made a face like she had no idea what he was talking about.

Talia said, "Done."

As they made their way to the stairs, he said, "I told the assistant director that I thought they should look into jackets left around the stadium. Discarded."

"I'll tell her."

Talia said, "The guy with the laptop told the other guy, the one in charge, that all their devices—the charges—were in place. Could be that they hid them in jackets, and if they're using a radio signal, then they could set them all off simultaneously."

Rain jacket bombs? He could hardly get his head around it, but there would be time enough to pick everything apart later.

Mason touched her shoulder. "If you were close enough, could you find and isolate the signal and make it so they couldn't set them off?"

She reached up and touched his hand. Held it on her shoulder so he didn't let go. "Maybe not in time to keep anyone from being killed when they're set off." She halted on the stairs. "That's why I added a few lines of code. Things to interrupt what they're doing."

Dakota turned to her. "Like what?"

"A funny dog video instead of the broadcast."

"The doggo parko one?"

She almost smiled. "And a few other things, just to make it

harder. If the laptop guy is good, but not incredibly detail oriented, he might miss a few of them."

"We should get the stadium evacuated before the Secretary of State gets on stage."

"I tried that," Mason said. "The assistant director of the Secret Service from DC isn't going to make the call without conclusive evidence. He and Stanton would have to be convinced."

"Like people being blown up? How's that for evidence?"

He shrugged at Dakota's question.

Talia said, "What if I can prove there's a threat? Make it look like something is happening with the screens, as if they're being hacked. If he thinks an attack is imminent—"

Dakota cut her off. "An attack *is* imminent."

Talia lifted one shoulder, his hand still on her other one, holding her close. "We can maybe force him to make that call. Hopefully before someone gets hurt."

Mason scratched at his chin with his free hand. She let go of his other, and he let it drop to his side. She said, "What is it?"

"I don't like the idea that you'll get blamed for anything else. This might all have been just so they have evidence to pin on you. A scapegoat."

"Does it matter, if people are safe?"

Mason wanted to kiss her, but stayed where he was.

Dakota's phone buzzed. "Maybe you won't have to." She lifted her gaze from the screen and looked at Talia. "Fire alarms are going off at the stadium."

27

"This is your doing?"

She glanced over at Mason in response to his question. Gave him a wry smile, as they walked toward the stadium. "I had to keep busy doing something, otherwise it would've been obvious I didn't intend to do what they wanted me to at all. So I layered in commands all over the place."

"Clever."

Dangerous, too. But neither of them mentioned that part.

They fought their way through, the crowd streaming from the stadium thinking there was some kind of fire. Or another problem.

"Victoria is on the lower east gangway." Dakota walked ahead of them like the teacher at a field trip. She stowed her phone back in her pocket. "They're escorting the Secretary of State back to his motorcade."

Talia looked at Mason to see if he thought that was a good idea. Maybe not, but there wasn't much he could do to argue about it. She liked that he was the kind of guy who took the world as it was. Some people spent their whole lives fighting for a change. And maybe there were times they saw it realized, but most of the time things just didn't work that way.

He seemed content to have his quiet life. To be here for his family, at least for now. Maybe he wanted more later. Like when Rayna was grown and out of the house—when she didn't require as much from her father. He probably had goals and things he wanted to do. The list of places she still hadn't been was extensive, and she was looking forward to her next vacation. She was going to Cologne in Germany, then to Italy on the train.

Did Mason like to get lost in strange places?

An older couple walked between them. After they'd passed, Mason snagged her hand. He tugged her close enough to say, "What?" without shouting. "What's that look on your face?"

"Do you know that 'cappuccino' is a universal language?"

He almost laughed. "What does that mean?"

"You can basically walk into any café or coffee shop in any country in Europe, and if you say 'cappuccino,' then they'll usually know what you mean."

"Sure, assuming that's what you want to drink."

"I've learned to love them."

He grinned. "You like to travel?"

"Definitely. Bustling streets with stores all in a row. Or tiny hill-side towns. Cobblestone is a plus. Those places where you have to ride a bike and you wear one of those scarves and it blows behind you in the wind."

"I can see the attraction."

She didn't know what to say to that. Perhaps he meant for her to read between the lines, or maybe not. She could banter, but didn't have the brain power for deep thoughts after the day they'd had. How did he? He'd nearly drowned. Then again, maybe this was nothing but banter for him.

She wanted to know. But how did she ask which it was?

"I—"

Dakota cut in. "Are you two going to make googly eyes at each other all day, or are we going to catch this guy?"

She twirled around to her teammate, standing there with a

giant grin on her face. Talia's cheeks flamed. As though she'd been caught by her mother doing something she shouldn't have.

"Let's go." Dakota turned away again, and they followed her.

Inside the breezeway, a suited man with a badge on his belt strode over. He called out, "Agent Anderson," and made a beeline for Mason. "This your doing?"

Talia said a relieved prayer to God of thanks for the fact they weren't still holding hands. What a disaster that would have been. This guy—whoever he was—wouldn't have taken him seriously after that.

Before Mason could answer, Talia moved past him. "Is that tablet connected to the Secret Service's network?" She reached for it before the man, who was behind the first guy looking like an aide, could react. "Thanks."

The first guy blustered. "Agent Armst—"

"This is one of my people." Victoria strode toward them.

It was all Talia could do to not rush to her. To launch herself into the director's arms like a crazy weirdo reuniting with her long lost sister, or something.

"She's on loan from the NSA."

Talia could have sworn Victoria actually winked at her. Then the gleam disappeared from her eyes, and she faced the DC assistant director. "The Secretary of State is away with his detail." She turned to Talia. "Now find me Yewell."

"Yes, ma'am." Talia moved away a couple of steps and got into the tablet. This was her forte, not all the other stuff she'd been forced to do. She found people. She did the tech work for this team, and she got the results they needed to bring the bad guy to justice.

She heard a new voice—probably the aide. "It has a passcode—"

Talia waved one hand. "I'm already in."

She got to work trying to figure out where Yewell was. Security cameras? That would mean a program to find someone whose face matched his. She didn't have an image of the man. But she could probably get one.

She chewed on her lip as she fished through the Secret Service's real time updates. Then she found one that had come from Stanton's team. Hadn't they been on the search for Yewell, while she and Mason and her team tried to find the hacker?

What a nightmare that had turned out to be.

"I'm just supposed to hand over control of this operation…"

She tuned out the assistant director's arguing with Dakota and Victoria and ran through what Stanton's team had come up with. She found a sighting on the street. A man matching Yewell's description getting into a car outside the building she'd been held in. Was this how they'd found her? Seemed like there was enough time in between that they could've found out another way. Or maybe it had been Alvarez. It didn't mean Stanton was dirty, even if it was possible. A thin chance didn't come close to being proof.

They had bigger problems right now.

"Sir, if you'll just—"

The other guy cut Mason off.

More arguing.

Talia found a signal running through the network connection in this building and out to the internet via Wi-Fi. "It's still active."

If Yewell knew everyone was being evacuated, would he…

"Oh no."

She heard the others gather around her, but no one said a word. No one was willing to break her concentration. Talia sat on the ground, set the tablet in her lap, and started typing upon the on-screen, awful keyboard with her fingers like it was a regular keyboard.

God, please don't let me make a mistake.

"If I can just…" She found the connection.

Devices placed around the building, a thread.

She worked them apart. One by one.

Severed the connection between them so that they could not be connected to from any device remotely on the—

An explosion ripped through one corner of the building.

———

THE RINGING in Mason's ears competed with the sound of screams like it was a sport. He blinked. Tried to get his eyes to focus while he straightened his arms to push off the ground. Talia was huddled underneath him.

She looked up as he moved, blinking herself.

"Okay?"

She made a face he'd seen Rayna make. "No. How many times are you going to do that?"

Mason said nothing. She was okay. He helped her stand, not that she needed assistance. More because he wanted to reassure himself that she was all right.

Victoria and Dakota got up. Both headed toward the source of the explosion. Victoria waved her arms. "Everyone clear the area!"

"Oh, no."

Mason glanced at Talia. She looked up at him, but his attention was on her hands.

The tablet was shattered.

"I can't find the signal now."

"You think more bombs will go off?"

"That, or it already went through and I interrupted it enough that only one went off." She bit her lip. "I hope nobody was badly hurt."

He glanced in the direction the bomb had detonated. Smoke laced the air around a pile of rubble. The assistant director from DC was in a huddle with other agents. He waved his arms wide as he spoke to them.

Sirens rang on their approach.

Good. They needed more people here to help.

"You saved lives." Mason tried to reassure her. "That's what we have to concentrate on."

She nodded but didn't exactly look convinced. "I need a—" Talia shifted before she'd even finished talking, her glance far off where people moved around. Fled the scene. Helped others. "That's…"

She took off. He saw it coming and moved with her. Looked to where she was looking. Who had she recognized? He glanced back and saw Dakota over by the blast damage, on her phone again. She mouthed something he didn't need to be told. Like he was going to leave Talia?

When he turned back, Talia was a few feet in front of him. Mason pulled his weapon, checked how many rounds he had left —not many—and readied it. Just in case.

"Hey!" She raced after a man running away from them, carrying something in his arms. A laptop?

The guy stumbled. He dropped the laptop, which cracked against the concrete. He swore, swiped it up, and kept running.

Mason forced his legs to move faster. This guy wasn't an athlete. He closed in, gripping his weapon in one hand, and launched himself at the guy in a sideways tackle. His shoulder hit the small of the man's back. He wrapped one arm around the guy's waist as they fell to the ground.

His arm hit the ground first. Pain spiraled from his elbow, snaking up that arm. Mason twisted so the bulk of his weight landed above the man's hip. Then he rolled. The man rolled with him, in front, all the way around to Mason's left.

He got up and held aim on the guy. "Give her the laptop."

Intention sparked in the man's gaze. He didn't want to give anything up.

"You've done all the damage you're going to do." Mason stared right back at him. "It's over."

The muscles around the man's mouth flexed. Some kind of a reaction. Did he think he was going to make more progress than one explosion?

People stared as they moved past him, the downed man and Talia. Cops would be here soon.

The assistant director elbowed his way between two people and came over. "This Yewell?"

Mason shook his head. "One of his people."

"He's their tech person," Talia said. "He probably sent the signal that set off that bomb."

Mason kept his attention on the man on the ground. "On your knees, hands on your head." He still hadn't given up the laptop. It lay across the man's lap, forgotten. Maybe it had been broken to the point of being useless. But maybe not.

The man shifted to his knees.

"Sir?"

The assistant director nodded. He strode around to the man's back and glanced aside at two approaching cops. "Cuffs!"

Mason shifted closer to Talia, still facing the man and not taking his gaze off him. "Think you can get anything from that laptop?"

"It's possible."

The man made a face, evidently not thinking much of Talia's statement.

"I don't know if there will be enough time. Or if it'll lead us to Yewell."

Dakota strode over. "Yewell's people hit the convoy as it left. This—" She waved at the commotion around them. "—was simply a distraction at this point. Set off the devices here, and cause confusion. Get the Secretary of State on the road."

"Stanton?"

"He called Victoria." Dakota wasn't happy. "Yewell is still out there, and Alvarez is unaccounted for."

Talia shifted, but he couldn't comfort her. All he could do was keep aim on this laptop guy and bide his time until the man was in custody. When Yewell was found.

There was no time to relax. They still had so much work to do. People were hurt here, and those responsible were still out there.

Mason thanked God that the bulk of the crowd had left the

stadium because of the fire alarm. Before the explosion had ripped through one section of wall. Then he prayed no one had been standing right there when it happened. Likely there were casualties. Ambulances were already loading up the injured.

Dakota folded her arms across her chest. "A witness said it was a jacket that exploded."

Mason didn't look at the assistant director. He didn't have time to say he'd told the man as much.

The cop handed over cuffs, and the assistant director had the laptop guy stand. Mason held his gun aimed at the man as he was secured. Watched for the slightest twitch of muscle that might indicate harmful intention.

He wasn't willing to risk Talia. Not now that she'd proven she was precisely who she seemed to be. Mason hadn't been testing her, not intentionally. No one thinking of entering a relationship should do that. But as people learned to trust one another, they demonstrated, in both big and small ways, that they were trustworthy. And she definitely was.

Strong.

Vulnerable.

Classy.

Funny.

There wasn't an attribute Mason looked for that she didn't check off the list. He wanted her in his life. For sure. Maybe even permanently.

The assistant director turned the laptop guy around and started to walk away with him. Both cops went too. Mason lowered his gun. Dismissed from his assignment here, he hauled Talia close to him. She rested against his chest and wrapped both arms around him.

After a minute or so in the embrace, she leaned back. "I need a computer if I'm going to find Alvarez." She paused a second. "Assuming he's still with Yewell, I should be able to use that to track him."

He nodded. The threat here was done. The man and his

laptop were in custody. "You're sure no more bombs are going to go off?"

She nodded.

On to the next thing then, he supposed.

"Just real quick before we go…" He stowed the weapon, then lifted both hands and touched her cheeks. Mason pressed his lips to hers. When she moved closer, he deepened it but still held back, not wanting to get carried away.

When she leaned back, he said, "The Secret Service office?" Surely Stanton would let her on one of their computers. Or he'd be too busy to notice until afterwards.

"Let's go." She turned away but not before he caught a glimpse of a smile on her face. She grabbed his hand and held it as they strode back to Victoria and Dakota to explain what they were doing.

Victoria nodded immediately. "Good."

Dakota tossed him a set of keys. Mason caught them in mid-air.

"We'll keep you posted." Talia set off.

She pretty much tugged him along in her haste to get there to find both her friend and Yewell.

"How are you doing?"

She blew out a breath as they neared the car. "I'm about ready to collapse. But this is almost done, right?"

He nodded and pulled the front passenger door open.

A shot rang out.

Before he realized what had happened, Talia collapsed into the car. She landed awkwardly on the seat, gasping.

Blood on her hands.

28

"Get in."

Talia curled up her legs, nothing but a reaction to his order. It was all she could do given the pain slicing through her left side.

Mason had crouched below the window. She ducked her head, so the shooter didn't take her out for real.

He needed to move. Go around the car, or get in the back. Weren't they leaving?

He didn't get in. Talia shifted in the seat, even though it hurt a lot. She had to grit her teeth to keep from crying out. Then again, no one could hear her. Why not let out all her pain and frustration?

Mason raced along the pedestrian area in front of the stadium. Away from her. She saw him duck between two people, and then he motioned to Dakota as she raced after him.

Victoria pulled the door open and crouched. "Okay?"

"I think…" She had to take a breath.

Victoria didn't wait for her to finish. She crouched and tore a hole in Talia's blouse. "A lot of blood, but I think it's just a deep graze."

Talia could hardly even work out where it was located. Her

entire left side burned like fire against her skin, moving through to her core. Magma, rolling down a hillside. Lava bubbling between rocks in Hawaii.

Sweat rolled down her face.

Victoria got in the driver's seat. She did something under the steering wheel. A panel popped out. She pulled two wires and touched the ends together. Before Talia could process the fact she'd hotwired the car, Victoria pulled out into traffic.

She made a U-turn and cut off at least half a dozen people and headed for...

"Where?"

She yanked the wheel hard to the left, then handed Talia her phone. "Find Alvarez."

Good. That was good. She needed something to focus on instead of the fact she was bleeding. And it *hurt*. The car straightened. Talia swayed with the motion and gritted her teeth. She found the app she'd downloaded to all their phones, just in case, and loaded the page for Alvarez—the burner phone Victoria had saved as his in her contacts.

A puzzle. That was what she needed. Otherwise she'd be trying to figure out who had shot her, and why. The hacker was dead. Laptop guy was in custody. There wasn't anyone else in Yewell's group who had a personal interest in her.

Or had it been about the team in general?

Victoria hit the brake. She threw the car in park and was halfway out the door when she said, "Stay here!"

Talia watched her go. She saw Mason and Dakota with a couple of cops, standing around a dead man. Dakota crouched, rolled the guy to his back, and took a picture with her phone. Mason motioned to her. She stood and handed the phone over. He said something, one word, and then came over to Talia.

He slid into the front seat and showed her the phone. "Recognize him?"

She stared at him rather than at the phone he held out.

They'd been kissing only moments ago. Now it was all about dead gunmen, and they were back to being scared for their lives.

"You okay?"

She looked at the phone screen instead of answering. "He was one of the men at the office where you found me. The one in charge." She shook her head. "Wasn't he there fighting you guys off when you came in?"

"I've never seen him before."

"So he left when you guys showed up and came back now to try and shoot at me?"

Mason shrugged one shoulder. "Maybe we'll never know."

She wanted to groan, but didn't. "This whole thing is turning into a convoluted mess."

"I've never had an operation turn out like this before." He shook his head and let out a long sigh. "Are you okay?"

"Victoria said it was a graze." Though, she felt like she wanted to hurl. But that would hurt. She probably didn't look much better than that made her feel.

"You're bleeding on the seat."

He got out and jogged to an ambulance, then came back with an armful of medical supplies. He squeezed a packet of something gooey onto gauze, and then touched it to the graze. Talia sucked in a breath.

"Sorry."

"It's just cold."

He taped it down. "We should get you to a hospital."

"In a minute." She didn't want to spend more time wondering why that guy had shot at her. What they needed to do was find Yewell and get Alvarez back.

For the first time, she was genuinely worried about the US Marshal. Maybe he wasn't okay. What if Yewell didn't let him go, or actually hurt him?

Victoria pulled open the rear door and climbed in the back seat. "One day you're going to have to teach me how to do that location stuff."

"But then you wouldn't need me."

"No chance." She buckled her seatbelt.

Talia said, "I have him."

"Good," Victoria said. "As soon as we get Alvarez and Drew back, I'll need to call the sheriff's office in Malvern County and let Ellie know that Drew is all right. But I need to see him for myself first."

Mason rolled down the window. "Dakota!"

She trotted over and got in the back as well. He put the car in drive and pulled away. Talia made sure she didn't move all that much as they drove across Seattle toward a warehouse registered to a trust.

Victoria's phone rang. Talia handed it back to her. While her boss spoke to whoever was on the other end, Mason reached over and held Talia's hand. She was glad for the reassurance. It helped to distract her from the pain in her side. What he'd done had helped, but when she moved and the edges of the wound shifted, it wasn't going to be good.

She was a little worried about passing out, actually. "I don't get why that guy shot at me."

"Hang on," Victoria said. "I'll put you on speakerphone." She shifted, then said, "It's Stanton. Tell me again what you just said."

Talia shifted in the seat, teeth gritted, to face Mason on the driver's side. So she could look at Victoria without twisting the wound on her side.

Stanton's voice came through the phone's speaker. "It was a total mess. The attack on the convoy was fast, and it was hard. They had to have known we would be using that route."

Victoria said, "And the Secretary of State?"

"Their force was overwhelming. Given how fast our guys were being mowed down, it was inevitable that they got through to him. As much as it gripes me to say that."

"And?"

"He was taken. They swept him off into one of their vehicles. At least seven Secret Service agents are dead. I barely got away."

He sucked in a breath. "But I'm in pursuit. I know where they're going."

Talia looked down at her phone, and the location of Alvarez's cell. She gave the address, and a general area."

"That's it. We're close, and I'm going to need backup."

"I'll call the FBI," Victoria said. "Welvern is recovering, but I should be able to get through to the Director and get us some backup."

Mason frowned. "The route the motorcade took wasn't public knowledge. It wasn't even decided until the last minute. Do they have enough men to have stationed some at each possible route, or did they get passed the information?"

He thought there might be a mole in the Secret Service?

"Agent Anderson?"

"Yes, sir."

Stanton was quiet for a second. "You're there with Victoria?"

"On our way and ready to lend a hand. Get this situation squared away." He glanced at Talia, then focused on the road again. "Talia got winged at the stadium but it's patched up, and we're headed to you."

"Yes…good. Glad to hear it." Stanton paused. "Let me know when you get here."

———

"You need to—"

She cut him off. "Stay in the car?"

"He's right." Victoria slammed the rear door and went to the trunk.

Mason crouched by the open driver's door. Talia didn't look happy, but she also wasn't arguing. "Be safe."

"I should be telling you that. You're the one walking into a building filled with an overwhelming force of armed gunmen." She took a breath like she was trying to control the pain. "But I need you to get Alvarez and that other guy back, so I don't have much choice but to push aside the fear. Do I?"

"And the Secretary of State."

"I care about the people I care about, and that's how it is."

Mason wanted to smile, but didn't because there wasn't time. "I'm not going to tell you to stay here. That might get you killed. I need you to do whatever you need to do to stay safe."

"Copy that."

Victoria passed a radio and earbud headphones to Talia. She handed another to Mason, then turned on her own pack. "Channel two."

"Copy that." Talia keyed her mic.

Mason got his turned on and slipped one earbud in.

"Mic check." She kept talking, and he walked a few paces away while he listened through his earpiece, then adjusted the volume.

Mason said, "I read you."

"Me too." Victoria went back to the trunk. She tossed him a vest. When he'd strapped it on, she held out a rifle. Extra magazine.

Mason nodded. "The FBI?"

"They'll be here momentarily."

Five minutes later, they approached the warehouse along with a group of FBI agents, armed response agents, local police officers and SWAT. Even state police had shown up. If there had been time, Mason might have taken a moment to let it sink in that this was a multi-agency operation. And it seemed very much like Victoria was the one in charge.

Stanton hadn't shown up, but there wasn't time to wait for him.

Victoria got on the radio. "All positions move in."

Not wasting any time. Mason respected that. Each position reported in that they copied, and everyone moved. They breached the warehouse from every entrance, even a couple of windows. It spread them thinner than anyone would've liked, but he figured the main fight would be congregated inside. Where they'd end up once they got through the stragglers on the way to the huge central room where Talia said most of the cell phones were currently located.

A man turned the corner at the end of the hall. Mason saw the gun and fired. The man fell. Each person breaching the building had been sent an electronic photo of Alvarez, and one of the man with him. Someone named Drew Turner.

Sounded familiar, but Mason couldn't place the guy.

His group turned the corner, and he took out another guy. The SWAT officer beside him took out a man as well. They kept going, that steady half-walk-half-run that ate up the feet of space between them and the main room, but meant they didn't rush headlong into a situation that was going to get them pinned down and outnumbered.

Speed and caution were the name of the game.

He prayed Talia was all right back in the vehicle as they approached a set of doors. Mason veered to the side and motioned for everyone to hit the walls. Then he peered through the tiny glass panel on his side. The SWAT officer did the same.

A round pierced the glass on the SWAT guy's side, and pink mist sprayed into the hall. He dropped to the floor.

Mason moved. He shoved the door open, already firing.

Older guy with a rifle. Down.

The one who'd killed that SWAT officer?

Mason scanned and put another guy down. He heard boots enter behind him, keeping track. They needed to get this done. They'd be able to assess the damage later. He didn't like losing anyone.

They pressed on as a group. Encountered resistance again and again. The last door before the warehouse was the worst. Mason and his group nearly didn't make it through. He was fast running out of ammo.

Talia got on the radio. "Charlie team is pinned down in the west hallway if anyone is available to assist."

Mason glanced back at his guys. Two police officers shifted and glanced at each other.

One said, "Yeah?"

The other nodded. "Let's go."

Mason keyed his radio. "Help is on the way."

Talia said, "Copy that."

He turned back to the hallway ahead of them.

"How many of these guys are we going to have to put down?"

Mason nodded, entirely agreeing with the FBI agent's sentiment, knowing it wasn't an actual question anyone wanted to answer. But there was no time to voice it. He was right, though. These guys were like ants pouring out of the woodwork. "Ready?"

"Yep."

They breached the doors hard and fast. The collection of men and a few women in the room turned. At the same time, two other doors were breached. The middle of the warehouse was bare except for pallets and piles of boxes.

"Guns down! Hands on your heads!"

"FBI!"

"Seattle PD!"

"Secret Service!"

The circle in the middle shifted. Handguns and all manner of rifles swung up to greet them, even a shotgun.

They all dove for cover as gunfire erupted. This was going to turn into a bloodbath quickly with them around the edges and the targets in the middle.

Mason rolled and came up behind a pallet.

Bullets ricocheted off the floor beside him. The noise in the room was deafening as shots were fired, one after the other. No pause. No time to gather his thoughts or make a plan.

He shifted and took a look. Lifted his gun and fired twice. A gunman dropped. Beyond him, on the far side, a law officer with a vest—the protective gear being the only way to tell the good guys from the bad guys—ducked behind cover.

"Keep your shots clean!" Mason yelled it twice, just to make sure. He didn't want anyone getting taken out by friendly fire.

Wood from the pallet exploded above his head. He flinched and gritted his teeth. Splinters were bad but getting your head blown off was arguably worse. He looked around for a better spot, while all around the warehouse people were dropping like flies. Would they actually be able to do this?

He keyed his radio. "Anyone got eyes on Yewell?"

Talia responded. "Room off to your seven o'clock."

He glanced in that direction. "Cover fire!"

He didn't know who it was, but they yelled, "Go!"

Mason raced for the door. Bullets sang past his head, but he kept it down and kept going. He barreled into the room so hard the door splintered. Gun up.

A group of guys. In the center, a man sat on a chair. The Secretary of State. Yewell and three of his men surrounded the man. Alvarez and his guy were both on the floor by the far wall, guns pointed at them.

"Stand down."

Yewell grinned.

"I'm not sure we're going to do that."

Mason spun. "Stanton?"

"You just refuse to die, don't you?" His boss looked at him with so much disdain, Mason had to wonder why he hadn't seen it before.

Alvarez and Drew both jumped up and slammed into the men holding weapons on them.

The Secretary of State yelled at his son.

Stanton swung out. Mason blocked it, then slammed the butt of his rifle into his boss's face. He crumpled to the floor in a heap.

Alvarez and Drew stood up in tandem, like they'd choreographed it. Unconscious men at their feet.

Alvarez grabbed a gun. "It's over, Yewell. Your plan failed."

29

Talia watched them walk Yewell from the warehouse. She let out the breath she'd been holding. Mason came out, walking a handcuffed Stanton by the elbow. She cracked the door and got out.

The huddle of people was at least a dozen. Several law enforcement agencies, but that world was a small one. Local feds knew local cops, especially lieutenants and captains. They milled around, getting caught up with what had happened.

The group pinned down in the hallway had been helped, and they were out now. Dead bodies probably littered every square foot of the warehouse, and more were walked out of the building in cuffs.

Talia moved to meet up with Mason. "The assistant director?"

He made a face while Stanton shifted to glare at her. Mason said, "Don't even think about it."

Stanton grunted. Mason handed him off to a couple of FBI agents, explaining who he was.

She turned to watch as Yewell was brought out, followed by his father. Only one of them had been cuffed. Victoria moved with them, explaining the severity of the situation to the FBI guy in charge of the scene. This man represented a serious threat, and she wanted him in federal prison ASAP. The Secretary of State just looked shell shocked.

Mason touched her elbow. Talia glanced over. He made a face.

"Yeah, she's pretty intimidating when she needs to be." But Victoria wasn't what she wanted to talk about. "Are you okay?"

He nodded. "You?"

"I'm good. Ready to get out of here, though." She needed a shower and two days of sleep. After that she was going to give Dakota back her tennis shoes. "I'd like to check on Niall."

That was assuming Mason intended to accompany her where she was going next. Maybe he couldn't, or didn't want to. There was probably too much for him to do here. Paperwork. His boss had been arrested.

She had no idea—

Mason shifted, close like when he'd kissed her. "Can I drive you? If it's all right with you, I don't think I'm okay letting you out of my sight right now."

Well, now. That was sweet. And sweet *always* needed a little sassy. Like a cherry on whipped cream. Talia stuck out one foot and put a hand on her right hip even though the movement made her left side spark with pain. "You're the one that got abducted. And nearly killed. And nearly swept away by water in a tunnel."

Mason grinned. "And shot?"

"It's a graze." She waved at him. "You look like death warmed over."

"You look beautiful." He gathered her in his arms and kissed her, until someone close by cleared their throat.

Both of them turned to see Victoria, standing there with a very smug smile on her face. Behind her, Dakota was outright laughing. Her fiancé stood beside her, the dog at his feet. Apparently they'd all shown up, and she hadn't even noticed.

"How's Niall?"

Relief flashed over Victoria's face. "He woke up pretty groggy, but they're hoping that things will start coming back fast."

Talia still wanted to see for herself. "And Welvern?"

"He's good. Called to ask me if I've managed to steal away his entire team yet."

Alvarez walked over, tall and slender. Beside him was a muscled man—not as big as Mason—who stuck his hand out to Victoria. "Drew Turner."

"Mr. Mayor." She smiled. "Of course. How's the sheriff?"

"Good. Thank you."

Talia gaped. "What…"

"You've been distracted." Victoria's eyebrows angled together. "I wouldn't have expected you to run a background check on our undercover friend."

Like Talia needed a background check? She said, "Northcorp Inland Holdings."

Drew's head jerked around to her. "Are you Talia?" She nodded, and they shook hands. "Small world."

"That it is." Victoria glanced between them.

Mason said, "I feel like there's a whole story here that no one's told me."

"I'll catch you up later."

Mason took her hand. "I'd like that."

Dakota made a noise. "Is he gonna come on board with the team as well?"

"What if he did?" Talia challenged. "What would be the big deal about that?"

Before Dakota could say anything, Victoria cut in. "He isn't." She held up a hand to Mason. "No offense. But Mason has a *lot* of work to do now. After all." She grinned. "He's the acting assistant director of the Secret Service office in Seattle."

Talia blinked. "He is?"

"I am?"

Alvarez snorted. "You guys are clueless."

Well, it wasn't like Talia hadn't figured out everything up until that point. Besides, the hacker had incriminated her in a security breach. He couldn't get into a relationship with her when she had that hanging over her head, could he? The hit to his career, and reputation, would be significant.

"Whatever just happened on your face," Alvarez said, "didn't look all that good. But I'm thinking you don't need to worry about it."

Talia felt all of their stares. She didn't want to be the center of attention, but here she was. She needed to say something, so they didn't try to fix all her problems. It was what they did, and she loved them for it. But trying to convince them she was fine never worked. Too bad it seemed like they were going to keep doing it anyway.

She lifted her chin. "We caught the bad guy, didn't we?"

"And then some," Josh said.

"Everyone is alive, or they'll heal. Right?" She looked around.

"True." Victoria smiled.

"So why are we standing around here? We should go celebrate!"

Dakota laughed, strode over and planted a kiss on Talia's forehead. "You're right. Dinner? I'm thinking stuffed-crust pizza."

Talia said, "I'm thinking steak."

Alvarez slung his arm around her shoulder. "I second the steak."

Mason stood watching them, a big grin on his face. "As soon as we get that graze stitched up, we can go get steak."

"Graze?" Alvarez looked at each of them, then her. "You got hurt?"

"It's a *graze*."

He spun to Mason. "You let her *get shot*?"

Mason lifted both hands. "I didn't—"

"Calm down." Talia tugged on Alvarez's shirt, then tried to shove him away. "Don't think I won't stun gun you." Where was her device? She had no idea. But when she found it, Alvarez was going to learn she was serious.

Talia headed for the car, listening to them argue behind her.

"How bad is it?"

"Dude."

"Someone tell me." He didn't sound happy.

"Let's just go."

Josh said, "I want a loaded baked potato."

"I gotta get home. It's a long drive, and I want to be there before Ellie goes on the night shift."

Talia glanced over her shoulder. "Bye, Drew!"

He waved over his shoulder and walked away in the opposite direction.

"I'll drive."

"No, I'm driving."

"I'm the one who has the keys."

Neema barked.

Talia's heart swelled as the voices blended together. The team was in one piece. Life went on. Things would go back to normal. Cerium was a problem for another day.

Mason got to the car door first and held it open for her.

Dakota said, "How come you never do that for me?"

Josh sighed. "Would you really let me?"

"No, but you're supposed to want to do it anyway."

"I do."

"Oh."

Talia grinned. She lifted up on tiptoes and pressed a kiss to Mason's lips. "She's totally jealous."

He laughed.

"I am not!"

———

Continue the NW Counter-Terrorism Taskforce series in *Fourth Day*, turn the page now to find out more…

Hope you enjoyed this story, please be leave a review at your favorite retailer!

Sign up for my newsletter and stay informed on new releases, participate in events, and get free stuff!
https://authorlisaphillips.com/subscribe

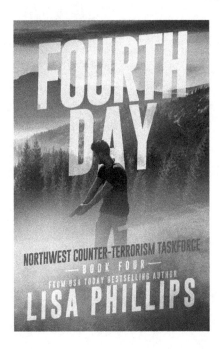

A dead woman returns. The trap is set.

Allyson can't get caught up in feelings. Not when there's work to do. The night her phone rings, the voice on the other end changes everything. Drawn into the latest Northwest Counter Terrorism Taskforce case, Allyson has to figure out where her loyalties lie. Sal knows things are changing with the team, but he isn't sure what's next for him. As soon as he clears this one last investigation he'll figure it out. Trouble is, finding Allyson might be the hardest thing he's ever done.

The Northwest Counter Terrorism Taskforce is on the case.

Find *Fourth Day* at select retailers:
books2read.com/u/bzd6dz

ALSO BY LISA PHILLIPS

Northwest Counter Terrorism Taskforce series:

First Wave - Book 1

Second Chance - Book 2

Third Hour - Book 3

Fourth Day - Book 4

Final Stand - Book 5

Find out more

https://authorlisaphillips.com/northwest-taskforce

Or, buy the complete series at a discounted rate!

Northwest Counter Terrorism Box Set

ABOUT THE AUTHOR

Follow Lisa on social media to find out about new releases and other exciting events!

Visit Lisa's Website to sign up for her mailing list to and stay up-to-date, get free books, and be included in special promotions!

https://www.authorlisaphillips.com

Find out about Lisa's books based in LAST CHANCE COUNTY at
https://lastchancecounty.com

CPSIA information can be obtained
at www.ICGtesting.com
Printed in the USA
BVHW030848020123
655391BV00015B/50